hearth wild /
post cardiac banff

hearth wild /
post cardiac banff

charles / noble

THISTLEDOWN PRESS

© Charles Noble, 2001
All rights reserved

No part of this publication may be reproduced or transmitted in any form or by any means, graphic, electronic or mechanical, including photocopying, recording, or any information storage and retrieval system, without permission in writing from the publisher. Requests for photocopying of any part of this book shall be directed in writing to CanCopy, 1 Yonge Street, Suite 1900, Toronto, Ontario, M5E 1E5.

Canadian Cataloguing in Publication Data

Noble, Charles, 1945 –
Hearth wild

ISBN 1-894345-29-0
I. Title.
PS8577.O32H42 2001   C813'.54   C2001-911007-3
PR9199.3.N545H42 2001

Cover photograph by Ernie Kroeger
Cover design by J. Forrie
Typeset by Thistledown Press Ltd.
Printed and bound in Canada

Thistledown Press Ltd.
633 Main Street
Saskatoon, Saskatchewan
S7H 0J8

Thistledown Press gratefully acknowledges the financial assistance of the Canada Council for the Arts, the Saskatchewan Arts Board, and the Government of Canada through the Book Publishing Industry Development Program for its publishing program.

hearth wild /
post cardiac banff

CONTENTS

Recap Beside Himself	9
Coffee	10
Fenland	12
Writer Horde	13
Around the Corner	14
Recap's Cabin	15
Apostrophe Piercings	15
Coffee	16
The Plot	18
Fenland	18
The Gym	20
Jon in the Underworld	24
More Banff	27
Bar in the Underworld	29
Friends and Anomies	32
Horde of Writers	34
Tunnel (Vision) Mountain:	
Another Woman Spotting	39
Coffee	40
Fenland	43
Jon in the Underworld	48
Jostle Again	55
Hegel's Cows	58
Gym	60
Hegel's Cows	63
Bar in the Underworld	65
Hegel's Cows	81

Coffee	83
Hegel's Cows	92
Fenland	93
Hegel's Cows	100
Aesop Asymptote	101
Hegel's Cows	118
Old Girlfriends: Rebecca	120
Goldilocks Guys	123
Jon in the Underworld	131
Dr Rock in Store	139
The Determination of Rebecca	147
Tain Gets Out of Banff	151
Horny John	158
Pretty Lights and Uncanny Vistas	166
Clarence Under the Scaffolding	170
Banff: The Hole Jon Left	173
Seeing Stars	194
Rock and the Fenland	204
Stable of Identity	208
Playcefire As Alley Cat	211
Brunt at the Town Party	222
The Kite and the Anchor	231
Mountain Painter in the Prairies	240
Rock, Playcefire and Recap in the Mall	259
Alice and Recap Go to Dinner	262
Recap Is Captured	263
AFTERWORD	265

The Tain of the Mirror (*tain* names the tinfoil, or lustreless back of the mirror) explores that gritty surface without which no reflection would be possible.
> — from the introduction to *The Tain of the Mirror* by Rodolphe Gasché.

Tain Bo Cuailnge, the Irish epic, was of "A shifting world of darkness: unholy Ireland."
> — from *How the Irish Saved Civilization* by Thomas Cahill.

Recap Beside Himself

Blind siding into the reflections of the day Captain Recap, or "Cap", or "Recap", crossed the parking lot full of empties — bunk incarnate, sleepy eco-footprints of invisible hands — behind the three tall spruce trees and fence back from and buffering Banff Avenue. He carefully placed his right foot on the worn beam and swung his left leg, led by its sore knee, through the designated break in the fence and then charged across the busy sidewalk.*

Jostling and fondling the tourists on the other side of the street he said "sorry, your fault" quite audibly.** The stream thickened with fresh whatever replacement suckers. Immediately Recap, ever the imposter boy, changed his tune. He wended roughly through like old Earl "the Earthquake" Lundsford,*** bumping and rolling with his

---

* Among his fellow forgetful witnesses then he dodged them, and with a nod to Ionesco, finished them as callous rhinoceros, and then he called up the pavement before he let it shimmer and needlessly mirage itself at some remove within his figuring, internal caterpillar tracks that continuously blended the opposing inertias of rest and motion†.

† He dropped the subject and disappeared in heightened showing forth.

** (but no one in the noise fair heard this portmanteau'd chipperiness since it went right into the coupling rut of seasoned expectation)

*** (which ghosts or piggybacks, which itself rimes the tacklers he usually got under, *lunge forth*, if anybody remembers)

shoulders. On through some more knots, mixing his metasports, he cut with his Gordian know-Howe elbows. Nearly in front of the Grizzly House he pulled up at one of the aliens bumped out of play, scissoring its legs, lying on the ice-welted concrete in the cool, snap spring. Pulled up and for some unreason pulled up the gasping fish, hoisted it onto his shoulder, then leaned into the crowd with the makeshift battering ram.

In the heart of the war zone, helicopter-viewed, none of the cotton combatting ants seemed to notice his particular and usual coffee bar which he now headed for and sure enough, but for a few regulars, the place was empty and so was his shoulder. The freed up alien broke into the air, took on stubborn airs in this slightly backwater street and caught itself in its own sweet alienation.*

Coffee

Recap, or "Cap", had a cappuccino in his parallel poetic or the "open work" of the Italian Eco. In reality he had an orange juice however much a coffee man he otherwise was. Rolls or more like croissants with egg inside and cheese melted on the outside; muffins, bran, carrot raisin, apple cinnamon etc; chocolate chip, macadamia and butter cookies; chocolate cake, puffed wheat squares, cheese cake,

---

* From the superfishall abyss† a refractory fish has its moment out of time, or tourist ecstasy. Trout pout and all, it hooked itself deeper, felt the better off the hook for it, breaking the light out of the light into an arch rainbow self catch, metaprison out of prism, free falling in and arising from underhanded light so usually merely spearing water quanta. A brain out of its depth, bursting with real illusory dimensions, no argument brooked.

† See Baudrillard re the superficial abyss but don't forget Nietzsche re women or Oscar Wilde's "only the unintelligent don't judge by appearances".

broccoli soup, all in this order, a catalogue he could do that would eventually blow the lid off and blow his cover too, in this narrative of his hand in the cookie jar, could do but could not do and keep everything down, as he wouldn't look at the "girls" behind the counter, she the daughter of a couple he shared a landlord with twenty-five years ago, if not the house as such which was divided into suites and rooms. They had lived in the converted garage.*

Toast would do, three butters if they were soft, otherwise two hard. He loosed the G & M *Report On Business* onto the next table, not without guilt for the receding property relations vision regulating the proper section one headlines and the establishment of horizon. He could hope for the triple agency in the hands of the infiltrations of what he might call the "basement tapes", ie the naïve however arcane advocacy of the imaginary business fifth column, not introjected from the *ROB* but right there between the lines in the richer cultural section.**

---

* (that itself had had a moon, down into the next epicycle another garage, as it were, that in turn was the centre for what would have its howl eat back up to and match the material lunacy in the real sky, even as aural would swallow aura, ie there floated on the gravelled driveway a dog house that the female dog, named Benjamin, *taut* to move on the end of the chain when the unfailing autodidacts from the elementary school heaved rocks at her)

** Hope for uncanny humans with no clothes or the clothes to become the man/woman, as the consumer demographic goes, to a degree where for all practical purposes the consistency would converge to completeness. A hope that is, that is truly unleashed in a sense Ernst Bloch's *Principle of Hope* would say: all the encyclopedic fallout from the long bomb of modernity is rosy-fingered by the archetypal dawn, ie of civilization. To say advertising genius in its creative bend over backwards to scoop real values, however much already a tag for what is fallen, in order to appropriate the better judgement at large, might for the wrong reasons right everything, including the wrong reasons.

Let him rest and let him look at the reflections in the salient, from the street in, windows: in effect looking out on the sidewalk and around corners and so trying to follow too much over and above what was, on paper, fixed to be read around more corners than a vast but vulgar geography could ever offer.*

Fenland

What a joke, the Fenland trail. Recap told it over and over. A slightly sloppy fairyland garden or theme park. Yet the bog growled louder than retarder brakes, and elk crashed through the forest on all sides. A little arched bridge within the trail, as opposed to over Echo Creek and out of the loop, was missing a 2 x 6 too much for the retired Parks water plant employee not to notice. Thirty years at the filtration works and never late a day. Two bikes, one with a basket for groceries and a saddle bag for tools, made by himself out of a woman's purse, and one fancy mountain bike for touring and exercise. One day to measure. The next to stand down and hammer the board. No one else would have fixed it, no one will ever notice.**

---

* One day yet, vulgar will have its say and given the chance establish its judgement day balancing of accounts even as it will lift and back off its own rhinoceros, its own rindy randy eros. But, appropriation gone wild, rhinos R us.

** Unless you see him above the Zeno once, which of river course was crushed forever by a collapsing twice, the water man standing in the choked dry little stream with hands on — the arch of your foot bridge. The fenland trail, Recap told it over and over till he lapped himself into a joker wildness.

Writer Horde

The rhinos were writers. The heard in the lobby of the Eric Harvey Theatre. If metaphors were sexual juices or what nots or kumquats he'd stick — yuck, yuk — to the first fluids, the milk of species kindness, and the place would stink more than a dairy barn. Recap just about said "diary bar". Good rhinos, good writers stomped through here.* Sitting around in the high humidity of the Sally Borden Sports Complex away from the freezing mountain air they looked for the telltale sign of a sorrowful Canadian, "victoid" (they slummed) of the serious.**

Her voice so husky and slow and low it was not believable at first. Then it became so — unbelievable. Held in a delicate equilibrium and thrown into question, it begged the nature of strength. She would quit smoking if he would start she said. Her light body smoked heavy and when she felt faint she went to sea or Bosnia. Banff was not to be, a piece of empty or moveable Faust.***

Choked by the hyper mobilized hordes the two of them took support in the very out-from-under-them, mindwalked on the black boxes of one another's unassuming

---

* Psychoanalytically really, how can a nose gotten so down, both to sniff and to sniff, the ground and itself respectively, get so up like nobody's business, yea, and like nay, none of your business.

** Get it out, thematized, uttered and outered so to walk on your own sore spots, free to begin like a goat in the spring or a murderess, say nanny for the nonce and topical nuance. Now askew and perpendicular to the shattered and the chattered he asks you. That everything's been said was the height of the bar till it at last called.

*** The old Goethe springing on spring after spring and wouldn't tell his daughter it was Hegel who had come into the cottage and was rattling away. She was simply ecstatically swayed by an absolute development swaddled in such unlikely Swabian accent.

assumptions, the blind spots of being out of character writing it but then again put back in, per the principle of nail bed estimation and the magic pad erasure of general disorientation. Hordes, by a "set of sets" lodged in the continuous minds that *go* by, and go *by*, distinction. How he loved small talk over the perfectly prickly nails. They recoiled themselves and uttered becoming humilities.* He put his hand on her hand and a confusion overruled. Her liquid eyes broke on his prominent not being there. They returned to the idle pines whose fallen needles had become innocuous matting.

Around the Corner

Over the top of the paper beyond the shade of the building in the winter sun she eased into a walk, puffing, endorphined. When she entered the shade and turned toward the glass door her floating stooped to actual slipping on the dripped-up ice bell. Slip conquered with slop, of limb, limb beyond limb, numb as the dumb simultaneous beautiful smile Recap caught off her balance, thrown over the slant of the news. The window of vision picked up after the interlude of wall and he watched the tight[s] wiggle disappear into the Rembrandt interior of the mall. He sipped his juice.

---

* Then this was benched by pretentious cracker barrels. Ah those moments and then all was gone a nesting and they walked along the edge, no cliffs, maybe not even a narrow Buberian ridge, though not ruled out. Just that constant ironic breaking out of fiction. Fiction breaking out and thus interned, they broke out of it in turn.

Recap's Cabin

Another high-sided silage truck stuffed with lurid downhill skiers screamed by, bass motor and air blast. Early mobilization blues. Captain Recap drew shut the curtain and could only imagine. The field trial Labrador cowered under the table when the fire siren fired up, all confused with the idiot whistle of the back up bobcat. He drew the curtain again, saw things, and jumbled his computer sights with the high stepping skiers boarding the long slide of immediacy down the alley, besieged by ever intermediate slopes of pre-reaction.

A huge five ton garbage truck he thought slammed into the corner of his cabin. Dog jumped, bristled her back, barked. The power knocked out. Again he looked out on the parking lot. No wreck of garbage after all. Raven bunched on the snow under the transformer. Magpies half the size, fifteen or twenty, swirled around, cautiously inspected the stunned carbon copy of its former self, beak above the snow like a telegraph key. On the way to his friend's ex-wife's funeral he detoured to the bird, its sheen sullied after the greased, short lightning of its curtailment.

Apostrophe Piercings

"O wolf, hang on! Do you get the double hook of it: interrupting you, encouraging you?" The call of the wild envelops all the codes, is the friction out of which they arise. "Go now wolf".• Ernie's photograph cuts off a winglike part of an erratic, a holy exponent and cliff-hanging

---

• "Gwan" ospreys. "Gwain" go the nights of old envelopes, old letters. "Go on!" we don't believe us. The end of Kroestch's *Alibi* unpacked.

boulder-than . . . The photograph's outcrop. Riding the click we take us. To the end of the valley of the ten peaks. Up on a pass above the summer-surviving snow to ski back down with hiking boots. Affords that play of perspective, folded and manifolded.

And beyond that? A terrible lack of usage, of words, a terrible usage come down. Desolate and anonymous — terminus for the flip to fortified, comforting thoughts, factored out like rocks from the vaster process singular thought connotes, itself shorter than circled fire, in-shore-er of fire. Convexed and concaved, though out of the cave anthropologically and presumably/presumptuously, platonically, we see Alex Emond meadows, Ruth Secunda* starry-eyed coyotes, and hear at this remove the almost human cry of the embedded, overdubbing train. Later to read of the hard pre-tracked wolf cub kill.

Coffee

Husky *éminence gris*, the grey hair thick and the mind too but with convictions, Dr Rock he was called, though no autochthonic presenter of self however inclined to re-present that sort of self at times. Conservative we might say and rehearse associative "conservation", remember John O. Thompson's** "comedy is conservative", as mitigations.

Captain Recap instantiates himself in a sheaf, is tossed

---

* Two (very different) Banff artists, though Alex's dog Sky, as photo-painted by Allan McKay (another Banff artist), looks like, if not a coyote, a feral dog.

** Canadian emigrant to England, in reverse to the other poet John Thompson, and author of the poetry collections *Echo and Montana* and *The Gates of Even* from which the quotation is taken.

into a timely harvester, a moving one as opposed to his grandfather's first threshing machines, or as an innocent insect car looking cross-wise is taken into the past by a fast train.•

Rock was already at a table and engaged in debate, not quite toppled into unilateral spiel, "steered into something I know something about". Recap was guessing. It turned out Rock was in his information-gathering mode, asking the young waitress about her younger taller sister. And this was not what it might seem, well maybe some innocent flirtation with these universal otter daughters.

He took his time to consider Recap and his predictable-but-always-something-different-about-it arrival. Recap considered Rock's daily bundle of potent ironies, the kind Wallace Stevens considered too much with us. The latest Liberal outrage: helicopters coming home to roost, their superficial slagging of Presto. Recap rose to the debait, recited indeed the niceties of manning a new image. Recap kept his cool by running hot and Rock laughed his nerves around the room.

When finally they got bored they went on about their ongoing sports injuries. Out the frame they did go on, physically lugging and lugging big books around, back and forth

---

• Recap: taking the *tain* he combined the separated towns of Banff and Foxhog, whose adjacent prairie fields he farmed, colligated his points of view, his personal pronouns, sitting at the centri-petals, leaking to the press of the killing enthnospheric new world order of weeds who would be gods at as much of a loss as this, this *this*, ingrown this-all. Even in a radical dialectical action there's always a conservative moment. Dr. Rock would want the pejorative meaning, though twisted to the good in his *dis tain* and ironic radix.

to the library, back from the bookstore, even trading a few. Rock's wife put brown paper over the dust jacket of what Rock took, which was only what he would read right away and so the book would come promptly back, pristine re the layer of paper and unpristine re Rock's undelayed delayering. That is to say the book's brains would be sucked out. Recap waited for Rock's recap, when he would nail it down as he'd lash his laughing to the walls whose ears would maybe later complete his sentences.

The Plot

Here it is: the time of a town, pre-narrative desires and such, upthrust in the wilderness, the plot, of land, in prehistorical ruins. Subjectivities in search of the ticket stubs, Dr. Johnson's naïve kicking, though not knocking, rocks, the atomistic firsts that can't be isolated.*

Fenland

The path of poetry. Not. Stop the press/sure of foot. Poetrees off the beat, in themselves, just trees. Really a short path, self guiding, and with the memory ahead each incidence is almost coincidence with the departed-or-the-now-never-arrivable, of course begging the resolution.** In

---

* Re Johnson's refootation of Berkley: Peirce, with his trinitarian categories, would second Johnson, but then he would third Berkley, of course only after he first also refooted† him.
 † Read "refitted" too.

** And so each walk is the path of poetry in the sense of embarrassment, full of itself, flush with its own dissolution into the forgone and so useless alright and then no good at the other end, by definition, if nothing more than its own infinitely disintegrating incidence. The repetitions mount, peak into different induced horizons and each trip around presents an altered gain, is a gain no matter how obsessively you finger the blistering images with a footfall you forget.

forest of the foresight the trees are their own recitation of fire. And a trace of forest fire dogged the path, muted the retriever's golden steaming pile. Onto the presence of Mr. Cigar. The joggers, pre-limping by on all twos so to scoop the 'scoping of possible injured knees, looked a little green, a little snotty. Recap got the drift. Mr. Cigar nowhere in sight and yet he lingered potently, the contrail roughly coincident with the needle-matted, root-veined path. One cigar does a whole one and one third miles. The cruel irony of Mr. Cigar trying to get away from it all, to fade into the tree-falling philosopher's absence.

There he was, the bastard, petting the retriever, worried about the lesions on her back. Recap always liked cigar smoke and in the haze, caught again some hotel lobby from the point-no-point of a kid's sunken and hence grander, treasured hope. And if we say "hopes" we grant fragility a notch or two inside the grand, taking it down but chalking it up to how we constantly climb out of the seeming constants. We say "we" here as a fudge, candy to be sure, dedicated to the parents of the sweet here-before, but also to the ghosts who necessarily leak through the frame. Dedicated to the Dedekind cut.*

In the open here, dear reader, Mr. Cigar is such a nice man, darn, we knit him wittingly not pickingly into the

---

* Cut a line on the screen where all presence dies and yet is reborn as representation through thick in thin†.

† Cut a line and choose which side is closed and isomorphic with a real number, then take your chances with the other side slid endlessly open.

greater cloud of glory but in the meantime we take our leave, overtake him and take him as he is.

The Gym

No need to brace against the cold early morning air with anxious weight-lift nerves, in fact it was balm to the simmering bomb. Body beautiful would be the concept the tectonic intrusions of a refractory skeleton would defuse. Recap looked up at the sublime shell-shocked earth, sea waves transmitted to total inscape unescape landscape, crusty, arch, broken arch, and characters, were they to come down from sublime industry. And industry indeed as the cosmological imaginary-cum-tourist gaze regulates the endless in-the-stars spiritual/material trade-offs. David Thompson had seen sea waves, breakers, when he first regarded the Rockies. Some sea, some highway. Hector, the geologist, half a century later rhapsodized over how formations, as present physiognomies, were at one with their becoming (as embedded in the word), the stratification wonderfully not obscured by igneous rock. Recap pulled away from the geo-grip and with the aftershock stepped into the orders of little echo grunts.

Brunt grimaced at the mirror, three feet away really and another three irreally. His face a consummate red, the gritty grin getting fiercer even as it slipped but then slipped into hilarity's grip, its letting go. He was supersetting shrugs, seventy-five pound dumbells in each hand. At each shrug Recap blurted out "Idunno". Brunt finished and burst out laughing. "Trudeaumaniac" Recap shouldered on.•

• Recap had never read *Shrug*, a book about Trudeau, nor had he read Ayn Rand who annoyed him because people often heard her name when he'd mention Hannah Arendt.

After a professional wrestling career complete with non-fake ambulance rushes to the hospital, a bad marriage, a flirtation with steroids, Brunt wrestled peacefully with below-5%-body-fat even as the expression "all the rage" flipped its elements and pinned them under it. He was the most disciplined thorough lifter Recap had ever encountered in his own oscillation between the narcissism of immediate looks (the irreal never-arrival of the self as an "unreconstructed" other) and the narcissism of power [lifting] where the "looks" are dropped in favour of a pure pushing outward [at the poor world] and then as this declines to "looks as if he could [be pushy]" which itself is inclined to the look turned back, *featuring* itself.

A sort of rearranging the deck chairs on the ice-slippery ego. Of course the oscillations are never mastered and eventually the moment of boredom arrives, mocks, under the martyrdom looking for a time to happen,* the lost insight of a Mishima mind flush with the sculpted body's convergence to suicide. That is, the boredom, remainder as new seeds for *reminder*, smothers the point of death's smothering, and its lack of direction is perfect antidote to dire direction, or is what Goethe got on with [life] with life-in-stages, that is boredom as another muse, its cranking action. But of course the heavy bubble world of the gym is simply shrugged off.

The maturest transformation within the never-say-die frame of lifting is the weekly pushing of the weakly flesh onto the shore of wavering age. No ego here anymore other than its parody, wherever the real ego has flown to. Just

---

* Reminiscent of Hubert Aquin who postponed his suicide a day at his wife's request because of an appointment she had.

the up and down of desperation and gasping laughter. The irony is always there and here kicks in. The weight-lifting body engenders an absurd astral body. And Brunt floated on his in the here and now even as Recap celebrated, having been childishly encouraged by the video he'd picked up in a bargain bin that claimed the older guys, yes claimed the older guys have it. Power lifters get stronger as they get older. Seventy year old cancer survivor squatting over three hundred pounds. The over all champs of course in their forties and fifties.

Recap slid the plates onto the bar and then paraded around the mirror-drained/mirror-stopped room, swinging his arms, then stretched his joints by pulling on the power rack. He watched Brunt lifting for the mirror results, his rolled up short sleeves circumcision-like, exposed the striated deltoid bulbs. Recap turned away from this display and wondered at the smashed through-the-mirror embarrassment. The double hook, like the upper arm's floating anchor, of possession-dispossession (how Sheila Watson would take this lowest common denominator of putting forward for the glory!, how indeed, it's hard to figure considering how her last novel was her first, low modern jumping over high modern into what we can't thankfully label anymore).

The refined interior hand of the will flung the inventoried muscles into the mirror, operatic butcher shop.*

---

* Every perspectivalled image was now in the hands of the constructivist sculptor as he only knew, insinuated into a reflex as well as the sinews. And as intimate meat cutter, lifted out of himself, incrementally, for that stab at a return to a base, undiminished, completed, displaced into the mirror.

Never to find that fetish again, rarest commodity over against the unfulfilled flesh in this arrested stage, to say its dismemberment in the crisscross, sissyfuss-haunted and hunting narcissism. And then the whole room was skeletons that* had futilely to recapitulate the evolution of the will-in-muscles. Recap knew suddenly the embarrassment was overcome by that other embarrassment, the super rich reach of the omniscient, for our purposes, screen. The first embarrassment was lost on Brunt, rightly so, stuck in the flickering promethean depths of the butcher shop window.

Recap was alone now among the body parts. He pulled himself together and waltzed around sheepishly. He imagined Brunt trekking over the bridge and up to the Banff Springs where he worked as a chef. On the strength of Recap's field-evoking, gym-dead/gym-borne magic pad that undercut/clearcut [body] development even as it arose, he saw him make his way into evidence of greater forest, walking closer to the foot of Sulphur. He imagined he was finishing his baked, cooked up industrial bread, was rooting for the ingredients even as his astral body had its way with the munchies. Heart-broken Frankenstein, heart-broken monster, face to face, and the mutual loss was good in the Hemingway way, in the profound surface as our supermen say.

These minnows have no teeth but do have little projections at the corners of their mouths that have the sense of touch and smell, called barbels (Ben Gadd). Their knees were weak,

---

* The free and infinitely pinpointed human antecedents are levelled by the fantasy of transparent and exhaustive third person shell, hardened beyond to a relative pronoun's thing, and the thing's thing was the ego's fly into the negative anointment.

coordination gone, senses all rainbowed and Rimbaud in the worked-over echoes of the workout in its narrow gorge of blood. They swallowed inconceivable sensations and their pride, uncorked in the stream.* And what almost dominates in Mary Shelley's book is the wonderful mountain landscapes of the Alps. She didn't hang with those Romantics for nothing, and there on a cliff, forgiving mirror of a monster's face, rappels a tale, going with Goethe who took his turning points to difficult mountain tops in (and out of) order to decide the beyond, this side of suicide.

Jon in the Underworld

Recap sat with Jon in the underworld and was at a loss, pun intended, just when there should be so much to say. Jon sitting there in silhouette in front of the light in the latticed window in Catherine's house, Recap thought of Jon's sense of rightness, sense of drama. "Ah Recap, you can call me up but can you place me, can you find the still point, 'distracted from distraction by distraction' as you are?" Recap placed him there because that was where he was, contemplating the literary history and the general history of Banff, and taking stock of his own place.

No matter how big were his big poems he was bigger and was meant to cross over into bigger poems, not death at fifty. *Headframe* Birk Sproxton said we're still learning to read him. Recap realized, say, that "Winter Journey"

---

* (and into their own magnified Renoirs, halfway between the father who said his life was "a cork in the stream" [as opposed to his still lifes, any pictures being the general case, and cork-lined, as it were] and the son, whose pictures move [meeting the stills where "move" is moved up to *emotion*])

didn't work read aloud. All that travail, fatigue, tedium, needed a different reader real time. A silent study, intermitten suspension of the attenuated suspense. Reminded Recap reading *The Naked and the Dead*, all that slogging in the jungle adding up to rime the tedium of the read, an oh so delivering naturalism, it worked and it didn't and then it did. But Jon's slow journey needed a slower read and it worked wonderfully in the *longue durée*, as Bruce wrote back, sending Recap his own short historiographical send-up. Recap needed to get out more, from in this journey of Jon's.

> *A mile more: walls of rock we cannot climb*
> *confine the river's and our course.*

And that house, so woody warm. How was it his chair was always so uncomfortable? Roughing it on the push back of dead cellulose, nay his own private Hindu Kushion, to speak of mountains and an elsewhere than the Rockies Jon also journeyed to. The ungrateful living, the band he belonged to. We, banned to the actualities, complain.

Recap: Earle Birney in the other room on the couch singing from those crazy poems, "Roll out the barrel". Mrs. Paris was there. Cyril was not but was there in the archives when Earle remembered for the tape recorder and remembered he and Cyril as kids. Recap told Mary that perhaps the sun would rise tomorrow and she scoffed loud enough for everyone to hear and laugh. He reddened like the dawn and inwardly cursed David Hume.

The next day Earle was down at Bruce's on Bow Avenue, another Catherine house, sitting on the floor smoking pot. He talked about Suknaski's poems stashed on mountains in little cairns. That guy Treble was around then, the folksinger from Minnesota, in fact he lived in Bruce's house. He used to get off the stage, well the stool, and walk around the tables improvising lyrics, more like notes, so to speak, toward lyrics, at the Grizzly house on those Sunday folk nights when Bruce's ex-wife's brother and Recap would drink beer they brought in in their percussively clinking paper bag. One night after Treble had broken up with that young woman reminiscent of the "Laugh In" Goldie Hawn, she came storming in the backdoor dragging some guy from the bar and hardly said a word as she came right through and out the front door, crestfallen it seemed because Treble wasn't there. Treble never drank, was eminently sober for such a crazy minstrel.

Lots of fun but there was angst in the air. Recap: Bruce slightly drunk and playing a particular song from Recap's Country Joe and the Fish album to his wife over the phone, one of those messages called up that requires it to be already in the human, not the mechanical, receiver. Bruce would also play his game around this time of asking you to name the person you'd most like to see walk in the door. Recap would squirm thinking Bruce wanted him to admit to the old flame he hadn't gotten over. He lied and said Norman Mailer, knowing Bruce would believe it. Funny how as Recap went off Mailer Jon seemed to tout the writer all the more and even tried to embarrass Recap by tricking him into revealing his bad judgement at parties. But Jon substantiated his fandom with recollections of listening to Dwight McDonald and Mailer debate on the radio back in the fifties or early sixties.

Recap thought it ironic at first, the affinity, thinking of Mailer's Hemingway persona, brawling, drinking etc. But then it was only as of late he was beginning to appreciate Jon's gutsiness, not necessarily Mailerian, but what was now needed around here. Bruce said he would go for Jane Fonda through the door. Recap sighed at the time. Bruce of course, typically, met her later in New York and wasn't impressed, naturally, over against unnatural expectation. Then Jon at the television festival found himself packed in behind some short woman whose steel-like buns with a tilt and twist of his head, because so close to fondle, he was just able to discern. And yes she turned out or around to be Jane.

Years later Bruce told him a good one about a friend he had in New York whose first encounter with a naked woman was seeing his aunt when he was nine or ten. He had accidentally come upon her as she got out of the shower, and Recap couldn't help think of Bruce thinking Eric Fischl's "Bad Boy". She didn't seem to mind, not hiding as she dried herself. Big pause, duplicated from the original, and then he adds his friend's uncle was Arthur Miller. A rather transcendent piece, so home alone.

More Banff

Canmore was open more and more to more as the millennium approached, and then Alice driving from the once coal mining town got and gave more Banff than Banff arrived at gave. In fact she saw it for the first time a particular time so much she decided to write a play about it. Recap didn't know if he believed she would write the play. The question became a fiction in itself. She pronounced she would have it produced at the Banff Centre. Not for the Canmore festival coming up Recap asked? The visitor she would have come to Banff in her play would be Italian. Well that was not hard to guess. Alice was Italian and proud of it. But that sounds only half right. Measures like this are wrong. She was too cosmopolitan to be anything but easy on the issue. Yet Recap remembered her saying she was ashamed of the heavy homemade bread she brought for school lunches when the other kids had the Elvis stuff. He confused it with the Caterina Edwards novel about a young Italian girl growing up likewise in Calgary — Alice, recapped through Caterina not lacking gloss herself in the Venetian blind of *The Lion's Mouth*.*

Banff Slide. That's what it is till mountain airs, ie pretensions, wake us and we drown. And let Eliot play chiasma with Joyce's *Wake*.** "Great things are done when man and mountains meet; that is not done by jostling in the street." And Jon adapted Randipole Billy's lines to name his weekly column. Recap waited for Alice to arrive and she never would in this play of arrival.

Recap then headed quickly for the store. Sunday evening war zone given the holiday on Monday. He jostled, became undone, and in his *outfit* again scooped up a done-in skier too weak to wait in line for the restaurant, carried him around the corner to another one, got him in and

---

* The included [Cat's?] mouth [mouse?] of course backs the lyin' up with truth. Behind that, somebody really did go to Venice.

** A heap of projections, not broken, but complete to teeming, somehow distinct *and* inseparable, Gödelled to the outside of themselves, the key rings from all of Canada and the tourist world tossed in and converging on the uninhabitable turf if that's what you can call the lichen "sandwich" that Rundle is under the moon and grandly off and along the highway from Canmore to Banff.

seated. Recap swirled his cape and escaped. When he got back Alice was waiting, Go-dot-ted on the landscape, her all-seeing rushes spiraling into the black hole of Calcutta room floor. She was high and restored to the "Mountainside" (her store's name like all names, with time, transcended itself). From behind the one-way mirror that had stopped any facts from getting in the way of the truth of Alice's art crimes, Recap-decap, dense dirt on nothing, stepped and now stopped the radiance from opening [the] night, ie put a lid on the rising Canmore star with a dark remark lite. "O that first expansiveness springing from the budding playwright's taking heart and part". Through the parking lot they walked toward the Lux theatre. "We're all displaced monsters" he said. Alice said her bookstore was full of self-Alp books.*

Bar in the Underworld

The late seventies in the Buffalo Paddock lounge. The early light from over Banff Avenue streaming in. The bar was empty and Tain had another and it was not the seventies. It was the underworld and a night life at least. She had reappeared, working at his favourite bar. She was wearing a long off-white dress with a kind of cape around the shoulders when he first met her quickly averted eyes.

---

* Recap opened up his senses, ie of *covering*, ranged, with tin ear to the ground, over the earth's "shining mountains†", repulsive *tains*, someone called Tain whom he could and couldn't expose — but again, opened to *cover* as the late breaking mountains on different scales turn into sheltered Italy or Swiss [Mary] Chalet. The monster is overcome, in/by himself or by the good Doctor Recap, or is Recap overcome by some tain of sheer upthrust creation?
† What the Stoneys and Cree called the Rockies.

She came into view again from behind the wall that shielded the bar from the entrance and the first table, and her shoulders were bare now, nicely tanned from a day at the Cascade Pits he surmised having seen her cycling back. He had met her on the sidewalk a few days before for the first time in months. There had been a shy, coy shy perhaps, new wrinkle of a twinkle in her eye. This then must have been it.

At the end of the night she came over and just started talking, about the new job, as if he had asked. She had given him even that, staked his first move for him. She stepped between the table and his chair to take the ash tray and her dress caught on his legs just below the knees and he was on them and electrified. Caught, and so was his tongue. He mumbled and trembled and couldn't even clear his throat. He was devastated with certainty. A field was playing him and when he left, his real heart hurt from the magnetism. Could this be good news, he thought? Yes and it was so strongly sourced he bided his sweet time, which in time turned to sweat.*

Finally, long after, at the rottenest time, he phoned, almost unconscious with self-consciousness. Self-Alped and cold-hearted at the same time he sealed his fate, even then perhaps otherwise open. His mind had gone around so much on what to say that when he called and she answered he shut her out with his crystallized script.

---

* Frozen in that force he got behind the accelerated moment which began to shed its own parodied moments, each falling further behind even as he fell further in. Yet anew she made room for him but it was time to make time and he couldn't somehow in a reactivated force that made his heart race.

Begging the question and the end with a ruthless humility. And what could she say, practically married, even though she ended with some question in her of what to make of it. He was strangely relieved, before the slide to a long sadness. For the moment now he dropped the fake warmth and basked in her fake cool. Or so he thought at the calm centre of the cruelty sprung between them.

Tain looked over at the buffalo head on the wall, then ninety degrees back to the windows. The bar empty except for him and Jimmy who sat alone in the corner next the drapes above the street. He couldn't tell if Jimmy was smiling or brooding in his beer the way his mother in Ireland warned him against long ago between the wars, closer to the second one. Suddenly he let out an agonized howl he deemed into defiance mid-note, half imitating "London", the big, raw boned senior in his red and black plaid woolen shirt and whose operatic outbursts you could regularly and regulatively count on in the Eddy once.

Those insult to injury mornings at the end of a long night of drinking, beyond the pale in an embarrassment of time travel, simply stop at the wrinkled prospect of another, not drink, but day, with morning then in a seductive wink, not this eerie retro awakening. All things being equal, anybody lives for the unruly sun, "busy old fool",* especially a farmer in the dark about the after-dark but not about the far cry from and to the earth. Tain walked among the wacky props of the bar, tapped the bar within for the wake-up call, laughed at the tame nightlife. Of course he'd

---

* Assuming you're done, not Donne.

gone to seed but going full cycle underground to get there, the same moment with different spins. He was neither sentimental nor regretful, rather was both and removed. He thought how easy to be one of these puppets now, tear away, do it right and string that girl-woman along till time comes to free the mutual recognitions. Ah the '-strapped puppeteer's world!

Pick any anonymous Saturday night, the heart of it. Sometimes it was there and sometimes not, sometimes it was installed and then stalled in a Wednesday. He would stagger home, hit the can where he would assiduously aim to clean the mould off the bowl with his piss drill. And the next day sitting in there, not constipated just irregular what with not bothering to eat properly or at any particular time, he would make puns that didn't make him laugh even to himself, like "I don't give a shit", after sitting there for an eternity. Or standing and swaying over the bowl trying to urinate but unable to he would look at his innocent and solemn penis, hector it with "you little cunt!"

Friends and Anomies

Everything was in his dark blue eyes, charismatic, penetrating, willful and knowing, and attractive to women over and above the playful dimples. Hooratio Fierytail was not a devil but devilishly good at what he did. Which was land on his feet after jumping or being pushed out of impossible predicaments. He was the first to point it out. Recap, now in the mid nineties, wrote this right ratio off to a surefire fate. Fierytail was always able to revise the past in the necessary Nietzschean sense, as the past was picked up and flung into the present whether you liked it or not. Yet his life was mellowing and Recap noticed that, although his revising was converging to a made-up mind on some basics, he was more inclined to reflect on and laugh in sweeping ways about our lots and so to make them for a time remotest motes. Recap took to calling him Playcefire, partially for a new rosiness in his outlook but mainly for how he'd gotten a grip on himself, turned himself around within his own same fate, played with his drive now even as he steered its restlessness. A long way from the hearth or that time behind the Cascade bar where his wife waited in a tree for him and then dropped on him when he passed through the gate. Or the time in the same backyard when Recap held them apart and the wind spat back her own spit she took for Fierytail's, at which nerve her anger redoubled.

 Hooratio, alias Playcefire, sat in the coffee bar wearing glasses now and read his paper. Recap put his down and fetched a juice and a blueberry-poppyseed muffin. As usual the reflected comings and goings in the street in the inset windows beguiled him. He sat down and looked up in time to catch both a half familiar face directly through the glass and Playcefire's middle finger lit into it.*

 Button button who's got the button. Playcefire's stories always came with the proviso to button the lip. Recap pushed on with casual God sips.** The respective newspapers rustled and shifted so the multiple views could all find elbow room

---

* Recap looked puzzled so Playcefire gave a quick thumbnail sketch, and made-over up-to-date Banff was thus set back an indexical remove from the re-entering story, storing — in its very distortion — the town, and which then dispatched itself to the glass, seen through and around.

** Recap, with the etymology, liked to use this expression in order to raise gossip even as he enjoyed lowering God.

and both save and avert their faces. The two general viewers avoided the political differences. In clipped code they invoked and immediately suppressed, say Clinton, say tender buttons, say you don't say. With his Wallace Stevens cat life Playcefire lived in a more leaping world, say than Recap in his whistling rabbit realm, yet how Fierytail took on the chin, blow by blow, the daily ironies of TV politics, had Recap reeling.

On the other hand maybe these guys and dolls were anachronistic on the side, in a low rent eternity. But how is the simulacrum, its incoherence not even comprehensive, as consolation, ie since we ask after it? It is perhaps the first (outside[?] of the mother) secondness to absorb itself into the would-be beholders' firstness.* Resisters to the electric wares become resistors to what, wattage — what age are we the "childermass"?**

Horde of Writers

Recap was aware of the potential for professional jealousy when he sat in the audience hour after hour listening to the star writers. Festivals seemed like such a good idea on

---

* Secondness being Peirce's category for what bumps us and indicates an outside to the ego. It goes without saying the thirdness of thought, including its self-criticism, also collapses where the simulacrum exists, or lives in a secondary way its negated secondness. This collapsing is what Hegel, in his triune moments, criticized in Schelling's deluded thirdness as the night when all cows are black. ("Crazy" Hölderlin, the poet, was the other of this once so close, student triumvirate.)

** The novel *The Childermass* was Percy† Wyndham Lewis' first volume in *The Human Age* trilogy, his fallen echo of *The Divine Comedy*, (though a fourth volume had been planned).

† Something in the tough-mindedness of Lewis is reminiscent of Peirce, pronounced like the *purse* part of "Percy". Of course the novelist Walker Percy wrote about Peirce and was a great admirer.

the one hand but on the other the occasion had a crowding out effect on the real action of literature. Yet the idea of occasion* appealed to him more and more the older he got, somewhat like the Arendtian idea of rising to historical moment, raising the voice as it were, in the sense of recapitulating its development as well as getting it out and heard, (Robert liking Recap's idea so much he used it for the title of his book**).

Underneath the stars, their capstones, were good writers and Recap was pleased to listen and even to concentrate and if transported so much the better, absorption theory aside, especially if the transport overcame the stalled and suffering body. But finally his concentration grew diluted and then it diffused out to meet the beckoning surround. As overcome as Recap, his friend Fred came over and, too much for words, they followed a telepath down the foot of the mountain to a bar, this wordless understanding mighty esoteric for writers who like to stick to the muddle of language even when conspiring not to have their cake but to prove the barley sandwich.

Leaving their writer selves at the door but neither coming back to romantic life they simply took their leave as they entered the bar and left to chance whatever was

---

* The rebel hates the occasion, rebel without an occasion, and in a sense half of a writer must avoid them even while the other half must fall in to the rising. That dilated happening, Godot to the good, the unbearable lightness of waiting born and reborn, worthy of "willing one's fate". But just in the straight life sense, occasion seemed the right idea and, too, inevitable. If you can take it, the anticipated attention, you take it in to you and you go over it, again, but in the sense of past the mark to a bracketing which implies an over and done with, a missing the mark (or occasion) but also an overdoing, or in fact occasion *in fact*. Of course you have to do *doing it up right* right.

** *Raising Our Voices*, a *remembering* novel by Robert Hilles.

left. A lot it turned out. A few rhetorical whines, a few catch-ups on women, then nosing into the maze of gossip and nuanced placings of personalities, then retracings to figure out what they were talking about. Long remembrances, tit for tat, the mutual tax for getting the treasure off their chests. And finally as oblique as it gets faint assessments of some of the readers they'd heard, almost as rumour had it, so anti occasion it had gotten. Fred and Recap trailed off in their exchanges, paid up and then went their separate ways home, Recap to his cabin in town and Fred back up to his room at the Centre's main residence, Lloyd Hall.

Recap: a reading years ago in the Donald Cameron building. Not the one when Sid and Jon read and Jon declared it was the battle for the Rockies. The turf was up in the air, but so much so Sid responded he didn't see it as a battle, at least not bottled up like this. Recap: the occasional seasoning of a bit of rutting one could take as evolution's ground-up roots, in the finer, soupçon sense of *course*.

The selected recollection: sitting next to Jon, in the same room as the turf-in-the-air time, listening to a reader in front, and after each haiku-like offering, to a few bars from a flute player behind them. A sweet tension formed in Recap's tingling brain tain but then quickly grew to giggling in his body. The same for Jon, doubling and more the problem. Somehow through extreme physical wrenching, shutting not shouting out, they made it through the evening.

Half a year after the festival and drinking with Fred, Recap once again mingled with some of the writers up at the Centre. One time after a long day in the artist colony studio she, who had resorted to Bosnia again and was back in Banff, asked Recap if he would drive her out of town for awhile. She had to get away from writing, from coming back at things so. She needed to see some prairie. They drove the old highway into the Stoney reserve. He looked at her slim edgy body, a fragility turned inside-out amounting to strength, a field of presence. Her voice low and slow with a hint of husky, commanding response. Yet she joked and teased and lit up a cigarette. Yes the first time ever in his new vehicle he admitted to her. She pleaded her case with a sly chuckle but agreed they should put the windows down.

Recap: the Treaty Number Seven book Walter had a hand in but which mostly presented the recording of the elders' and others' own oral accounts of what was handed down of what happened in the fateful 1870s. He remembered that three bands of Stoneys from three different regions were given only this one Morley reserve. Something to do with McDougal's convenience and rewards.

"Buffalo" she exclaimed when they passed the sign indicating the preserve. So they followed the next signs, the alienated, non-indexical ones, needless to say. On the dirt road the dust came in and turned with the smoke. He slowed down and she finished her cigarette and he touched blindly the windows up. The road forked and they hesitated, then chose, and then their arm of the fork forked but they found their way to the south in the lee of a foothill topped with brush and rock, pulled up to the fence and got out. The air was fresh in the July still light evening. Her long summer dress billowed slightly and then clung to her legs in the breeze and she just stood grinning and humming.

Or was it a kind of diminished keening he heard? But she was so happy to feast her eyes on the herd. Only a remnant of the long, not so long ago ones, but certainly bigger than any he'd ever seen. Various sized groups, and individuals set off, calves with their mothers and young ones frolicking, mock butting each other. A strange sound, and a half pint galloping over to an adult. It seemed every phase of development was there. In captivity with assured feed an ironic then, planned parenthood seemed to be out of the question. But you could see continuous evolution, if you sorted out the random selection.

Driving back toward the mountains, darker now in the still bright sundown sky, they met two teenaged girls on the dirt road who stole looks at them, and they stole back. Slight smiles crept over their Stoney faces! He and she drove on still half-retracting their looking and in this land above the flats they seemed almost not to know where to land their vision, or lack of, more impossibly. Through the reserve town of Morley heading to the Trans Canada uncaptivated people turned and saw them.

He told her about the Calgary judge who'd put over a domestic assault case pending a general investigation into a string of cases and alleged corruption in the band council. Recap introduced it clumsily, implicating himself he felt at the level of tone or perspective however handled. Her voice rose and raced a bit and in careful grammar judged back all these judgements coming down. With her size and cigarette and quavering force of address he was somehow reminded of Sheila Watson, her allegory of the disappearing of the black shiny dogs, bone by bone, claw by claw, into the prior prairie. They drove faster down the numbing number one and he said nothing till she said something that restored him back to before the story just told. They arrived in calm and silence at the walk winding through the kept fir trees below Lloyd Hall. There seemed no right thing to do and they looked at one another and smiled and said good-bye.

Tunnel (Vision) Mountain: Another Woman Spotting

Coming into his own now, huffing comfortably up and around the switchbacks, pacing and projecting the long traverses, the final steep climb with one little hook back up the other way again, around a corner and then the distorted last little big vista before the last long traverse to the lower end of the ridge, he ignored all the useless haunting views back across the valley, Sulphur and up the valley highway-wise toward Lake Louise. His eyes were getting stiffer he meta-recognized again as he looked ahead and met a tall athletic woman walking down toward him. He knew who she was, the one he saw cycling or not but in cycling duds all the time.

In some un-detailed way he was sure of her and could see her smiling but looked down because her face wouldn't come defined and he thought in a rarefied mood increment it rude to recognize her yet. When he could be sure, he looked up and noticed her smile becoming more tentative as she nevertheless said hello. In harmony with his overbalance on the incline of mountain he smiled enough too much and intoned enough familiarity to betray he thought a delayed and long simmering reaction to her sudden but natural-feeling smile and first hello in the bookstore weeks before. He remembered seeing her in the coffee bar in the summer shortly after the first time he'd noticed her. He had been behind at an angle and marvelled at the grace of her long neck and finally when she left he had feasted albeit furtively on the animal grace descended into the rest of her now erect and moving body.

At the Rundle end of the ridge he stopped and turned back as was his habit now in perhaps over-consideration of his dog in light of the cliffs, the deceptive gulf to the trick trickle of river and miniature golf course. He did however double take the view down to the roofs of the Banff Centre buildings and to the bridged river and over to Sulphur and to the rest of the valley.* And yet again as he descended with a vague sense of reward he grew absent-minded with a feeling of parachute lift and the expansive valley came into being and being his, so particular, even as a mood dissolved the fix on anything.

Coffee

Dr. Rock sat down, his stolid body thudding into the chair, and dismissed what Recap was reading in the newspaper. His latest book read was rolled up in his head and he wanted to unroll it into another part of his brain or out and back again, independent within his repertoire. Or was he filing some kind of precedent or pre-figure in Recap's head for backing up some future argument thereby made easier in such involuntarily collaborative and ceded memory.

Rock had been reading the nineteenth century diaries of young North West Mounted Policemen and was excited by the good writing of the young recruits in such raw

---

*Taken by this picture, as it were, with futility he invited distraction and yet by the very slipped-in and slept-in underwriting remained removed within the campy frame.

survival conditions. He went on about Jerry Potts. Actually fairly quickly for these recitals Recap got into the rolling out and mentioned the Treaty Number Seven book he'd been reading in the context of heroizing the police. How even McLeod, who'd won the trust of the Blackfoot, in the end betrayed them, had been merely paternal till the treaty got signed and the government got what it wanted.

Rock began to laugh as he conjured up a sympathetic picture of Potts. Recap butted in with how the oral historian elders had said, time and again, that, but for the odd word, Potts couldn't speak Blackfoot and that at Blackfoot Crossing it was obvious to everyone that he was drunk over the three days to the eventual signing. He'd been a poor translator and even poorer and selective in attending to what various chiefs were saying. In fact a lot of what was said he never recorded, Recap continued. The government terms were already written down before the historic meeting and he was ill equipped to understand the Queen's English in such convoluted legalese. So for instance the First Peoples were never given explanations of what ceding land meant. Recap encapsulated "they held out grass and said the white people could take that under the right arrangements; they held out dirt and proclaimed this could not be owned by anyone".

Rock rolled with this and lifted the view to a contemporary scene, a lecture he'd attended at the Centre. An RCMP constable had talked about the nature of cults, had given a criteria in point form for how to spot them. Rock said he considered the points one by one and came to the mounting certainty the Mounties perfectly constituted a cult. Recap laughed somewhat hypothetically at the irony,

Rock not giving him the complete list of points though more than he himself was usually able to give in like cases of remembered ironies that go a little flat without the bubble and burst of the specifics. The idea and Rock's own dominating laugh were enough though.

Recap: Rock laughing quoting his own laughing into laughing again when he arrived at the coffee bar one day. It was at one of those times when Recap thought Rock a little hardened by it all, by whatever processes in his past, by the nature of Rock. A new, more hapless Rock, nay helpless-with-cosmic-stitches Rock, quickly filled him in on his latest misadventure. He had gotten a rather intrusive, and American, Recap noted, get well card for a close friend who regularly ended up in hospital with an incurable but so far quite serviceable disease. The card proposed the patient was screaming now but would be more when he got the bill. When the card was opened an energetic cry was generated. Before he was able to sign it and take it to his friend the friend died. Recap remembered Rock had carried the news strangely that day. He sat down quite usually at the table where Playcefire and Recap had been talking. He let them go on and then talked about other news for quite a while before he told them of the death.

Rock had thrown the card in the garbage and then later had dumped the garbage in the dumpster in the alley and went on down town to run various errands. In the late afternoon he came back down the alley toward the big garbage bin where curiously a couple of police cars and a fire truck with lights flashing were parked. Apparently the card had slid out of the garbage within the garbage and had opened. Someone had heard the muffled cry and called the police. Of course they thought someone had discarded a baby. Recap said he knew poets who would give their eyeteeth for such a story, a realism in touch with its own folds of irony and allegory. Rock's wife had declared she couldn't even let him out of the house without chaos descending about him.

Fenland

By the time Jon died, Recap had settled upon this forest refuge, timeless even as one by one new trees fell into the fen, and once again within the famous resort he resorted to the easy trail, arrived at the beginning of the loop and began to pace it off. Every hundred paces he folded a finger back on the glove he had removed and when that one was done he started on the other glove. He was holding a couple of fingerless fingers when, as happened more often then than lately, he met the Jackie O look-alike* walking, listing to one side, trying to restrain her huge "so dominant" rottweiler bitch, which had once attacked his Lab who now treaded cautiously and with the hair on her back standing up. Recap had given up trying to talk to her much anymore and hardly nodded as he passed counting to himself. Though he didn't give up looking at her long legs and her Jackie O features, her black tights and black top she always wore even when he saw her, rarely, in the coffee bar.

Playcefire, his usually piercing eyes dilating to a fool's mock despair, had decided to start running one day even though he had a bad back. The back seemed none the worse for wear when he ran now so he thought he'd better

---

* (one of the many temptresses from the town who, unwittingly or not he could never be sure, teased him)

get at it. Recap had taken over a year off from running till he'd learned from the doctor he had "theatre knees" (trouble keeping his knees tucked in) from biased quad development, and had then figured out how to correct them. But he'd been running a mile or so three or four days a week for quite awhile when Playcefire came out with him the day that lead a few more days later to Recap's gloved count-recount. Playcefire wasn't sure he wanted to run right around the loop the first day and so ran counter clockwise with the idea he would at least turn around when he met Recap and probably before.

Recap had said the bridge over Echo creek to the Vermillion Lakes road was pretty well halfway. And so when he reached the bridge he was surprised to see Playcefire already thirty or forty yards back from the bridge heading for home. Recap picked up what he already thought was a pretty good pace and then where the path widened and turned away from the creek through the tall spruce trees, lungs burning, he caught and overtook him, and was glad under the anxiety of competition for the enforced exercise.

When Recap reached the bridge with his second glove almost fingerless he started over again counting Playcefire's half. He either ran or walked the trail almost every day. Counting was no labour but kind of fun, barely diminishing the vast and redundant wandering one's mind did during these regular, familiar walks. The wandering simply retreated a bit as though a shadowing wolf had moved deeper into the forest. On the next day he decided to time running the respective halves and ended up timing the greater round trip, ie from the cabin in town and then back, and also once he was doing it and "it" wouldn't stop he timed all the segments, from the road into the forest to the beginning of the loop, this at a walk, and from the cabin to the road where that segment to the loop began.

He didn't feed all this information back to Playcefire but he did relate to him, a bit sheepishly, though he lifted the sheepishness into his own pre-empting parody, the differences in the halves. Playcefire's half was a good two hundred paces shorter. He thought innocently enough that Playcefire would not be unpleased to hear this scientific nail-down. Of course the telling and the transparent transparent telling on himself didn't work. Rock and Playcefire jumped on him mercilessly. They went overboard to Recap's mind, had him putting up big signs with distances noted, perhaps traffic lights and scoreboards. Recap protested it was just a matter of being a legend in his own mind not on some map.

Kidding aside something was changing in the nature of his friendship with Playcefire. Recap knew he'd been held up as some kind of model, unrealistically and at times he thought as a screen for some other more complex and screwy projection.* Now he felt he was being seen as an untimely reminder, as an obstacle and as eccentric and feckless according to an idea of norm Playcefire more and more hewed to. Recap thought of their psychologically complex discussions and arguments about money. Once Recap, Polonius-like, had simply stuck to the old "wisdom"

---

* (especially since Playcefire was more the victim of his own "fierytail" then and Recap's pontifications were counterpointed by the darkness of drunken tains in/out on the town)

of keeping money and friendship apart. Now he thought this unquestioned separation a touch abstract. And although the intertwining was still risky, there was something exemptingly special case about Playcefire's mixing them.

After a broken marriage Playcefire was progressing through various motives and stages of being a parent, till a kind of equilibrium of the blood love from the beginning was being reached with the tough love now, a forever working out. He lived under the arch of the impossibility now of ever seeing his own real parents. An arch beginning somewhere prior to him and hanging over him in incompletion. Only now with this new resting and arresting love for his children could he extract that pot of gold which had been so far the gulf between his unknown parents and his actual ground, which had been his brilliant, heart-of-the-matter mastery of the godless age, or slave world, the ironic pragmatism of effective worldly substitution with its built-in delay of disillusion, built on the split of demand and supply within the initial and the inertial human individual endlessly rolling over and then recapping itself.

The pot of gold, perfect standard for the measureless measure. The untouchable cache always cashing in or out with indifferent difference from itself. The parallel world of hearth was an inch away from this endless touring of the inventory, and the thought-experiment gold played the mirror going faster than the light of its glitter.* Recap

---

*The inventory played the Turing test turned back on the human and, by passing the buck, added up, in this race to the black gold, to passing the essentially deficit-human-as-passing-for-human, ie in its endless cheap supply of itself it remained hidden and worked its effective false magic.

thought of the tourists touched down, willing to be beheld in profile, in single file, in filling out general forms fallen to the giddy absurdity of good times. The drop dead looks from being in the shoes of the visitors were priceless, the fine waste of an abyss the mountain heights brokered.

They were the slaves who held the uncheatable answers, who recognized everything in their unmastery, whether or not they knew it through to a last man or judgement. Playcefire had said to Recap, to put them on an equal footing, that he too, as a businessman in Banff, was a farmer. In the hit and myth of perspective he extended his hand to the street and said that there was his crop strolling to the harvest.

Outside the loop the more he was in it, timeless in the Fenland as it were, Recap went around again and met an English woman. She in fact stopped him and asked him which way it was back to Banff. She knew she was on her second loop because things were starting to look familiar. Recap told her to keep going and when she reached the next fork to take the "right path, ie the path on the right". Continuing on himself he passed the halfway bridge and then the next bridge over to the parking lot. As he neared the beginning fork he saw again the young English woman with a good start on her third round.

Recap thought of Al Purdy going back to his early years to the time he got lost in the bush in Ontario going around in more desperate circles than one could ever manage in this noise sponge, saturated with muffled motor and tire whine, and regularly stepped on by trains signing horn-whistle on top of the clickedy-clack and Doppler rhythm roar. He set her right again and said under his breath "I guess you're finding it a little too Purdy in here".*

Jon in the Underworld

Jon moved away from the windows and sat behind the table that was not completely emerged from the trees it had been. His expressive, swarthy face changed suddenly, cheeks and lips producing an equine sound as he coughed from a rhetorically hoarse throat to interrupt the noise that was a silence so to turn attention into a returning authority. His glasses were as owl's eyes. Enigmatically he intoned in his readerly voice "it's the wide open possibilities" to nothing in particular. Recap had been thinking of the earlier times when he sat here while Jon held forth on some worked up topic, that week's *Crag and Canyon* column or a theme he was exploring for a poem. As Jon's topic rose out of his blacked-out psyche and soared as though a broadcast, Recap felt frozen and restless in his own actuality, reduced to a tain occluded from its double, the tain that would create the wormhole to his own kind of emergent and evanescent light. "The actualities are choking everything out" he said in reply in the here and now of the underworld. He thought of the Cascade Plaza Jon lived

---

* Recap considered how a going over again jumps you up to form, to the knowing that is the buoyant negative. That to some degree to be stuck in the impossible content is to the same degree a glory. The immediate, usually inhabited and negated by the mediate (of course the reverse moment also occurs), somehow, for this accidental tourist, ground any larger fractal down into a set's complete incompleteness, precluding the economy and rest and vista she could have otherwise been set up with, and without zooming off to a bad infinity.

long enough to see and condemn and of all the busy new construction since.

He told Jon about how when he first came to Banff Jon's telling discourse used to send him back so much there was nothing to say but everything, and the reasons were two and related. Recap had been in his moment of expanding creativity, with the implicit metaphor of big bang — Gell-Mann claiming it had been one of those pejorative phrases that went over to the other side and never looked back, something like how "politically correct" went from recognition of a tension in the left over to the right as a wholesale undialectical negative — onward to expansion.*

Jon's studied knowledges and formal dialogues cum monologues in coffee shops, and in the taverns, good havens, were at times a tad demanding and anyway amiss to Recap's mind, primarily, "primarily" underlined, because of the clash of the first, seed world and the old world

---

* Jon jumped off his beloved mountains to cosmogony with relative ease. Recap was more inclined to think of seed in expressing the position or *moment* from which one dissolves the world and then births it out again as some fuzzy clone out in the sticks, ie from any old cell or synecdoche, but all important was the synecdochic action presupposed, and of course the most thorough re-creation would converge to the creation, thought to be dead, in the sense of deadly present, in its extant tracks, but of course never more than partially present in this less-is-more, unconscious re-creation, immediately, as opposed to mediately unconscious through futile, hyper-conscious re-creation. This obsessive self-world creation crowded out or demolished and cleared away the other factored-out and fallen-into-line world. Recap still believed this a true moment, if not the truer first moment, but a moment that can fall into a vacuum if uncorrected by the objective world which is of course recognized as frozen but also as of fluid origin and therefore of fluid possibilities.

observed, in the two senses, of a rule or custom followed, and of "perceived".*

No prisoners are taken, no big base maintained and everything is hush hush. That is, Recap had nothing saved to say in these objective discussions. The irony the other way is that the objective justice done to the world is done with the action of a giant rollover into a parallel world holding company, a world of knowledges both detached and, here's the irony back across the irony, also commingled with its life-giving, life-lifted samples, the otherwise re-topologized, almost zero sum, lyric intensities, the tains that refuse their obvious recaps.

Recap pondered the newer yet emerging irony of his own words now said through Jon's silence and silhouette, as Jon had moved back to sit in front of the light from the latticed window. Of course alongside the knowledges Jon loved the local lore and the essential stories. Recap at first had a hard time believing that this essentiality lived in Jon's mind, relative essentiality albeit. But then as the years went by Recap noticed one by one those around him who had been here any length of time, and not referring to the pyramiding gorby** syndrome, were becoming transformed. All the non-literary types too, perhaps especially these, were becoming characters, alas bottom up literary types.

At first they were objects of benign condescension, and we're not talking the heroic characters of the outfitting

---

* And incidentally because this first fight against the world is guerrilla warfare the world is, with some irony and *saving grace*, Wittgenstein be warmed, left as it is, *mutatus mutandi* , in this re-topologizing lyric converging to a tain state.

** ("Gorby†" being the term for tourists or recent arrivals)
  † Origin obscure.

and guiding era to whom Jon didn't condescend, though one must remember him switching his historical interest to the women, Mary T. S. Schaffer, Alma Mills for instance, and finally reserving hero status for the animals, the moose as touched by Carl Rungius. Recap wondered about definitions here, much like he wondered about the consistency of Jon's eccentric centrism tangent unto "geology is destiny", proclaiming reassurance in the fact that these mountains would be here long after mere man, a sentiment[?] possibly derived from or reaffirmed in Levi-Strauss' *Triste Tropiques* which Jon so admired.

Recap's intuitive unease triggered the memory of Murray Bookchin•'s doubts about the overthrowing of humanist presumptions with, again, hard-earned humanist values or assumptions, the universal solvent, as it were, meets the universal container. Once out on the farm, ensconced in the silent eye of his blaring diesel and in an ignorant-of-its-force moment, he had heard on the radio Jon declare that there were forces out there that would "pounce upon this tender body [ie the wilderness] like a sabre tooth tiger". Recap laughed out loud on the prairie at Jon's unhappy metaphor, blessing "the forces out there" [ie the developers] with something more feral, evolutionarily speaking, than the present day wilderness. But such was Jon's excess, his wildness.

In time these town characters were a solace to Jon and if they would stand or sit down and talk he would take

---

• The anarchist theorist who criticized the bio-centrists who were on the same slide as the anarchists away from the central centrality but who had slid too far out in Bookchin's books.

them as they were and talked only as a listener talks. He was an author in search of a character, sometimes for his own.* Recap would give anything now for the parallel world that was the world, not Jon in search of character, for he had surely at*tain*ed that fate, but Jon as author of the parallel, the researcher, the recapitulator, mountain retreater, his clearing out and clearing up. The clearing of the air, the negative that knowledge needs. Recap would give anything for the unforgiving hardness of Jon's ambition, for his restless mind and his last words as the challenge of the route to the roots, the intimations of fossils on the tops of mountains.

Recap: in the wildman winter of '72 they had been ahead of their time. Bruce had just been divorced so they invited Jon over for a stag supper on Bow Avenue one evening. After supper with no dessert and no conscience or foreknowledge of a just desert, Recap vacantly sat down in the desert that was a breakfast room, no mess, no furniture, reflection of Bruce's obsession with "clearing the table",** sort of a Susan Sontag debriefing à la her closet*** living in Paris.

---

* And this is as human as it gets: character as responsible moral actor and character as taken into legend, not at bottom a matter of status but the willing sacrifice out of life's negative and blind safety, ie to be flung into the centres at the periphery as contingent examples of one, ani-mating the holes that are our memories emptying into the present. Those are characters that were our wasted and puritan attentions.

** See the etymology of "dessert".

*** The literal meaning, no figurative pun, pace (or peace!) Pagliat.

† Means straw. Is Camille an all-pupose scarecrow protecting the out*lying* fields of stuff we're made of, or one of those dolls maintaining, like W. Lewis, the awful vacuum all interiority vanishes in?

Recap had once rescued a box of assorted, very good books that some hip-era sojourner had left behind. Actually the sojourner, a rugged college wrestler from the States and avid Northern Canadian outdoorsman, was the romantic-idealist son of an executive high in the Coca Cola empire. Bruce had been about to chuck them in his efforts toward degree zero house.

Suddenly Bruce's immaculate conception, which could almost do without a house, materialized. He caught Recap off guard with a dirty, well a half-clean trick. He poured the soapy dishwater from the spaghetti pot down over his long hair, his shirt and into his crotch and over the rest of his pants. The way through misery is to compound it and so Recap arose, like the drunk that fills the hole in everybody's mind, walked out into the twenty below air and two feet of fresh snow, soaked to his shoeless, rubberless, rudderless stocking feet. He ran down the alley onto the street and came to a crisis in logic, at least that was the way Jon put it and what Jon most liked to emphasize in his later re-tellings.

More impressive by far in filling this hole, in fulfilling this role, would be to walk, take as long as possible against wanting urgently to return to register the impression. Freezing to death seemed minor compared to the empty communion with and diffusion to the expanding stars. He was dying to get back and be reduced to a presence reduced in turn to the drama of being stopped short, to being an opacity for others' projections, which of course in his absence he fulfilled better than ever he could by going back. In wanting to enjoy their enjoyment he would cross himself, quite unlike Christ, rather as fully and foolishly, if fatefully incomplete, human, a reflection trying to cover its backside, confused with it.

Finally he walked in the front door with stiff, but still wet, clothes, whereupon he stripped completely and continued on out the back door again. Logic was slow to catch on or up as he rioted into a run and then remembered to meander and then once again, in a slow motion, swaggered in the front door. So effective was this compounding it leaped into Bruce's sense of Camus' judge-penitent logic. He also stripped down and ventured into the January night.

Hysterical to stave off hysteria, in time he too scrambled through the front door. They laughed pretty hard a while longer and then looked at Jon who was laughing even harder. The unspoken logic was palpable as Jon's pumped-plump face, the one someone called Frank Mahovlich narrow, fell and he penitently slipped off his shoes and then the rest that followed, according to the distinct but restless logic. He pushed open the back door, paused heroically on the icy stoop, descended like some kind of Olympian, and then, gracefully and tragically, fell like a tree, face into the snow. After rolling over he flapped his arms and legs and of course one-upped them with an elegant angel.

For months after, they competed in the sharing of this shared experience. Months after still, it was revealed that Catharine's secretary had happened to see everything from behind the garage where she'd parked her happenstance, a word Jon would have used. Jon especially enjoyed this one-upwomanship. Her only remark was that she'd wanted to participate (compounding never ends) but felt she'd have corrupted the innocence. Probably they wouldn't have been above damning the innocence. Double negative subjunctive shivered into the warmth that gave them all away. The core of mock misery turned out — to be *on them*, discrete butts *and* continuous underwriters.

Jon was very formal about many things. Their respective names. About handing themselves over to authorship, especially how this rolls over into the unintentional, express amusement of the impressionable limit, the limitless muse happening by. One of his remarkable gifts *is*, his hearty, last laugh from the wings. The unflappable frame, Recap thought, that freezes and so frees us. The unmoved remark that lifts the discussion with all the nerve of Minerva's owl, its rollover of innocence and experience.

Jostle Again

Recap pushed onto the sidewalk on Banff Avenue from the parking lot and found himself to be walking through a giant wheat field, well at least as high as a good crop of rye.* The heads looked him in the eye as though he were the grim reaper bringing everybody down. Recap didn't feel all that grim but he kept a straight, introspective face to keep up appearances, ie so not to be caught as a lost soul or as what's left when the soul's flown, a lost body, though that of course was what he would rather have been, to be finding himself lost, soul not upset but taken aback and body newly quaint with its little needs, not desires, in this camped-up base.

But he wasn't introspecting in the way he probably would have been were it not for the stand of nicely ripe

---

* Had Playcefire's metaphor gone awry in some perverse magic [realism]?

spring wheat. He could barely see the shops and restaurants for the heads leaning with plump, good bushel weight seed. It was all pretty familiar given his years of conditioning as a tied to the land, dyed in the wool farmer. The farm reality died abruptly in October and went underground but could be called up anytime. The farm sector reality, the ground's nose in the know, was absorbed in elliptical sun-circling, a same eating same, even say any yearly anomaly, so that only weeks after completion of harvest when people asked him how it had gone he often couldn't tell them.

He was embarrassed about this and so would make a point of memorizing the complexion of the just past season, even though of course he ate and slept and dreamt each invigorating, labouring day. Increment by increment as the crop came down, came in, the season was sculpted into the next season and, as quartered earth time, cooperated in washing out the division just as it washed out the crop colours.*

The memory though of the specific just past season was outrightly consumed by the archetype. This process was universal with farmers and with the general populace, though perhaps especially with farmers and this "especially" even though or perhaps especially again in light of the death of dark, and of unseasonable seasons.** Of course the rescinding of memory occurred as lethally in the

---

* And yet somehow a degree-by-degree boiled frog leapfrogged free and the present cooked itself as much by opposable seasoning as by its own raw resistance.

** Rising out of this absorption of course are the clipboard field plans and record-keeping. And one doesn't forget the year the bank foreclosed or even just sent the sheriff around. And yet that ideal erasure is fostered by the labouring vegetable world echoing the great celestial circle.

routinizing cities, but Recap left this for another day to reconsider.

Was he extreme in this farming out his farming to the dark side of his hemispheric brain, or more ideally now and slightly out of fashion, to the workers of his subconscious? In fact this way was the way of myth, not modern scientifically attended to myth nor as parodied religion that half works, and then indeed fulfills the prophecy pretended to, nor as adventitiously literary nor even as generatively literary, though this gets closer. But myth as the trick of life in life, trick because it is otherwise death in life, that myth of modern deracination or, on the other hand, beheadedness, take your pick, as another useless choice.*

That is, the life within life emerged into being greater than its matrix. Recap's farming lessons amounted to a lessening of life, ie he went to sleep in the matrix. It was more like walking into a movie or magic realism. He wasn't always dangerous, mostly he just had to be turned around from time to time, so that his liabilities could be gotten around. His abilities lay in enduring the long hours of round and round the field. And here we must admit the situation was not as pure as implied. Recap was bifurcated. His surplus value was not reinvested in farm know-how but spent on history comprehensions, history assaults, history

---

*This life-in-life process must be a virtue-involving Alasdair McIntyre "practice", must be in fact according to his criteria, must in fact be deep and rich in order to absorb one drastically enough to be a life reborn. And here's where something went wrong for Recap when he went myth or, as a myth, this sense worked for here of concrete, ie whole, in Hegelian terms, action. A proper farmer was historical, ie he remembered the yearly variations as not just lessons, though that of course, but also as good anecdote, fair enough, and maybe yet to yield a lesson. And then the lessons yielded a life.

punctures. Insofar as the farming task at hand never went smoothly, involved breakdowns and vicissitudes of field and weather conditions, his over and above the call of duty reveries often themselves got punctured back.

In other words breakdowns, he'd often Heideggerianly proclaimed, inserted you into the primary process of a practice as actually being practiced. The break, with a twist, after a clearing negative, became the lid you pulled down when you submerged into the machine and the task, as these were still stubbed by and stubbornly governed by the natural ground. Of course this awakening was not always as dramatic as a breakdown and Recap had been known to cuss same. All it took was the usual flicker of body tonus and the balance of nature's unforgiving consistency of fluttering irritants in the sky, and the usual resistance of the rough-in-the-diamonds hard copy of the land. This to tune him into the video Plato'd banished him to. But there in Banff he was stuck in the absurdity of wheat on the street, accelerating in the heavy curve of Playcefire's words.

Hegel's Cows

Drop up, to Banff, vacation heaven. In 1971 Recap went to heaven. At*tain*ed heaven? As if you ever could, and considering Spinoza's caveat on supereminence, negative theology etc. Heaven attained, you would lose the vault and Recap would have his work cut for him. But of course! Here would be clearing house indeed, a clean slate crossroads. In heaven there would be no heaven, no roof, ie Recap would have to *do*, even as Tain would leave his mark re, ie, the slate.

Recap had vacated the prairie. Was not "here" so much as not there. Camping it up with the "little Egyptian bump,"• humans aping humans, avoiding the fire in the rock. Recognition is over (above, again) and after itself, leaves the back door open to inflation and diminishing returns. And then the earth urn is owed the infinite *kindness of strange*. Camping *as*: enjoyment through the back door, make that backwoods. Hardship buoyantly displaced. Chopping wood as likely: dosing: REM ember, cliché cooked up into Ra archetype.

1994: Recap's topsy-turvy life, as Tain on the street by night and as Recap underground by night redoubled into day, was coming to a watershed, well a cabin, with five deluxe windows where light graded light and instances of Tain returned in elusive, quick change artistry. He moved out of his old house. A few months later, somehow, they tore down his basement suite. Later again in his new bed one morning he felt periodic vibrations in the springs. On the way to the high school community gym he saw the pile driver planted firmly in the corner pounding the bedrock where he used to sleep.

Out of the fire into a cabin — now he was cooking, right/downtown. Twenty-seven years in Banff and he was saluting drugstore cowboys but wouldn't hug an elk, become a tree or even a Daphne. Turning on his heel he created shade with his hand, on faith reckoned the sun's dark spots, gravi*tains* from unattainable Beatrice. And

---

• A financial term Recap associated with the Reichmanns, derived from a belly dancer's movement but applied to takeovers in which the assets of the target company are moved to become a piece of the action in its own acquisition.

between total order and total disorder was the complexity that reigned and healed.

Patrick Lane out on the prairie masturbating, putting his seed into a wheat field. Pathetic phallus he. Kroetsch the old buffalo, as Marty and Suknaski used to call him, fell in love with a curvaceous rock as a boy going to church. Dream rub.

Recap looked out the windows of his cabin, mountains gal-orious. The graduality of distance kinked into sublime leap. Hegel would have called these folds, or *per saltum* breaks, a metaphor for the transition of bad into good infinity. The land standing up and showing itself to itself, well as if to say, Por-ridge Purdy, look at me! Mountains to Al were the colour of Monarch cereal (that moniker in the poem coloured by the coincidental meaning).

Gym

Recap hit the mountain with his left arm tucked into his side instead of extended to break his fall, a learned reflex after the many years of either sore or tender elbows from pushing and pulling weights. He almost cracked a rib but was only aware at the time that his breath was no longer his, ie knocked out of him. Never body-check a mountain. Even a little one like Tunnel. It was early spring and most of the accumulated snow had melted from the path but it had turned cold again and hard ice patches had formed and then a light snow had dusted them.

Halfway down the mountain he knelt on the path letting out an eerie dry hiss from his lungs. The usual panic rose to the outer edges of his mind, here contracting quickly to the grip that he was and that somehow had him in it. The retriever raced back to his animal squeaks and jumped on him and licked him. Finally breath again and then the aching rib and muscles in his side and around his back kicked in. He walked gingerly the rest of the way down in the cold cloudy day, the kind of day he most liked to, more than survive, thrive in, by a funny kind of logic that both accepted and rejected its presence.

He could barely get out of bed the next day and only by a hard won special technique that involved putting one hand over his head to the wall at the head of the bed and simultaneously hooking the back of his foot on the edge of the mattress. Nevertheless he went to the gym and somehow got down on the bench and was able to lift the barbells off the uprights and bring them to his chest. He forgot the pain after the first rep but then couldn't get off the bench without Brunt's helping hand. On subsequent days he managed to do most things, but was especially not able to do squats. Though in lieu of, the leg press machine served him well.

At some point here, a few years after Jon's death, Brunt had lost his weight belt and one day Recap said he was pretty sure he knew who had stolen it. It was some guy obviously just starting out, young and quite slight but kind of quirky and fierce in a smouldering but not disagreeable way. In fact Recap had been struck by him, that toughness incongruously thrown together with an innocuous looking body and had enjoyed talking to him. He'd been friendly but definitely was not one of those guys who talked more than they lifted. He talked about what he'd once been able to do, sure enough, and talked about what he had to work on and was pretty gritty about getting on with it.

How easy for impressions to shift. On the strength of his wearing a weight belt like Brunt's, after he'd said he needed one, Recap quickly turned a perceived quirkiness into a crookedness. He had to tell Brunt what he figured. Brunt, dedicated lifter, working out like clockwork, was not in the least upset. Although Recap had known, for all the focus, that he had a good sense of humour. And from whence did it come? That space of being, Recap thought, freed up through tying oneself down.

And perhaps that inevitable darker side, the cruel roots of humour coming into bloom here specifically from the righteousness of the disciplined body in relation to the lassitude and dilapidation of others. Yet these roots were just as likely to yield the reflexive feeling of self futility, cruel roots indeed. A square one kind of logic with many slippery moments. Recap often thought that the base line of weights was a process of taking control of the normal mood swings, deliberately depressing oneself, ie pressing weights, bowing a line down so that it would spring back, the daily climbing back to square one as tri-oomph.

Brunt, who from a distance looked even bigger than he was because of excellent proportions, had a well-defined jaw, not square but rather like Superman's, smiled beatifically, and had lately expounded a kind of eastern philosophy, said that there were bigger things to worry about than a missing weight belt, say like marriage problems. He talked a bit more and Recap learned after all this time that Brunt, much younger than he but well into his thirties, had been married and was the father of a girl he was not allowed to see. Recap thought of 'roid rages, thought of the show biz life of a wrestler. He didn't know what to think. And they fell to going with the energy and managing their raging, albeit conditioned, hormones.

He wasn't necessarily interested in the content of Brunt's new found philosophy but he was interested in the step back from his detailed awareness of nutrition and knowledge of body, muscles, blood, nerves, dynamic loops etc. With a twist, he was nerding to a body of knowledge, into and out of the tain of the mirror. For in the opacity there was the emergent light of types, levels and their numbered relations, the implicit acknowledgement of givens if not unknowns, freed-up and freeing up. Recap liked this new body builder who was defining himself out of the *mere* definition of muscle.

Then another day Recap walked into the gym and the quirky guy was doing squats, what he said he couldn't do till he got a belt. He had a belt alright. There was Brunt with a belt too. Before Recap could say anything Brunt laughed and said he had found his at home. Recap redefined quirky as quickly as his next breath. Quirky enough himself, through a kind of restitution action that allowed him to make these drastic judgements about people, he presumptuously confessed to the guy that he had branded him a thief, told him as a kind of joke they might embrace, a sort of phantom third party or trust fund in which they could place a limited and tentative back-to-square-one friendship.

Hegel's Cows

Wilderness, interpellated creature of civilization. Mountain peak, the uninhabitable, teasing Aristotle out of the meanest impossible goal and into his level best activity, the recapitulation of what he knew, endless descent into the valley where the Plateau of general ideas caved in to the times stood on their heads, ie where balloons grow out of pins, which means, at a guess, the resultant mean between time and eternity is mixed up, as in both crazy and cooked, as can be seen in the fact that it takes some shade of clock face to contemplate Plato facing faceless eternity.

Propping God up to ferocity in a feral city we want the vague hearth in, defying, defining. Hegel said the more Spirit withdraws into itself the more it is drawn out to become its other/Nature. But still, how so consummate or hug? Tim Lilburn has it — beheld by an animal. Re the grizzly: Marty drew near, roughly defined as vicarious horse fear, another example of the absolute's triune pornography*.

Bottom up: John Glassco remembered Schopenhauer saying the conscious falling rock would will itself to fall and would be right. Hegel said it was Leibniz and nuts, ie the conscious falling rock would be something else.

---

* Towards a general theory by way of, say, McLuhan's pornography as any too-much-of-a-page-turner and then Baudrillard's meditation on science as huge blind-alley detour of endless unveiling, cut off from the vertex that would see its whole thrust is but and better a gesture cum synecdoche. From another side, the difficulties of fallen-ness and finitude would be dramatized were blind-folded God to be conveyed on a regular flight to Hawaii. At the shucking of clichés, grass skirts etc, and then at the superconducted removal of the divine scales, a cosmic blind would roll up catastrophically, taking its window with it. The special theory of porn per se regards an innocence, misguided albeit, at play in the fallen male, his futile implication in the demanding part that would see it, and see it one again, stand for the [w]hole†, folded in on itself with Leibniz. And may the sacred and profane be twisted through the constant, pivotal psychology.

† Substitutes are in order re flooding same, eg finger in the dyke.

Before reading Sharon Butala's dwelling on dwelling Recap read only an excerpt, and therefore of course dropped in as an expert to behold her dropped-off Peter, her green and not green, con-*vert*-ing among constellated cattle, catalyst husband. But there! Recap slept, with no wife/writer to behold him, over the hill in the diesel cab, his head on a plastic bag on the steering wheel. At supper he went in with red Safeway letters mirror-assed to his forehead. Ecce homo.

Butala's man sleeping into nature, perchance to rub the wrong way, out. In-a-sense the dream descends to the top of the morning, symptom of the asymptote. The rest is restitution in a cloud, a bottom up.

Every Milky Way star is a crème de la crème retreat. To be in and pore over the Big Pitcher — Dipper, whatever. Peirce said perception is always hypothetical, sensation its limit. To go beyond is to dream back, or to find the body, incarnated perception, evolution's recent hypothesis, full blown animal, and in one leap an origin is — avoided. The species already uppity. Our *end*? Up in the air. Alter conditions and the walking hunch could stiffen to a stage, walk off itself. But O from the pataphysical future see back the Kantian wood, the crooked tower — the unbelievable vision!

Bar in the Underworld

Recap stood off to one side next to a stack of 2x4s while his friend Mel chatted with his new landlord. The carpenters were finished for the day, long now into night. There were piles of dust and old plaster around the huge room. The ceiling panels had been removed and the air ducts and wiring were exposed. They would call it "Two Crows" and then, within a few months, the "Wolf Street Café", rehearsing the rapid name changes that otherwise went with the turn-over of businesses (riming that of customers, albeit more slowly) in Banff.

Recap: the year, around '76 or '77, the place, Ticino's, was the night spot to be at after the regular bars closed. In fact everyone started leaving the bar early so to beat the line-up. A year earlier it had been the Grizzly House that had had the dance floor and disco music that everyone fought line-ups over. Once Tain had come to this former here so early the place was practically empty and he hardly even had a buzz on. That was the month he had first met the capital Her. So he was pre-dazzled and nervous as he sat there ungodly and ungodly early for the disco action. He was feeling a little transparent and telegraphic but hung in and braced himself. But then she glided into view.

He'd begun to think it might be her night off. She was wearing a low-cut floor-length red velvet dress but it was always her face that captured him. The radiance that night was unbearable. He tried to keep calm, keep a straight face. It was like being in a movie that overpowered with tear-jerking emotion but it was not tears he was fighting at that moment. Though one could certainly weep over such a sight that afforded both all insight and no insight. The objectifying was no simple sexist reduction for there was, as Levinas would say, something infinite here, a presence and at the same time a hole in the presence.

A smooth young face with a deadly wrinkle, for even a so-called vacancy was, in a blink, a look back, a fleeting expression that gave and took away the presence, made possible the presence. Tain was good old fashioned smitten. But then fashion was here again the possibility of a look (in a new one, and as both looked at and looking back), a fallen window, fallen into place. Any place could stand a face lift. Her radiant and ground zero revealing eyes, smile, stole the show and the world fell away to black. He forgot where he was. Actually he was having a heart attack, at least he was surely heading that way in this overwhelming confrontation.

She came nearer and smiled at him on her way to the tables behind him. He suddenly realized there was a howl in his throat. He'd not actually broken down "in front of everybody" (two kinds of "together" together!), but he was every bit shattered through and through and visibly trembled. What strange reaction was his flow of blood, his body tingling even as his genitals shrank, the ultimate withdrawal and declaration of good intentions. Could such honour be autonomic?

It wasn't the repression of sexual impulse but the release from the localization. Generalized but not abstract. Wholly concrete even though it seemed to strike down time and body's space. *The Romance of the Rose* (part one), alive and well and living in the disco, as guarded a garden as ever. Her light red hair and deep red velvet dress, the slight flush in her cheeks and the darker red of her lips. His disease, the disco/ordinating of his limbs, the inbreathing, the reverse tightening in his crotch. In little parcels of desperate breath he let the howl out. Rather than plan his attack he turned to cope with the destruction.

A year after Mel had been conferring with his new landlord in the half-built new place Recap looked in at the new piles of rubble, plaster and splinters of wood. The long diagonal Rundle stone walk was gone as was the parallel board walk that lead off through arches into the various sectioned off areas, each done with a different motif, murals and reliefs on the different walls. Poplar branches laid side by side made up one of the ceilings. The boardwalk created an interior exterior, quite enchanting even though one had seen it day by day constructed, take form. And now all cleaned out again but for little piles, empty like a large basement with dust motes floating in the light. The Wolf St place shedding its indexical name for a franchise one, no *No Logo*-ly, "St James Gate Olde Irish Pub".

Recap: Tain's favourite lounge* was also no longer, nor were all the magical nights, all the aching moments, all the quiet despair. Tain would sit at the curved bar and over the course of the night he would catch himself in the mirror behind the liquor bottles, stupefied but nevertheless composed and ready for action. Way downstairs in the Cascade bar would be a sea of drinkers, shuffleboard players, pool players, young first timers and groups of older tourists and the odd middle-aged local couple. It had been a huge single space divided minimally by pillars and one long two-sided bench, a great divide but easily seen over and run around at both ends.

The walls were covered with huge murals, not great art by any means but not unloved by the locals. Someone had drawn a football just past the end of the outstretched leg and

---

*The lounge where in '78 his knees got brushed by Her dress, where he awakened to his second chance and was paralyzed by the sting of her delicate, though, and through, delegated touch.

skate of a female figure skater. One night in '71 after a day of jackhammering another few increments of a basement in the side of Tunnel mountain, the neighbours threatening to kill him over the noise of the compressor and constant rock dust, standing on the street staring at him with hands on their hips or throwing snowballs at him, Tain looked at a boulder in the mural away across the room and his hands instinctively gripped a phantom jackhammer and began a muted ratatatat.

A year or two later Tain had been in the mostly empty bar on another afternoon drinking with Jimmy when suddenly through the back door from the alley they heard a commotion. They usually laughed anyway at the sight of Little Tommy but something very curious was going on this day. He was carrying an empty bird cage coming toward them in his sprightly little walk, leading Big Eddy behind him almost as if on a leash.

Big Eddy was big, tall with very wide shoulders and with long arms and huge hands. He used to tip old cars over as a stunt for tourists when he was younger. And had once carried an engine block down Bear street. Little Tommy was English and had been in the army and talked in crackling quick bursts of clipped words. He usually had a self-satisfied and droll look on his face. Sometimes he seemed to be in another world. You'd see him walking down the street by himself talking a mile a minute, cussing somebody up and down. His voice would carry over the median on Banff Avenue to the other side of the street. But even when he was addressing you he would look away and you didn't know if he was with you or just having you on, a professional clown on the job all the time.

He came up to the table and Jimmy, not one to be slow with a remark, get set, himself, just grinned a gaping grin and waited for Tommy to talk. "Looking for a good bloody bluebird" the little Englishman growled enigmatically and Jimmy and Tain came unglued. He repeated it, his head jerking this way and that around the room warily, like a bird himself. He was of course permanently barred. Jimmy finally said some teasing thing but it didn't seem to register as trouble was coming over.

Leo the owner in his thick accent told him to get the hell out. Tommy turned on him viciously, calling him a "Jew bastard" whereupon Big Eddy, always loyal to the Cascade, to Leo and especially Doug, the legendary ageless waiter, picked him up around the waist, birdcage and all, and carried him out and up the long flight of stairs to Banff Avenue. What passersby would have made of this barking and snapping emergence from the bowels of such a tavern is hard to say.

Another night Jimmy and Tain were half way through a night of drinking when a friend, a local, came over and asked them to watch the pool table. The bar was a quarter full of British army guys and a couple of them were interfering with the pool game going on. Jimmy didn't need much coaxing, his Irish ire was already up. Tain pretended to go to the bathroom and bumped powerfully into one of the army guys and then caught him roughly and with a wry look said "oh jeez I'm sorry". When he turned around, Jimmy, with his sheer presence, had a guy up against the wall.

Mind you he was mightily mobilized for the occasion. He held a pool cue like a rifle and he went through a rifle drill about half an inch away from the British soldier. Bang on the floor went the cue then up to his waist, one hand slapping across to grab it. His teeth were bared and he wagged his head with feverish energy. He'd been in the Irish army, not the IRA, and the British army and had been a boxer. He'd been in Holland late in the war helping to train the Dutch resistance. He'd told Tain how he'd taught them to keep low as they crawled, by lowering the machine guns again, then having the guns fire anew over their heads.

Tain was worried about Jimmy since it was only a year since his massive heart attack. He approached him and Jimmy gave him a quick look with a silly grin. The guy he had "pinned" didn't look all that frightened, though he should have been since Jimmy was still incredibly fast and would have been hard to hit. He could have been mistaken for close to eighty, as a fixed sight, with his bald head on top and white hair on the sides. He had a craggy face that a sculptor would kill for to capture. Once you saw him move he at once shed about twenty years from his actual age, just over fifty.

And this vitality, even though he'd broken his back once as well as his elbow so that he couldn't now fully straighten his left arm. He'd been found naked and unconscious outside a pub in Ireland. Someone had apparently thrown him out of a second storey window. He never found out who. And he'd been told in the hospital he'd never walk again but after a year or so on canes he just started walking one night when he was drunk, just by throwing his canes away like some faith-healed Christian and not some shit-faced boozer. Of course he was faithful to "[my] god" who especially for him worked in mysterious ways.

Before anything more could happen a captain in charge came over and grabbed the soldier by the shirt, banged him hard against the wall, balled into his ear, completely ignoring Tain and Jimmy.

One Sunday in about '73 Tain woke on the two mattresses that were his bed, barely a foot from the floor. Rather than the usual headache after a night of drinking and who knows what, he realized he was still drunk, that he'd consumed enough liquor that it took him a good night's rest in order to do justice to the resources of booze in his body, somehow in sleep to rehabilitate some brain cells so they could be ravaged again, give the ever ready alcohol something to chew on. The more he thought about it he realized he was high and hung over and in a way that it was the best of both worlds. He had the stimulated brain and not just the jangled nerves and he had, well the joy of already feeling good, sort of breakfast in bed.

He looked over at Jimmy who was sitting in the little blue chair near the closet listening to an old *Reader's Digest* record classic on the stereo, turned down low. He was also sipping a beer. When he noticed Tain was awake he asked if he wanted a beer. "Are you kidding?" Tain half shouted with his dry and raspy throat, giving him a mock dirty look. Jimmy laughed loudly and took another sip. He was still pissed too or was getting so with the morning beer.

Tain never drank on Sunday as a rule, that idiomatic expression singular for the way it definitely allows the exceptions. Not for religious reasons of course. But he was still athlete enough to want to maintain some kind of condition, ie to allow him the well-being necessary to launch a few push-ups and then dynamic tension exercises for his biceps, for which eventually he got some adjustable dumbbells. But of course drinking was more fun when you took a holiday from it too. No doubt vanity played its part in this rule.

It wasn't playing hard to get, he really meant to stick to his Sunday as a day of recovery. But because of all the booze in his system he continued to joke and verbally spar with Jimmy over the issue and also started going over the events of the night before, reconstructing them. Hell, just trying to remember them. Jimmy would prod him with "Recap, O chronicler from hell, let's have it". Between the two of them they slowly were getting their story straight, not for some hypothetical cop but almost as if rehearsing a play they hoped would please their audience. This was his mistake, although also the usual procedure, this going over the previous night of drinking to make sure nothing criminal had actually occurred, and of course there was some initial panic in the process because he often remembered the cops playing some part, just as the curtain rose, so to speak.

There was the time in the Grizzly House when Jimmy had thrown a glass the distance of a few tables over just for the hell of it as far as Tain could remember. Tain had rather unjustly gone over to the offended party at the table where the glass had shattered, hunkered down and put his chin on the edge, then dared the guy, a local bouncer, to hit him. Naturally the guy was unnerved at this second wave of ambiguous assault. Tain later got to be a friend of the guy and didn't usually act such an asshole, though he did love the theatrics of these ploys and what got stirred up by the action, not by any means always revenge and further violence.

By a sort of *Man In A Glass Booth** logic, not an inversion or Bottom carnivalesque of it, for that would be impossible, and not quite as a trivialization of it either, but perhaps as a minor corollary, the life within life drama aimed both at historical realization and the memory of the present, he became multiple and contradictory, violent and funny together. The violence was rarely actual, and then only as interrupting the violence already begun. It was a psychic violence. And when he had everybody's attention he

---

* The movie made from Robert Shaw's play that dramatizes first of all the problematics of basic realization, then historical realization and finally the realization of evil, which in this telescoping reaches a point, but a point that mushrooms. The main character, a Jew, masquerades as a former Nazi in New York after the war. He allows himself to get caught by Nazi hunters and to be taken back to Israel as a kind of Eichmann-like character with an *essential* difference in addressing this problem of realization: the victims who didn't know, the Jews, not yet or ever victims, who didn't know, the Nazis who didn't know, in the ordinary sense, or in the ultimate sense, the other Germans who didn't know (and of course one goes back mentally and puts quotes around the "know's" to various effects) and then the people looking back in time who don't know. A problem of technical vantage points and a problem of moral imagination. At the time, if you can say this, was there a panopticon, a quasi omniscience? Was Hitler situated here, all-seeing, demonically, if you can say that? The Nazi in disguise addressed and dressed these questions, and the question of banality. He recapitulated the history of atrocities as he dramatically relished them so to incarnate evil with an unbearable density, insult to injury to an nth degree so to finally trigger great cathartic cries of pain and disgust from the Jews in the court room who saw the Nazi through their feint reflections in the glass even as the "Nazi" began to peel off his clothing to reveal the numbers tattooed on his arm and as he ended his terrible litany of enacted evil. His moral imagination so real it was riven to the roots till he ended catatonic and Christ-like with his arms pushed up against the glass booth.

would take on the role of clown and sometimes just for good measure take on the others' sins, like the man in the glass booth and that other famous rabble rouser, though perhaps unlike the latter in his parking more in the means, or commission, than in the end, or remission, and unlike the former in his doing just an ordinary asshole, not to be confused with the famous "banality" which anyway the glass booth man transformed and black-holed into its opposite.

Of course it still left him feeling like an asshole and rightly so but he would always get over it as he recapitulated the night and assessed or covered his ass in the theatre of his mind. When the RCMP officer came into the Grizzly House and came over to their table he was extremely pleasant. In fact he seemed in a jocular mood so when he took out his book and asked for their names Tain forthrightly announced "this here's Neil Diamond", gesturing to Jimmy who was splitting himself, and then incongruously "I'm Chuck Berry".

The cop laughed too and they thought he was an okay guy. Perhaps he was shy, considering everyone in the whole place was looking at them. Or perhaps it was Jimmy's age, and the appearance of being even older, plus the craggy signs of character, in the moral sense and not in what should have been more evident if you knew him, the crazy sense, written on his face. Perhaps there was the behind the scenes influence of the staff because they did wonder who had actually called the guy in. They were sort of the resident clowns of the place and often sat with Peter the owner and traded jokes.

His mistake on this particular Sunday in his bed was to let this theatre business get out of hand when still full of the good stuff. They were getting too much of a kick out of themselves, in themselves. So he had that one exhilarating moment when he knew he was going over to the what, the other side? Or was it simply pushing off the mountain and down a slope on skis. It was like accepting a sexual invitation and abandoning oneself. He accepted a beer was what he did. In fact drank two in bed. By the time he got up he was really drunk and it was afternoon. They decided they should loose themselves on the town, offer themselves up.

Jimmy claimed the restaurant in the Cascade would serve them beer if they would only have a sandwich. Well Tain figured they could do that for them and off they went waltzing down the street, Jimmy in a little cap and sunglasses and actually not waltzing but shuffling along in quick short little steps and having trouble keeping up with Tain who wasn't all that fast a walker. The day was fresh not cold and Tain let his long hair and beard bounce as he walked. He enjoyed the breeze buzzing his Sunday, morning to him, buzz.

He was aware that long hair affected one's manners, little manoeuvres with the hands and swings of the head, almost a little feminine and noticed it affected every guy who wore long hair no matter how macho. Everyone at least at a subconscious level indulged this handling of hair, even though it was necessary most of the time, as when getting it out of the eyes or away from one's soup. Yet there was a definite feminization that was more than accepted. Tain greasily liked it for the way it played as bait for the "rednecks" around so that he could reveal his true belligerent hippy self.

But the point was it wasn't his true self. It was the relativity, the playing of what seemed a necessary role, mirroring the redneck back to himself, which again was not their true self, if say by mere circumstance the redneck were lent long hair and one could thereby say be relieved of his slavery to macho-dumb. And all this notwithstanding the relativity of the association of femininity and long hair, but understanding too that relative masks nevertheless swung into real mutual othernesses whose respective adoptions could be triggered by the, in this case, aforementioned mannerisms. And then there was the possibility that Tain was the real red neck whose true state he could only attain from the side of hippy culture, as its defender. He was saved from the burden of this thought by the wonderful fluidity engendered by that wonderful fluid, the golden goodness as they sentimentally and ironically, empirically said.

They sat in the restaurant for the rest of the afternoon and drank beer after beer. Jimmy told old jokes and Tain thought up new critiques of them in the form of new variations, or just the down right ripping apart of them after he reminded Jimmy how old and boring they were. But of course he wanted Jimmy to tell them so he could tell his parasitic jokes back and it was all only a ritual anyway as they only wanted to laugh and disturb the rest of the customers, not so much that they would get kicked out though. Herb and his friends were sitting down a ways and kept turning and nodding at them whenever their laughter got especially loud.

Then it did begin to get out of control, in fact it reminded Tain of the pain of not being able to stop laughing that time he took horse tranquilizer once unwittingly. He had bargained for MDA, the so-called love drug. He remembered once not being physically able to get out from the middle of a big bar down in Lethbridge for fear of breaking down into complete hysteria. With effort now, he and Jimmy were able to calm themselves and then Herb came over, like maybe they had some special drug they should tell him about, like he thought these were the sounds of enlightenment. Herb had even longer hair and was known to be a local guru, extremely well-read in widely different realms.

It was moments like this, this mention of guru, that would make Tain make one of his obscure puns that he would later realize was even more obscure than he thought, sometimes because as they say (telling phrase) there was simply more wisdom in the language than one ever realized initially, sometimes through getting one of the components of the pun wrong. Here he might have invoked Ezra Pound to get to "Kang-guru" only, in trying to re-experience the pleasure later, to remember it was "Kung" not "Kang" for the great Chinese wise man. Then again he was fool enough to have simply said "Kangaroo" with no pretensions whatever. He said nothing of the kind here since no one mentioned guru. Or perhaps Jimmy did, he would.

Tain encouraged Jimmy to tell one of his jokes and when he did Tain was reminded just how good it was, in fact how it might appear as a piece of transcendental thought. He first told about being late for work at a construction site and that when the foreman had asked him if he knew when they "started around here" had replied that he didn't know, "they're always at it when I get here!" Then he told Herb about getting hired as a foreman once. The boss had asked him if he knew anything about machines and he had replied "no, but I know when they're idle", then got the job. Also on the strength of this appeal he had earned the attention of a famous economist, at least he claimed he had, until he showed up at the great man's lecture, sitting himself down in the front row and proceeding to exhibit his drunken self.

Herb just stood over them, grinning and seemingly wanting to bless them but wondering if it was necessary probably too. Jimmy shook himself out of a lecture and said he was a mean man, that he meant everything he said and then laughed at his own joke. Tain and Jimmy were getting the giggles again and Herb was starting to get a contact paroxysm himself so he bade them farewell and went back to his table. They felt strangely relieved, not that they didn't think the world of Herb, but more the case of having had to feel responsible for their merriment, to give it some kind of meaning, Jimmy's statement notwithstanding. In fact they felt as relieved as if they'd pacified a redneck and not, as they had, disrupted a "hippy".

It was starting to get dark, and Tain thought as much but almost said "it's starting to get drunk" and then did say it. They ate their grilled cheese sandwiches as if only a duty but the food made them hungry even as they chewed and swallowed, and were finally ambushed by their own satisfaction. No longer giddy but at peace with themselves and slightly somnambulant, they sauntered into the street, and halfway home, stopped and sat on one of the benches near the spruce trees just past the Credit Union. They said little and looked at the evening sky. Then along came Clarissa on her bike and leading a half grown Doberman pinscher. She looked at them oddly and then started to laugh as she realized they were drunk and that it was a Sunday departure for Tain. They got up and continued down the street and Clarissa followed with the dog. They turned in to their yard and she went on down Marten Street but said she'd be back.

Jimmy was about ready to crash and Tain wasn't sure what he was ready for when Clarissa arrived with a bottle of wine and the dog again. She'd been impressed with how blissful and silly they were and wanted in on the fun. Tain drank right out of the bottle in a mock aggressive way. Jimmy declined the wine as per usual but he was really done in too. Clarissa grabbed the bottle back and took a swig. She was pinching Tain and Tain was grabbing and putting a leg pincer hold on the Doberman. Soon he and Clarissa were wrestling on the bed and the pup was jumping all over them.

Jimmy had rolled out the foamy and was lying down with his hands behind his head watching and laughing quietly. Soon he was snoring and Tain and Clarissa were getting out of their clothes. The light from the street through the open curtain bathed the room in the merest of light. Tain was beginning to realize that, though his body generally felt fatigued in a nice kind of way, his sexual energy was cranked up and concentrated where it counted, in that conventional macho sense, something fierce. The balance of stupour and stimulation over the twenty-four hours was coming out on the hang-over over-stimulation side. The room ebbed deeper into night and yet the light from the street, not the street light directly, defined itself more clearly and it seemed actually brighter than before. The opposite wall reflected and seemed to radiate among the shadows.

Below the window on the bed and where Jimmy was on the floor, in contrast, it was quite dark. The lovemaking was approaching tantric time if not essence, whatever that was, and the Doberman was getting involved. Jimmy woke briefly as he turned over but he caught the dog on the back of Tain's leg and the tongue licking the "enlightened" rising butt. He had no more energy to laugh but as he pulled the blanket over his other shoulder now he grinned abstractly and muttered "they're always at it when I get here".

Hegel's Cows

Begin with a minimal alien and its moment of ideality, no floating mind bubble (and what do you make of this figure from "hell"?) but rather as Hegel had it, to be simply always a part of something more, as in enjambed to unfolding and fudging new powers, to be complex and unfit in a fitting way. Ideal in the sense a point, a line, a plane are calculated fiction, successively scooped, as are the swallowing plains swallowed by: the lazy-bar-none. We start off with a start, 3-D infinity, bang! — little big bang.

Meanwhile back at the farm, how to saddle, sidle up to nature? To labour with her. To labour, rather than work which, after Arendt, produces from plans quasi permanent things, cathedrals or pyramids. At bottom Recap and his brother still actually labour, shovel, sweat between machines and the land. The realm of cycles, of perishables, there to labour and there closest to the wild animal as to participate — in the analogy. But no hug.

And the machine breaks. Breaks the grip gotten, out of hand. Altered material sacrificed to the moment of alterability and they take the enormous fall into lost scale, of land. Not airplane revelations but the loose finessed convergence of immediate muddling: metal bins, a haywire harnessing kicking over the traces of horse power, going down into the place and pace of middle, unlincoln* legs. Digging for seed they have otherwise, seeded, buried and lifted down. Dirt under the nails moons the untouchable sum. Then under the thumb comes the beauty of the dawn upon the hills, the plain hills they half remember and need again to swing, and miss.

Eighteen years farming on their own, including the eighties' droughts, and suckholed to the bank that preached to the converted species' specie, spread the ins and outs of the knots bank and brothers were each other in, nature's negative physicists assign time, space falling all over the seeds of itself and a prophet taking to the streets that roam.

Eighteen years releases the spring in the spring, catches the fall, the drama of winter teasing season out of season. The correlative of a life insinuated, even cloud seeded and instrumentalized but just the same a myth, lifting the tasks along with all the punctured epidermis and festerings on

---

* "How long should a man's legs be?" "Long enough to reach the ground." So said honest, but sly, Abe [honest, but sly, apocrypha?].

the fly. Happy in the blood the unhappy stud of history risen to reason that slips into its own resourceful pin pan continuum, now the funeral is home and arranged.

Walking further afield Recap's brother keeps, and keeps digging and digging what was just interred as blinking certified and will be long, caught in an umbilical beauty of green and dead gold, "Burnt Norton" graduation of in-turn time, syncopated threshold, seed, two-way mired, letting go its rustling thunder-stealing arrangement.

His brother takes after their grandfather who worked with soil scientists but never lost the love of the feel of bare feet in a freshly ploughed field, or as he historically converted to, cultivated field.*

Now they've largely abandoned even cultivation and his brother works with soil scientists, plant scientists. Don Gayton** demonstrates a proper science can be true to a poetics of earth. Hegel would have agreed in his "science of spirit", in his Swabian sympathy for the farm.

Coffee

Again going to his favourite coffee bar, arisen from the ruins of the old King Eddy tavern at the end of the eighties and to last itself barely a decade, Recap saw through the window, Rock, his boxer shoulders rolled forward, reading the *Sun*. He entered and nodded at Rock as he went over

---

* The grandfather's invention of the blade cultivator (referred to in *Wolf Willow*) that undercut weeds and stubble, left the trash on top of the soil to protect against erosion.

** Not that Gayton would necessarily approve of all of their practices, though open to constant re-evaluation, but he certainly sympathizes with the constraints farmers are under from cheap food policies.

to investigate the day's muffins. When he sat down with his juice and toast Rock was still reading the paper. So he ate in silence but for the odd grunt and clearing of his throat. Rock made similar noises and even spoke a few words that floated over toward Recap but like fighter planes testing the boundaries of international air space they seemed to turn back and were shown, ironically, to be for himself, ie he was talking to himself about what he was reading but threatening to disseminate to Recap, or as sometimes was the case the content just seemed for the moment that it shouldn't be contained.

Recap at these words cleared his throat a little more loudly and then when he finished the toast grabbed the *Globe and Mail*. Rock liked to flaunt reading or carrying the *Sun*, which went with his recoiling at being considered an intellectual. Yet one wondered, since his greatest sport was to corner intellectuals or at least the wannabes and try to destroy their positions with incontrovertible fact. He considered the *Globe* to be left wing. Recap roared that this, to the real left wingers, would be news!

Finally they both put their papers down and eased into conversation. Rock had a love-hate relationship with the reading of novels, but an unequivocal distaste for Canadian ones. He would make periodic resolutions that he would no longer read them. Often the attacks were ad hominem, ie he had known so and so down east, or had taken classes from or with so and so and, without too many steps in between, therefore their novels were trash.

And yet when pushed he seemed to have done some homework. Recap thought at times there must be more to this and wondered about his down east history. It often sounded, though often full of more substantive argument and convincing conviction, like good old *ressentiment*, though Rock otherwise and at the time, at times, seemed to be enjoying himself. In fact he was often downright chipper as he slagged away. Of course *ressentiment* allows for that, being that it is just the re-routing of energy, albeit in pretty twisted ways sometimes.

Some years earlier Rock had been reading The Tent Peg by Aritha Van Herk and was going after it from a gold miner's point of view. It was true he'd been up north and done a lot of prospecting. In fact he'd gone up just recently to try it again. He met up with a couple of old buddies. Quite a bit of time had gone by since he'd last been up there and last seen them. One was quite a character, a fiery right winger from Europe, living in the States now, who would send regular missives up to Rock on the latest of the Democrat or "liberal" follies.

He was a tough-minded engineer who lived pretty hard, in fact so hard he needed to get a new heart. Up in Yukon he would take dozens of anti-rejection pills every morning and then drink a couple of bottles of whiskey over the rest of the day. Rock, in contrast with the two buddies, the other of whom spent hours each morning untangling a ball of string, came off seeming the mildest and sanest of men. He came off and came back too, shaking his head for days back in Banff. He wondered about what a transplant operation, anaesthetics and follow-up drugs do to the personality.

But he had been fired up with how Van Herk had got it wrong about gold mining though he never did specify or get down to technicalities. "Where do I start" was his excuse. Recap strongly begged to differ and at moments like this would get more redneck than the genuine article, so to speak. It wasn't a literal mining or metallurgical treatise, he insisted, but a novel with other fish to fry.

By chance he'd read it along with Faulkner's *As I Lay Dying* and had suffered no decline in critical interest going from one to the other. Hilles had told him he had told Van Herk this and that she had replied Faulkner had been an influence. Recap took that in the best sense, in the inevitable sense, but of course Rock would have seen this in a one-sided, reductive and detracting sense he thought.

Jon had been acquainted with Rock's put down of CanLit and had finally, over the question of Farley Mowat, turned the whole issue to the base moment of "can you do any better"? And this rimed with Aritha's recounting Marian Engel's dealing with a student's cynical and naïve dismissal of some other writer. She'd banged her fist down on the lectern, or maybe even thrown something, perhaps a book!, and then proceeded to try to communicate how much work goes into the writing of a novel, the sleepless nights, the hour after hour, day after day expense of spirit. Engel had been impassioned and so was Van Herk in her reiteration.

Of course after the importance of this energy moment had been emphasized one had to be wary of the reductive moment this moment passes over to. And yet Recap thought that if this energy talked about were intertwined with real wrestling, or with openness to one's frightening possibilities, beyond the pleasure, though carried along, to the work of holding work and self together in this got-a-live-one moment one dared, then the "reductive moment" was no simple empirical hedge.

Rock of course was an empiricist himself and yet that's reductive too. He and Jon were avid subscribers to the *Skeptical Inquirer*. Rock didn't take kindly to being labeled or put in a box. For instance he liked to infuriate liberals, though he used this term in that American sense which made for some confusion in talking about the Grits, especially lately, with its blatant right wing positions, but he resented and objected loudly to being stuck with, say, an opposing ideological label himself.

Rock had told Recap of some scientist's account of ideology, that an artifact, that was in fact a tool that was used, became ideological when it was worshipped as a fetish. All of which reminded Recap of a richer Marxian account of it and then the richer ironies of Marxism being sublated into a mere ideology, which, with the Hegelian reference, raises it again into a rich historical question. And there are the contingent riches of the simply different usages current.

Of course Baudrillard finds ideology obsolete, an embarrassing usage. Rock liked to endorse various Reform, or *Alberta Report* attacks on the Liberals but when pressed about the fundamentalism, he of course was out of their camp in a flash. Down on the political religions of the nineteenth century and down on religion. Well there were still lots of positions to take and Rock took them but he knew how to roll too.

Recap did have one quibble with *The Tent Peg* and that in relation to the scene where the boy/girl or man/woman reflected on penises in the latrine. He/she said, upon observing them at the urinals, that in this flaccid state they were all pretty much the same. Recap, from his own experience, though it would hardly add up to a statistical sample, in contrast say to the average modern day woman, re the non-flaccid field, and from a book that arrived from the Book of the Month Club many years ago in his parents' home, was quite sure it was quite the reverse, ie tumescent penises "tended" to equalize. Small matter, and it was the larger equipment or the question of mining technique that [g]old Rock was claiming to find fault with.

Recap often thought Rock should write, even a column. He would of course find out what it was like to expose himself. But genuinely, Recap thought he would be good, that it would lead him into new reflexivities, whole new areas and regroupings and the picking up of threads, the return to pastures of new ideas or the prefigurations of new ideas. Well, would just intensify his already mobilized mind. He essentially did research constantly, as it was, sometimes just so he could better someone in argument.

There were secondary considerations here that were not stable, that in fact jumped their status into primary states. There was the pure pleasure of argument, with all the unforeseen connections and the discovery or rediscovery of what you didn't know you knew. You were inclined to reduce this to ego, as ego may be the big drive to research so that it can win the truth and may in the end, after all the absorption, claim it again as trophy, but in a beautiful (Keatsian?) self-overcoming the truth may in fact win out, after having borrowed the ego for its energy. Recap knew this dynamic always came into play and specifically recognized it in Rock, the love of truth, however constant/inconstant.

Rock in his best moments was a gadfly, in the Socratic way, walking around town with huge Chinese novels in his head, social conditions as they related to Elizabethan theatre that he'd remembered from some famous scholar he'd had as a professor at U of T and whose book on Shakespearean tragedy Recap had once read. Hell, Rock even read the Canadian constitution in the Meech Lake days. Walking around the streets of Banff loaded for bear, as it were.

Perhaps there was honour in this refusal to write. Recap remembered someone saying that when Sheila Watson was asked why she didn't write more she'd replied that someone had to do the reading, of all the writing being done these days. In fact when she died he'd heard Aritha give a eulogy on the radio remembering meeting her in a bookstore and how Sheila had deplored the general fall in reading habits and had made a fist to signify the call to read our Canadian books.

In an analogous way to how Rock would take an *Alberta Report* position but drop the religion, he would also take other redneck positions but implicitly at least criticize the property-based realities behind them, for instance the agribusiness on the prairies and attendant fertilizer and chemical industries. He was appalled driving across the prairies to see all the land ruined by alkali, that he attributed to chemical fertilizers. Recap had to correct him on this, at least as he knew the story in his area. It was not the chemicals applied but the inflexible practice of summerfallow that was causing the problem. Not allowing anything to grow in the low wet areas where the ground water flowed to.

On the days when Rock got Recap down on the question of immigration Recap eventually remembered the

Rock who lived up north, lived in a tent, read explorers' journals and observed the wild animals. A story of a squirrel running up and hiding in his shirt when he was sitting around his fire. It turned out a big black bear had been nearby of which the squirrel had been quite aware of course.

He told the story laughing, as if he could still feel the creature's tickling feet. Rock had talked about his idea of a garden, one of weeds, the weeds of diversity that is, not the weeds of a biological totalitarianism. Recap wondered teasingly to himself if Rock and Frank Davey would make good [flower] bedfellows, thinking of Davey's *Weeds*. Rock had thought it out quite elaborately, though Recap could only remember him talking about dandelion leaves for salads. And this made him think of Rock's ideas for inventions, just modest ideas like the neckerchief that with some button holes would convert into a bib-napkin, that Rock thought might especially take off in the cowboy market.

One thing Recap and Rock knew was that there was always more to learn, it seemed more all the time and equally they were aware of how much they were forgetting. No matter how prejudiced in an almost parodied way and actually cynical and seemingly really bitter Rock was, Recap respected the way he stood his ground and how his weapon of choice was open argument. Well, like anyone you had to open him up, but then he respected a good argument, backed up with fact. Recap remembered him admitting, perhaps more than he realized, that when he had been arguing about the stock market, typically, with a stock broker, he had shifted the argument around to "something I knew something about". An attempt to demolish the guy for the pure sake, or to test, by extension, the credibility on the other matters? And then how often one does shift to something one knows something about, with a mixture of motives and a mixture of results.

Rock the renter, the floating gadfly seeming always to settle in a conservative to ultra conservative position. And Recap the big land owner espousing liberal and left wing positions. Maybe this is why Hegel generated both left and right wing followers and is often characterized as having no base by Marxists and by a strain of Peircean philosophy.*

But Hegel stood his ground, was every bit as radical as Marx on property relations and knew how they affected the concrete, ie wholly real dimensions of reason. He was one-sided, in his sense of the idea, on the issue of revolutionary action since he was consistently radical on how the master-slave relation haunted all levels and areas of objective and subjective phenomenon. Hegel had searched the historical epochs for clues in balancing the sides of a question, in

---

* Peirce is a whole other issue, the stringent scientist and rigorous logician but the ridiculer of most scientists' unthought-out empiricism. Recap couldn't yet keep up with Peirce's rigour but he knew he was an ally, along with Putnam and Searle against the neuroscientists and the philosophers of "consciousness explained" who short-circuited first person subjective experience. Peirce was a bit tricky here, especially considering he once said he used the word "mind" merely as a "sop to Cerberus", and then considering this against Searle's *The Rediscovery of the Mind*, but somehow Peirce's championing of generals in conjunction with, at the level of firstness, his ironically conscious (at a very low grade) primitive "atoms", suggested his affinity with these thinkers, not non-, but neuroscientific-plus, as in a derived, oscillating dualism of "persons", you-as-them (and *even* as-it) and you-as-me. An affinity with Putnam for sure (pace Searle calling him a "functionalist"), given Putnam's championing of Peirce, given Putnam's combining of epistemology and ethics through the action of re-presentation and the acts of the will that thereby inhere. Recap thought this and further twists such as the Dennets of empiricism taking to their bosoms the Derridas of deconstruction.

avoiding dominance in relations, in propositions, even in the relation of one's reason to one's intuition. He saw in his historical circumstances only abstract (in his sense of one-sided, or split off from the whole) possibilities and was wary of forcing them into imbalanced actualities.

Rock and Recap in the here and now of the nineties stepped back from one another and stepped back from the latest developments. There were times when Recap would skim through the *Globe* and hope there was nothing of interest in it so he would be sooner free for the heavier matter of a book which sinks in the times and so curves and retards the flow of events into exaggerated shapes. And yet there were little folds of untimely thoughts in the newspaper too that had to be checked and one had to brush the times, in the trendy[?] sense of rub against briefly, but also meaning the individual strokes suggesting limit resolution too. After Rock left, Recap watched him walk down the street favouring one leg and thought the dancer's intentions were used well by the dance.

Hegel's Cows

Murray Bookchin the anarchist said there's no ideal (in the other augmented sense) state of nature to go back to, ie to take nature back to and of course no collapsing our ideality (in the other other sense — the awkward retroactive hinge signifying the ever ne-gating labour of this veri-ideality), no back to nature, Hegel's recipe for evil, the lethal but phoney choice for non-recognition, reconsidered as a face, and a faith, down. In our ideality we exceed the throw of the indices however much their point/blanks resist.

Our non-locality is irresistible. We flow out of ourselves. Peirce said our melodies of thought exist as signs carried through us, signs of signs, into the community of sing/sign-tists — to designate figuratively how symbolic language tops up the variegated feed of instrumental signs, which includes symbols semantically construed as indexical or expressive over evolutionary time, eg wing as air's art. An economy of spirit or ideality of signs exactly needs an aggregate of irritated memories and open public archives to behold all the necessary moves, all the necessary errors in the curve of truth — ride it as we will (to "picture think", partially, to split on *will*). The individual mind cannot hold itself but in the community we're beholden to, which beholds us, which squeezes even, in a mockery of love abandoned at the heart, in the longing "errors".

The centre of locality disappears, reappears in Toronto! Sharon Butala has those days on the ranch when she longs to be down east in a restaurant of writers. Toronto is the bad infinity, spiritual wilderness from which we place our good infinity. TO is TO the good because TO the bad, because TO is FRO — to harass in these Harris times, reflect Klein times.

Fenland

Big heavy flakes and the fenland is again a winter wonderland. Recap thought of Jon's line "Silence is born of the marriage of deep wonder and winter" that Recap incorporated into his dedication poem to him. Twice now people had come up and said how much they liked this line in his poem and then looked awkward when he told them the line was actually Jon's.

Over the little footbridge and along the creek Recap and his Labrador, the hyper field trial one, a footbridge herself, to, and in the same instant, moat or mote against, the wild animals, came to where the creek forks and where you get a look at the first Vermillion Lake where the valley is flat and where Jon in his *Indians in the Rockies* recounted the pre-history and history of the journeys going back a hundred and fifteen centuries towards the last ice age and up to the archeologists in the 1980s who determined this.

On a piece of grassland jutting out into the ice a coyote stood with muzzle in the air. It barked a couple of quick dog-like barks that then broke into a high-pitched howl. The Lab looked at him or her and then went on about her business sniffing Elk turds and eating bits of bark which, as later reported to Ernie* as her half symbiotic relation to the three-toed woodpecker who produced the bits, produced Ernie's "and that's how the dog got its bark". She was not a fierce dog but on the steroids had a fierce appetite and went about happily barking up the right trees.

Further along the trail where it diverged slightly from the creek they met Mr. Cigar coming the other way. He held his arm out, raised above his shoulder. He opened his hand just as they arrived and a small bird either came out of it or flew into it. It was so sudden that Recap thought

---

* Ernie Kroeger the Banff photographer whose photograph from his threshold series presents a cabin whose window's reflection shows the viewer what she might be seeing were she in the cabin looking out, namely, a forest, some of whose trees were taken in the literal sense to build the cabin. Recap liked the implications of the two black boxes implicated in the picture, the cabin and the camera, the tains, real and suggestive behind the reflections.

this, that is that it had been produced from his hand. Was Mr. Cigar a trickster? But no, he had crushed peanuts in his hand and the chickadees, or maybe the same one, flew out of the trees, landed, scored, and flew off again. They or it must have been storing the peanuts because they were always right back.

Recap wondered who Mr. Cigar was. He was new around here he could tell from the first questions the man had asked. He looked like he could be Brian Patton's* quite a bit older and shyer brother. His unaggressive walk, though a kind of benign stealth, was at odds with his cigar and the bigger gestures of the arm the cigar entailed.

Recap continued to walk and glanced at a stump, the work of a beaver that looked exactly like a beaver from behind and which had caused the dog to sneak zig-zag up to it the first time she'd seen it. Just before the bridge over the creek to the parking area they came across a younger and an older man and a woman who seemed to be the older man's wife. They were very cheerful and had been off the trail looking at a bird, a chickadee, and then asked Recap if he knew what it was. They were full of questions about the dog's shaved patch and made jokes as he explained it. The woman wondered if the dog would start lifting weights with her steroids. Recap said no but that he was thinking of sharing them with her.

In the back of his mind he remembered telling Playcefire's brother that he had been disappointed that nobody had ever accused him of being on them. The older

---

* Author of many books and co-author of *The Canadian Rockies Trail Guide* which includes the self guiding Fenland Trail.

man looked at the lesions and said they "looked like . . . " but he couldn't remember so Recap said "moss" and then his wife said "lichen" and he said "yeah you know, it grows on rocks". The younger man was more serious and, though shyer, asked if there were any elk around. Recap told him not today, that they'd been out in full force yesterday and the day before. Today they had taken a vote and decided on the river just where the creek flowed into it.

"How many?" the man asked. "Fifty or sixty" Recap replied. Some had been on the ice and others up into the trees on the far side. A big coyote was on the river too, circling by, keeping an eye on them. The couple apologized for teasing him about the dog so Recap decided to use a bad, recycled pun on them as a gentle, delayed rejoinder and as retroactively cueing their jokes. "Well, at the point where you liken the lesions to lichen . . . " and he trailed off, literally turning and walking on as he said this, hearing their hearty groans behind him.

The dog on the leash, he walked up Wolf and approached Bear where Mike had just come around the corner by the new theatre. Mike had been asking him regularly about his dog, in fact he said now "I always have to ask about your dog?" Recap brought him up to date, more than happy to meet his self-conscious eternal return of a gesture halfway.

Mike was still getting used to "life after life" as was Recap, in himself, and as he observed Mike and was in turn getting used to him, as neo-Mike. He still had the wild dark brown hair and the shades and a sort of tough John Lennon look, but there was a much gentler, reflective, smell-the-flowers quality to him. In fact there was an unnerving sweetness to him, even though Recap had always got along with him, and intertwined with the wild cowboy toughness there had always been a freaking sweet Jesus strand.

Pound for pound he had surely been one of the toughest guys in the valley. Recap had heard of his exploits with his fists from many sources but had never actually seen him fight, which would have been no doubt not nearly as pretty and romantic as hearing about it. He would have fit in with Wild Bill Peyto in the trapping, guiding and outfitter days in the late nineteenth century valley here. He had come from Ontario as a teenager in the early '70s but was a natural on a horse, and on bulls too. He was also a gifted carpenter and moved people with original artistic decor he figured out on the fly for various bars and restaurants that he worked on.

Recap: Tain had wrestled with him one time on the floor of a restaurant after hours and then once out back. He was like a wildcat and felt much heavier than he looked. Tain outweighed him and back of the restaurant had just anchored himself as Mike whirled the two of them around and then suddenly reversed directions, then again reversed, pushing in and then pulling away. Tain was just reacting but it was all he could do to stay on his feet, besides he was by far the soberer of the two this particular night. Also Tain realized in the spirit of play Mike was sticking to some unwritten rules, like no sudden punches or kicks, basic tactics in a real fight.

He was strong without any regular weight-lifting, just what working did to him, and he was absolutely lean eating only when he felt hungry and according to how he was living at the time. His strength though was his dynamic motion, quickness and the Judo-like use of his weight. Tain had seen him do cartwheels and back flips. Throw in the no-pulled punches and kicks and the man was lethal. But he had a sense of the ridiculous and the poetic too. He would talk in absurdist flights and then split a gut at some crazy intersection of thoughts and words, words diverted and bent at street level where the energy is chancy and multifarious.

On the corner of Wolf and Bear Recap could see Mike was no longer young though much younger than Recap and knew his knees and neck had had better days. The raw cowboy from the east talked much straighter now but you could still bring out that wild grin with the right allusion. Recap: once Tain and Mike had been horsing around early one summer Saturday evening back of the Magpie and Stump, in the parking lot. Neither had yet been drinking but Mike goaded Tain into lifting cars.

He would go ahead and pick one, like some kind of eccentric promoter. Tain would check the bumper out to see how it would agree with his bare hands. Winter lifting was better because you had gloves. He would lift till both back wheels were off and drop it, letting it bounce a bit. Mostly Rabbits, but he did a Pinto too, he liked that for a change and because it seemed to look heavier. He did them either facing in to the trunk like he was humping it and with his chin practically on the lid, or turned around hack squatting them.

He preferred doggy style because it seemed more of a challenge, like he were doing a curl. Sometimes he'd lift a small truck from one side. He went back to the Pinto after failing at something bigger. He was getting tired too as Mike the task master drove him on, getting more hysterical as they paraded around the parking lot negotiating cars, "fights". Tain said that this would be the last. He lifted it high and then dropped it heavily. He'd hoped he wouldn't split his pants and then realized he still hadn't as he turned around to see a couple in a tiny car drive by, not in the least worried, rather laughing they were and would have been saying, if they'd been in *Natural Born Killers*, "murder me, murder me".

Tain and Mike had gone their separate ways and then somehow ended up at the same party later that night, by this time both thoroughly pissed. Walking down the street in the early morning Mike went into his promoter bit and picked out cars on the street for Tain to lift. But the picks got bigger and bigger, an old Caddy, a tow truck and then finally an RV as big as a Brewster bus. Tain would get on one side at the rear wheel well and strain away managing to wiggle and then sway it some.

Mike in some kind of yin-yang sense of delicate balance, ie is in some refined, but then not so refined, counterpoint to Tain's futile efforts, started twisting all the side mirrors of the vehicles on the street so they pointed down at the pavement. Then he pretended to break an aerial off, Ariel and Caliban together, as he revealed the fancy restitution of the spring base. But he pretended a little too hard on the next one which wasn't spring but the air of winter and the crack of dawn. They ran down the street laughing not so much at the unfortunate deed but, on the other side of their running, at being caught up in the role of naughty boys.

Hegel's Cows

Walter Hildebrandt's *Views From Fort Battleford* and Sarah Carter's *Lost Harvests* dispel the myth that the Cree were unwilling to farm and/or incompetent. The truth is "we", the lately Europeans, through our own ceding — ironic for being the key hidden weapon word in Treaty Number Seven — we, through the moment we ceded ourselves to a state, reneged on promises of land, equipment, instructors and markets, undermined their in-good-faith efforts. As plain competitors we crowded them out, literally and economically.

Plain playing the bald truth at last, if we include here the exposure of the we-as-just-weeds fallacy, of the ecological shrug, a conspiracy theory that says to the natural, to the metaphor: weigh your turn as you turn a/way, ie into three senses. The first is licensed unlimited play — into the next two. The second is the thanks but no thanks, or rebellion even. The third is the new way or revolution, in turn the beginning of never settling for less than the play of truth: its innocent mind-of-its-own wrecking and reckoning, its drama, and its experienced ways in giving and disowning itself right in the right hands, how like the play of light, how it goes over, to play apart the whole.

Of its two minds it plays one off against the other, plays into each of their hands, then crosses them to play the field which is always out of its mind with the ghosts of itself. Some moment says the we-as-just-[ascendant]-weeds is the only gift we could give back but that it would come as useless and fallacious alibi in a too ultimate history that is best called "Broken Arrow".

These new "Indian" histories come to light, enter the legal system, devolve and evoke the once fatefully railroaded oral traditions, help bring about land claim settlements, bring about clearings of air for the "smudges" of these oralities. The real irony of that polysemic "settlements" over against the globitarian horizon is the new super rich nomads barely touching down for their de-localized hyper comparative advantages while refugees search for havens in the nowhere, ideality-gone-wild[?], world. Can the Swabian's cows be absorbed into the night of all black? How distinctly Frankenstein can it get, Victors-victoids?

Aesop Asymptote

Aesop Asymptote is of course a preposterous name, not to mention the namer or his falling into the trendy course of culture critique tending to tire of mere reflected glory and thence toward the very cachet of mathematical authority. A name is such an uncanny collector of the relevant, not to mention the irrelevant, and that, by its very hands off approach, its arbitrary particularity welcoming the sundry shadowy waters, a most unlikely cap-tain of endless associations.

Recap: this fabulous name only a preamble in order to get a purchase on Playcefire heading east to the prairie, to the agricultural heartland. A morning person anyway, farmer's hours appealed to him. He would be closer to Saskatchewan where he spent a good portion of his formative years. Things were looking up even as he pulled his implement hat down snugly in the strong Chinook winds. These hats always change a face, even level it toward a goofy everyman look, especially on so tight. It softened

Playcefire's controlling eyes, his intelligent eyes full of fire, always trying to place a possible threat or opportunity. He seemed happy on the farm in the spring and Recap called him Rosy.

One thinks of the guy at Rochdale College who was convicted and jailed on drug charges and is now a regular on the new morning show on CBC. Normal Mailer had known him in the sixties and seventies and came up to Toronto to his trial as a character witness. Somewhere Mailer talked about how you had to sit up and take notice of a guy with enough balls to go by and embrace the name "Rosy". Which makes one think about this thing[s] "balls".

One assumes males are perpetually in search of them. Or that we are trying to keep up to them, or then again, trying to flee them. Well obviously in some way they are there to stay and right under our noses, or correlates. If one allows that the "hysterical male" either underplays or overplays being male then one is on the way to realizing that one never hits the mark or groove, so to speak. And then in further consideration one realizes that this having balls refers to action and a sense of fate that equally applies to women.*

And of course one hears, either comically or pathetically, women accusing one another of having them or not. And the truth is they may have the advantage in this pursuit of balls since the literal reduction presents no distraction. They have a clean slate and wider field of action. But this is nonsense this figuring of balls. It is a

---

* Hemingway told Lillian Hellman in Spain "you have *cojones*".

matter of not being caught in your own, not reflection, for that would be a step or half step in the right direction, like Narcissus who didn't recognize himself in his own reflection, but in your reflecting.

The real point is being "not caught", for surely you have to wrestle with the fact of your own reflecting. It is a matter of realizing a world and its embedded, but also arising, history. You die into the world a thousand times, to leave off the legal or conscience allusion, though the guilt of the existentialists is pertinent, and finally you die forever opaquely into the earth, as well as, for a time, fluidly into the world or the minds of those who carry on. This jailbreak escape into oneself as fatefully absorbed into the world of others is surely the issue of balls and has nothing to do with a male prerogative or ability, though perhaps a male injustice.

Recap had phoned Aesop or a once Rosy, more accurately, Playcefire (but Rosy for here), over a debt that in Recap's mind was getting to be a little too outstanding. Recap couldn't be certain he wouldn't get repaid, actually he thought he would eventually, that is he would when Rosy was rolling in it. He didn't like that thought. He knew Rosy was a great juggler, was often on a shoestring, was an adept scrambler and paid off, with a sense of survival, on a priority basis which had to do with what most immediately, or mediately down the road ultimately, threatened the very game itself.

Recap understood this and admired the skill and this being on the edge, this actual holding oneself together. He knew from his own experience on the farm what it was like lying in bed not able to sleep for the knots in the stomach wondering what the bank's next move would be, what the market forces were brewing, what the force of nature would deal them. But by the same token, this view from the money side of things, where you often didn't know whether you were coming or going, ie not only where the money was going, either into returns or the melting air, but the not knowing what of this fanciful air you were investing in the concrete fiction of money as it actually squeezed out the future, gave Recap pause.*

He didn't mind making the small loan (Rosy had said after that "I can't come up with that kind of money" and *u*nequally "I'm not going to argue over a few dollars") for a short period, period. Rosy and he went back a long way, and what does a "long way" say about the nature of friendship, it had to be some kind of proof, unless James Jones' characters "Hammer" and "Nail" say something else. What does a "long way" do to a friendship?

Do differences, or to factor out to the two sides, do the shortcomings get ameliorated or just accepted, and if the latter, is this a generosity of spirit or a weakening of integrity in the separate selves? Or does joint history become too quickly a movie, seductive in its grainy quality, a parody or sentimentalization of the going over fatefully to the reflected world? And how does one sort this out from the mutual references that throw both back into the history, but as historians chiselling cracks in the movie, or say the blockbuster?

---

* Marx through Tristram Shandy and Don Quixote navigated the strange attractor possibilities of this air when he built a whole castle from the fact of the criminal: criminal law, professors and their compendiums of law, lawyers, police, locksmiths etc.

He did not mind making this "small" loan this particular time, though he minded when the time for repayment had passed many times over, trying to take into consideration the usual mitigating circumstances. But that was just the point, the circumstances were the exciting and dangerous circumstances of the entrepreneur. Something didn't seem right about lending to an entrepreneur, at least for Recap, who split himself in relation to his money that came from inherited capital and from his half-yearly toil, the toil that rose up flush with the momentum and machinery of the buzzed-up agribus land, and that also seemed gestures, still laborious, that danced alongside the essence of farming practice as modern capitalism, as it in turn toiled under the frightening vagaries of finance capitalism that so ruled the governments, the overruled governments of the day.

He would flip over to his other self and accept the money like an allowance. Perhaps he'd inherited along with everything else the thrift bound up in his mother's memory of, among other things, her Labour politician father defeated in the Social Credit landslide right in the middle of the depression. And also inherited his father's reaction attitude, not his reaction action, to *his* father's wheeling and dealing his great enterprizes, ie Recap's father had had to sort out and organize the chips where they fell, keep everything running day to day after their great time-violating founding by Recap's grandfather.

Third generation equals degeneration he sometimes thought, of himself, not his brother or sister who, in their separate ways, were engaged on something like fronts compared to his rearguard action. His brother on the farm actually combined both the father's and the grandfather's actions, starting things *and* keeping them going. But then he thought too that the action for himself stops here, not in a degeneration but in a decadence as the moment of ripeness which must be spoken of towards new ends. Frighteningly hi-falutin this was and so he settled for the meantime of endless research and then the search for its point.

He would have been more ready to lend to an artist or, like he did in the past, to friends that were simply down and out, out of work or in some way unable to. The problem was Rosy's sense of game, his living by his wits, his dynamism in the market place versus Recap's stasis at the base that he often felt was dwindling even as he worked contentedly to convert his discontented life into mental capital, as the new sociologists cum economists were saying, until a certain discontent arose from here into new uncertainty.

And this despite the productivity of the farm in the first half of the nineties. The great depression had haunted the eighties. Did they pass for their own mean ghost now? They did at the real gut level but it didn't square at the historical level and certainly not at the mythic level where comparisons to the thirties were being made at the time, except once in a while as correlative to his emotions. Hustling was a necessity for Rosy, and Recap could accept it as natural in the world as it was, suspendable though it was too and capable of being rethought, and/or as it was closing on something catastrophic, or as many said, as it was now already a living in the aftermath of ruin or a thousand years of boredom.

Recap had then phoned Rosy and had been made to wait for him to call back which he had forgotten to do. So when Recap phoned again it was late and he could tell, though Rosy had not gone to bed, he had probably been asleep on the couch in front of the TV. Recap alluded to not wanting to get angry but the allusion itself actualized the anger that came out in tone and insinuation. But Rosy more than rose to the occasion. A lot of things surfaced.

Definitely on a rant Recap thought as he pulled away from the receiver and Rosy's grinding voice. He heard the little "you little cocksucker" come out of the phone he now held out in front of him like an artifact, complete with new hot/cool comic marshallings. He put it around to the side of his head but back from his ear, not so much for the sake of his ears, though it was at drum-damage level, but as gesture to himself that he would let him react however, as long as he got his money back, and that he was not in the wrong and could rest on that fact. He knew it was just a matter of time till Rosy would hang up and he was resigned to not having a say anymore, took satisfaction he thought in letting Rosy have a less than satisfying gesture hanging up.

He pretended to laugh to himself when he heard the word "presumptuous", a word whose entry into Rosy's economy of words he figured he could almost date, and whose new possession had relinquished Recap's, as though an impersonator had just done him, had done with him. But the new life for the word just underlined its mocking, albeit unmagical, autonomy. Recap tried to re-laugh his distant laugh but who knows where the last laugh lies, in both senses. He couldn't read anymore that night even though he held his book in reading position for another hour. He was startled to hear a bold knock at the door around midnight. It was a cabdriver with an envelope which contained the money owed in the form of post-dated cheques and a letter repeating the telephone harangue in a more coherent and formal way, though it also reflected on the status of their friendship in a serious way, that is as a threat but too as an honest objectivity.

Recap soon realized his satisfaction was illusory as far as that night went, for he could hardly sleep at all and continually had to get up to piss. His body had taken all the violence through the phone after all and he felt it as a reflex he had initiated, which compounded the racing of his mind. He found out later that Rosy had walked the streets of Banff that night till three or four in the morning and had gotten up as usual just after six.

In the letter Rosy had said things were different now and Recap considered this. He phoned the next day after writing a letter in response but they ended up talking everything out on the phone. He apologized but tried to stick to his guns about legitimately wanting the money back, separating out the violence he'd unleashed to apologize for strictly. He later thought about the symmetry now in relation to when Rosy worked on the farm just after his brother and he had acquired a big chunk of land, just before the disastrous eighties. It had rained again and Rosy had taken off to Calgary for the weekend where he'd had a pretty wild time, drinking and frolicking in a jacuzzi.

Unfortunately he'd slipped on a ladder and badly gashed his heel. When he came back he could still drive a tractor but had had so little sleep he couldn't stay awake. Recap knew the feeling, actually the sweetest intimation of sleep there is, that lulling effect of the lumbering tractor in the muting cab, somehow heightened when you're fighting it. And they were on night shift which compounded Rosy's pretty serious sleep deficit. Recap sympathized at first, telling him not to fight it, just to stop the tractor and put his head down on the steering wheel, sleep for five or ten minutes, especially if he were ahead of Recap on the drills. Recap had almost twenty more feet than Rosy's rod weeder width and then his marker extended another twenty feet and so Rosy would have to get a good head start and make sure to lap him when Recap filled the drills.*

Rosy took the words to heart because in no time his machine stopped and the dust momentarily clouded around the tractor and then dissipated. Recap watched and after ten minutes the tractor puffed black smoke into the early morning sky and he was in business again. But then the frequency increased so that Recap was gaining on him and getting agitated about the fact. Finally Rosy stopped at the corner where Recap had been filling, which he had to do this round, and now his drill marker was right up the rod weeder's ass. He rushed over to the rental tractor and pulled the door open. Rosy woke suddenly and Recap started swearing and yelling at him. Rosy put it in gear and headed out.

---

* A rod weeder only works on summerfallow fields and is usually operated as close in time to the seeder (drills) as possible without impeding its progress. Though in the right conditions it could subvert the natural order, ie Recap had seen it pulled behind a disk drill, say, the idea being to make the death date of the sprouting weeds approach the birth date of the planted seeds, or even give the illusion of succeeding† (with the time-as-space metaphor seeming to contradict the direction of the spaced-out machine).

† Success with weeds is always illusory.

Days later when they were virtually finished seeding Recap drove him into town so he could rent a car and get back to Banff. They were silent in the truck and then Recap attempted to apologize. He knew there was something deeper going on that he didn't know how to talk about. He steered into the often true enough cliché about envying pleasure, the pleasure Rosy had had in Calgary that weekend. That his violent shouting was somehow rooted in that, combined with the push they were making to get the crop in. He felt ill at ease saying this because it didn't seem even half the story, unless things are simpler than we sometimes think and the prevailing wisdom coming down in the higher clichés of the day knew more about you than you realized.

Rosy accepted this explanation though he didn't seem particularly pleased. Recap felt that he'd maybe accepted it to such an extent that it might be hard to extricate himself from the tarring done by his own diagnosis. He knew Rosy had other things on his mind too. That the farm had represented something idyllic he was escaping to from Banff. As a teenager Rosy had worked on his grandfather's farm and remembered the old man's self-reliance and the good food at the table. He also remembered how he liked the smell of freshly cultivated soil.

On the other hand Recap and his brother had acquired the new land late in winter and had barely pulled together enough machinery and men to take on the challenge of cropping it all in. But then just after they were able to get on the land it rained heavily for five days. It was more than a week before they could get back on it and the weeds had already had a good start before the rain. By the time they got to some of the fields the weeds, kochia and tansy mustard among others, were easily three feet high. They were just learning about continuous cropping, and combined with the bad timing was their limited range of machinery. The cultivator could get through, undercutting the weeds, but the hoe drills acted like a rake and constantly plugged up.

Often alone on night shift, Recap was barely able to make two rounds sometimes, mind you they were huge two hundred acre fields, two miles long. He would stop and try to fork the weeds out of the hoes and then clear them to the side, and would crawl under yanking them out by hand. Sometimes he'd stop and just go to the piles in front of him and spread weeds around or carry them back to the last round. They were still green and heavy.

One night he arrived for his shift and everything looked good, set up well. The huge drill outfit was full of seed and fertilizer, the three ton seed truck was parked strategically and the day crew had spent most of the time clearing weeds right off the field, using an old 1948 Dodge truck which some of them got a kick out of driving. Recap figured he was good for at least five rounds before he had to fill. No stopping every fifty yards to fork and scream "fuck" at the top of his lungs in the wide open night-muted prairie. Somewhere up there there was a ghost chorus who could echo this frustration, not least of whom would be the Cree from the 1880s.

Sometimes he would scream at the tractor, which he'd forget in such a state to throttle back completely, till his throat and lungs hurt and the dumb machine defeated him in its drowning out drone, blasting his head when he walked in front of the radiator grill to go back to the ladder you climbed to get back in, to futilely start over again. This night he made the rounds in about two and a half hours since the field was much smaller, being cut off by a ditch and some wetland down from a dam. When he walked out the field at the corner and over to the truck he realized they'd parked it, load and all, in a soft spot, actually muddy once you broke the surface.

The truck had slowly sunk and now was tilted to one side. He could barely get a chain around the axle after he had unhooked the tractor from the huge drill hitch and unplugged all the hydraulics. He spent the rest of the night pulling the truck out, loading the drills with wheat and packing eighty bags of fertilizer and then cutting them open into the boxes. Everything at night was considerably slower because of the prohibition of the dark, whether making you cautious or in just trying to judge or even see, say if something were dropped or put down carelessly.

Rosy had idealized the farm but it must have seemed right, all that land, more than good moisture and the optimism on the prairies at the beginning of the eighties. The view back to the Rockies in the spring was overpowering. The snow capped peaks at Waterton, old Chief. Recap's mother could see where the recent slide had changed its profile. Mount Assiniboine could be seen slightly north from due west. Some mornings coming from the night shift could be massively depressing especially if things weren't going well.

After they started one shift and there was light left in the long day and Rosy's heel was still bothering him Recap had him drive the three-quarter ton down the field as he forked weeds into the box. When they got to the end of a two mile field he just forked them directly into the ditch. Recap didn't mind though Rosy was feeling guilty, just driving. In fact Recap was getting manic, trotting from pile to pile as the "crazy harrows" had left them. He turned what would have been later the hell of constant interruption, into a workout now.

Rosy had been stopping the truck and getting out to fork but Recap was racing and tried to obsolesce the truck's position almost before it arrived by amalgamating piles and firing the whole load into the box. Rosy would have to get back in and drive further up. Despite Recap's perverse game, the heel must have really been bothering Rosy because he was trying to get out as much for the fresh air, soil smell and sunset as trying to help. His sock was all bloody and so when finally enough field was cleared to keep the freshly filled drills busy, Rosy drove back to town so he could re-bandage his foot and change into boots.

Two hours later Recap was finished the rounds and stopped to fill again. Rosy was nowhere to be seen. It was light now but definitely not rosy in the sky. Low grey clouds were socked in from horizon to horizon. Recap's mood was darkening as he climbed out of the warm cab and went over to get the seed truck. With two you could back up the little merc with the fertilizer bags to one end of the drills so the seed truck could still get in behind them the whole way along, and then have two operations going at once. When he had filled seed he pulled the truck away and went and got the fertilizer truck.

Fifty-six feet of drill, eight drills, ten bags of fertilizer per drill. When he'd done that and was ready to go again Rosy finally showed up. It was getting really light and if he was lucky he could get one round done before the day crew arrived. The one thing more after the weed clearing that Rosy could have helped him with was this just finished filling, made twice as long without him.

Rosy had keyed on the red light on the microwave tower to find his way back. Only thing was there were lots of towers around the area with red lights and though it was grey it was not James Gray's *Red Lights on the Prairie*, even though Recap had been thinking the proverbially worst, that Rosy had been fucking, ie the dog. He hadn't thought he would fuck up on the red lights. In a cooler moment he could see how it could have happened. And later they did laugh about it. They didn't laugh about Recap's shouting that other night though. And Rosy nursed it for many years.

Recap wondered now if it had been Tain, Tain with a love for the darkness illuminated with quick and quirky flickers of thought, that Rosy was expecting to work with when he arrived at the mythic farm. It would take another ten years before Recap would slip into the mythic, when, as it was said, farming got into your blood. There had been more than enough years for him farming, over thirty by the early nineties, but not that many years being his own boss. That first year on the new land had historic and mythic dimension, that is he was ten times more active, in the sense of sheer labour possibly too, but in the sense of worrying every little acre seeded, every breakdown, every putting of the drills into transport and manoeuvring the whole length around a corner on the road and then into an approach or through a gate.

Jimmy's motto about machines, "I know when they're idle", applied. By a kind of athleticism and sheer will Recap insinuated himself into the operation, threaded himself through every anticipation with his nerves that hummed and as the adrenalin shot through his veins. But he couldn't keep that up in the next years. Especially after five and six bushel crops and two dollar wheat. The first year was like a military campaign but it was hard to fight a war twice. Ten years later with good crops and good prices and after a major confrontation with a major bank he had become mythic. He took it day by day, tried to get something done, got home and showered and was reading the paper in bed before midnight if he was lucky.

The myth had holes in it through which the light of historical day shone, extinguishing timelessness, but these were, not the exception that proves* the rule, as Hugh Kenner the part empiricist points out, but that which "tests" the rule. Rosy had projected the myth and hid out in its shelter, and basked on the patio by day as further proof of his holiday of work. And there were only two bad nights. The rest of the time he was a hard worker, spotted things that were going to break or cause trouble. He was a natural around machines, for seeing to their basic maintenance.

Recap for his part, on his side, was carrying the world on his shoulders that "Rosy" year, in the paranoid sense, worrying into the four corners so to speak. In actuality he was doing a pretty good job. He could taste the myth in a split second but the history pulled him apart however much he held on, held himself together. He just couldn't

---

* Illogical unless you try the word history to prove otherwise.

quite savour anything really in the moment, but then perhaps there was more quick savouring in the not quite. And he was saving it in some obscure way. It was a strange year, the first time around as his own boss. Later he let his brother tease him to someone else about how it "was hard to get good owners".

Recap was content to go mythic and let his brother become boss. Rosy had wanted him to be boss when he worked (was it for him or with him?), to be benign boss and live in a myth. Recap had turned out to be a hard ass, which is not a boss but just the lights on with nobody home, the absence of someone, desperately lost out in the contingencies, or back at square one, mile zero, with no recollection, a Tain with a fear of the dark. Rosy had grown to call him Recap the lecturer, one who would go over how they'd become lost, in these moments he'd lost his tain relief. Recap was rarely again a hard ass, though there were flashes in that ten years. He was perhaps a passive aggressive, a history without a boss and he was postponing the myth, except for and on the farm.

Rosy was in ruins, in the sense again of life-after-life, when Recap phoned him that night about the money. Indebted and out of myth yet decidedly a boss, frustrated with the world which had let him down, which it had, one could say objectively with a touch of better world on the brain. Rosy was coping, first things first, with what came in the mail, on the phone and through the door. A day in the trenches. He had done everything right he knew even as he wondered if he'd lost his nerve, the kind he had years ago when he would try anything, risk all. His plan had come to life and should have worked beautifully but for the knocking world. He reflected on the ruins and looked for his own reflections, not coming back at him now but as broken off, away from him.

The plan was perfect in the sense of perfectly acceptable, the present clearly arranged and the grab or greed of the other players, the tics and predestinations of them, had been elegantly entered into the equation. But some incalculable overbalance had emerged from the usual mess of forces and become a fate, and had come calling. And on the phone Recap had deployed his ploy and Rosy fell to hard ass. Recap was not impressed, well of course, as the idiom indicates, he was, but negatively.

What had he seen in the theatre of the phone?! Naturally he thought of the chickens coming home to roost, of his hard ass yelling at Rosy fifteen years before. He saw a reflection, but of neither he nor Rosy. A great gulf had fallen between them as they separated off, each into their consistencies, hard but healthy states in which to find themselves. As Hegel is diverted through Gödel these new consistencies opened them to the incompletenesses that being alive is, even as they carried the possibility of myth and its wonderful killing fields.

Recap thought of their discussions of women, endless discussions. Yet how much time they had spent between them, no pun intended. Recap for long stretches and Rosy for many short stretches. Rosy offering them too much materially, Recap too little, period. Their fantasies of women were of "the complete woman", their perceptions of women in other, real relations were sensitive, appreciative and complete. Their actual relations were their undoing, of the women of course too, to be fair, taking undoing in a brave sense. In the meantime they corrected their hopes with flirtations and disasters, Rosy more often than Recap whose hopes sprang eternally. But he thought that through these corrections Rosy, alias Aesop what's his name, must be getting closer to myth on the ground where the sun dispels itself and fantasies of same.

A few nights after the phone call Recap lay in his actual bed and took the bottom of the top sheet between his two big toes then stretched out his legs so that the sheet reached the end of the bed. Then he kicked the sheet out left and right all the while he held the heavy Hudson's Bay blankets. This is how he made the bed. It was his metaphor for how things might be, that is how one might overcome the aporia appearing between consistency, or distinctness, and completeness. To lie in one's bed and then make it, not withstanding the more probable meaning of more foundationally "making one's bed", yet the derivative meaning suited a day by day more derivative life-within-life. This was Rosy's practice, in theory.* Playcefire's comfort was the irritation that ignited in a flash the idea of travel.

Hegel's Cows

Real human beings, the kind with both idealities (the augmented one generated by hope), are the "necessary evil" for the new ghosts, *out* of the machine, and over and

---

* A reverse truism of course, one that tempts the reversal of the reversal†, especially as the will is wont to flag, in the sense of rearguard celebration too. A truism that dramatizes the great double hook of chance and myth's utter ironic dependence on it.

† (if the reversal isn't perchance the rub[bed-out] in bed with the made-up which be-leaves itself wide open in the original assaying)

over the horizon. Even the bad infinite needs the propped-up individual mediating mind, albeit atomized, like the minimal maximal consumer, just as the infotains in the maw of the Franken mirrors need human termini — to be beheld by what they harvest.

But if there's evil here it *is* human, the collapsed human as atomized out into spurious infinite progressions. If there's evil there's humanity with its good potential under the always spurious or false collapse. The good ratio of spirit, an infinite fold on itself, lets be generated these manifold falsifications of itself. The bad is the sign of the good, the good not necessarily the sign of the bad, as long as the rear-guard arrow of time exists. And a ripple of asymmetry exists in the inter-identification of good and bad such that good would be somehow bigger in its moment of "left hand to right hand" ignorance.[*] The ignorance from an expansive shattering versus the expensive ignorance of the shattering's immanence and imminence.

Human mediation dirempts into depletion/corruption of the biosphere and into our angelization cum a banality equal to the banality of the originators of evil, though the evil at the real human end be never banal (topically see Le Carré's, admittedly rather banal itself, *The Tailor of Panama*, for how banal fantasy invades and can do evil in the material world), and as Earth is enslaved, so it calls and takes on its greatest charisma, takes on more power than

---

[*] In the Sermon on the Mount the surmounting of self is a return to beginning as a Kantian end in itself. Can this end be distinguished from the "childermass" of the Frankenworld or be immune to Nietzsche's ridicule, his eternal return notwithstanding?

any of the other *so-called* higher realms, more than the potential difference, not the devil, behind evil.

On the other hand the complete return to Nature for us, not aliens say, but alienators — to use a kind of PoMo SF, or now, Hegeling, speculative word — such return would be perfect futility. Such return would be no return but the falling rock (above) — in reverse. Impossible, the temptation and attempt would just re-inscribe the banal origination of evil.

The conscious falling rock could never — banking on Peirce's "reduction up", ie deep down proto-feelings — balance, back into nature. For good *reason*: its knot/not into itself, and its knot/not into the singular semantics of a human being, ie to suggest reason's next-year-country community and its self-correcting experiments with realisms half pregnant with the untimely, even in the latest, always late, sensation from myopia groping its way to a mythopoeia. Good reason: its powerful recall, recoil, its eternal spring. We can't keep, and keep hope or a good rock-ignition down on the farm.

Old Girlfriends: Rebecca

There's an injustice done to the discontinuity between "girl" and "woman" despite the weight of usage now and politics. And for sure "girl" is pathetically inappropriate, nay, at a deeper level, sounds dead wrong. "Woman" is too *uber* and over (almost as ovaries can take her over), goes beyond the mark of respect and alienates. Though there is a powerful sexuality in the word, sometimes liftingly on the mark. "Girl" is something penetrating, with ironic other connotations here, which goes to the heart of the reference, as in, naturally, back toward origin lost in a tain, exceeded by the referent however much carrying it, with a further teasing-away connotation.

Recap, for one (in his own so innocent term), did love to tease the girls too. They grow up around "girl", are bigger indeterminately than it and the usage gauges how much they want to escape it. Of course sometimes to the extent and *extension* of "woman", which then seems somehow to overshoot into qualities of oppressive umbrella, a rime of sky, and in itself an interesting visual sign and thence complex symbol as one tries to get a handle on it without collapsing to the literal one, teasingly ambiguous too in itself. It remains, there is a gulf, so then neither works satisfactorily. If informality is on the road to intimacy then there is something of "girl" in that direction, the just right context and predication presupposed going with it, it goes without saying.

Friendships with old girlfriends are a pleasant afterlife and Recap and Rebecca were enjoying its fall to earth, that would be between five and a half and just under six feet up from it, their respective heights. Actually they had been walking on the winter-closed road up on and around Tunnel Mountain. The snow was deep in places but there had been plenty of human and animal traffic to tramp it down so that in most places they could walk together as they talked. They could borrow the old intimacy, not for new intimacies but for real conversation about what interested them in many, though far from all, realms.

They likewise moved in dimensions where power relations were not mentioned or mentionable because they had fallen away in this fall to new springy footing, garden of delighted weightlessness. The high wisps of cloud left the day bright, Stoney Squaw ribbed with dark trees and Cascade its usually shining self. Recap thought how as a child he'd taken "Stoney", short-circuiting the Indian band or bands (three), as simply meaning the stone of the mountain, which of course it meant too, harking back to the source of the band's name.*

He thought of how the world was more than willing to have a bit of fun with language and could conspire to keep private meanings in public circulation, at least as far as the wrongheaded user was concerned, which was both as far as the public world extended and not as far as even to enter it, since the unwitting stealth bomb user saw the usage's waves reach out to and conspire with all other usages and the public heard only their own correct usage and not the anomalous private one at all. He had been much older than he would care to admit when he suddenly realized that "useless as tits on a board" should be "tits on a boar".

There's something very pleasing about a closed road, almost as if it were more secluded than a never-was-a-road. Almost as if the road were a minus sign, that is less than simply no road again, as if the road, reincarnated, were a gain in the heart of loss, useful in the uselessness wheeling back to life, with the un-cleared snow turning a coursing negligence into a fine foray. The road remained as an echo or comment on the solitude thus come into being. The recognition of a sweet desolation requires in a recoiling way the inhabitation of the familiar to effect, to set off the

---

* "Stoney", from their Ojibwa name *Assiniboine*: "people who cook with [hot] stones".

minimum communion. The road closed is the road open to the possibilities that hover between five and a half to six feet off the ground.

The time passed quickly into new negligence and the effort of negotiating some taxing inclines on narrower icy paths went practically unnoticed absorbed as they were. And coming around the mountain when she comes, because that is the way of absorption and the world of possibles — that is, the new lies of the land and scene changes seemed to come upon them. They were surprised by winter, sure, what the hell, it's that deep, this memorable way.

But what is meant, they were surprised by the tourist cabins, surprising them in turn coming in from behind rather than the usual office way. In the possible world he and she were flittingly all the bunkered down visitors at once. And those were clay feet that were their parked cars, and shall we say, sticking out of bed. It was a tickling thought this possible interruption of the embedded, perfectly placed, displaced persons. It was not four o'clock yet, the sun still reigned and his thoughts were all wet. When they reached the foot of Tunnel and were back into town the jostle of it all brought them to their other senses, the realization they'd exhausted the possibilities for now but that their friendship was borne by the backing of an inaccessible but inescapable actuality.

Goldilocks Guys

The eighties were running out and about to run into the Calgary Winter Olympics. Jim F was in one of his Hyde states, that is hiding out from some catastrophe of insults, though there was that moment, at least in some of the earlier catastrophes, when it was more a festival. But in Recap's basement suite Mr. F was still in his nasty or hurling mode, seemingly oblivious to Recap and his increasing irritability at the lateness of it all. It was more than the three o'clock this particular night, it was the long lost source of some hurt. Some insult Jim F had suffered way back in childhood? It was the endless rehearsal of symptoms until they had become rootless and senseless however much they had their moment of pure carnival and comment on the easily seen-to-be mad world, the spinning insularity of a drunken, post-hippy Banff.

He compulsively dialed and redialed the telephone, obviously waking people up who promptly hung up on him, or then he talked in various degrees of put on and tones of being put off already, or he would stand in deadly attention to what the other person was saying. He would drop the phone and then bang it on the cradle on the wall so that it bounced off and crashed on the table. Then he would throw it at the wall. Recap had once seen him piss into a receiver. Here he was drinking a liqueur that Recap happened to have on hand and was starting to spew it on the table and wall.

Recap finally yelled at him but it was as if to a stone, so he grabbed him and turned his real anger into its own ad agency, growled and acted the symptoms of a madness greater than Jim's. This meant he had to lift him off his feet by the lapels, out into the hallway and up against the wall. He had to think on his feet what the next choreographic climax was going to be, which turned out to be sliding him along the wall and then falling over on the mat with him. He sat on Jim's stomach and thrust his hands around his throat. Jim finally looked scared so he let him up and walked back into his room.

Jim followed with his tail between his legs and asked, barely audible, if he could have his pack. Recap handed it to him quickly. Jim said "see you [pause], never" and turned to go. Recap started talking normally and apologized, with reservations about Jim having to get a hold of himself, that this was no good. They hugged one another in reconciliation. Jim talked sorrowfully and contritely for awhile and then started joking and then play threatening Recap with karate moves. He did Bruce Lee imitations, pulled his fist up just short of Recap's nose. Recap got annoyed again and said that he had to get to sleep. Jim left.

Just around noon the next day Recap answered the phone. It was Jim from the police station he was about to leave. Apparently he had gone into Smitty's when it opened at six and, after he had sat down, asked to see the waitress's panties, instead of the menu. Now he asked Recap to meet him at Sidestreet, the long narrow bar attached to the Rundle Restaurant. Recap hedged but said he might drop in for a minute. When he did he found Jim in a benign, most sweetly drunken state, funny as only he could be and full of boyish charm, and all he wanted was reassurance that they were still friends. Recap rubbed Jim's head when he left and told him to take care.

Recap: the famous episode of Jim F and Jim H. Jim H was a funny man too, much taken with older movies and could do imitations of Bogart and Cagney. He was also one to get into long nights of drunken irresolution. He was harder than Jim F and quick to actually fight, no playing around with fake karate. Recap had seen him with bloodied knuckles, skinned nose and bruised forehead. Face down once in the street with a small crowd on the sidewalk watching him. But he hadn't been knocked down, he was just thrashing around in a puddle an inch or two deep. When Recap got closer he could see that he was swimming, perhaps acting out Burt Lancaster's role in *The Swimmer*, who knew?

Recap steered around and kept walking but could hear Jim H's hoarse voice raging in the night air. He could imagine the veins in his neck and side of his forehead bulging as he raged, and Recap winced for the guy's knees and elbows and hands in their thrashing. He thought about the exaggerated swings of it all in Jim H's larger temporal scene. He would see him seriously running the hills around the Banff Centre and knew by his triceps he did regular push-ups or dips or maybe even worked out at the Sally Borden. His biceps were veined too but the menace in him, when he wasn't being a clown, showed up in his eyes and forehead.

Jim F and Jim H ended up carousing together one night. It was like adding gasoline to a fire. Recap imagined the scene of the crime as the same building where Jim F's old girlfriend had lived. When and where Jim F had crawled along the sidewalk behind a hedge to get to his erstwhile girlfriend's car so he could let the air out of her tires. He did let the air out and his girlfriend stood at the window and watched the whole thing, the guerrila theatre of the post cardiac blues.

But this time it was Jim H's old girlfriend that took the hit. She was out with her new boyfriend when the two of them got into her apartment. They drank all the booze they could find and then cooked up some kind of supper, beans as the main course. Then they lit a fire in the fireplace and listened to records. Both were musical, especially Jim F and had their critical tastes. Apparently they didn't like her music so started chucking the records into the fire. Finally they needed sleep, climbed into her bed. That's where she found them, snoring when she finally got home.

Jim F was a terrific musician. A hard player, he would often break strings on his guitar. He eventually cut a record and it was a wonder and an ordeal to keep him sober and get him into the studio when the other muscians were there. It was a terrific album, capturing his drive and that husky velvety voice that could suddenly rise up into thinner sweet timbres. Recap loved to sit in the huge lounge mid evening in the BPL and listen to him sing "Bojangles" over by the huge fireplace. Recap would drink coffee with a shooter of scotch at this time of night. Later he would drink in the Magpie and listen to Jim and all the other musicians that would come to jam.

He had seen Bruce Cockburn, Sid Marty, Big Miller, Gay Delorme, Dave Wilkie, Big Dave McLean and many others play there. Cockburn didn't play himself but some of his band did. Lots of great locals had played there too, including Chuck Tracey with his wry wit and quirky and sometimes retro tastes in jazz, pop and folk music. They'd had a wake there when he died. Somebody put together a tape of various of his own recordings of himself and played it between all the stories. He'd died before he was fifty, seemed to have basically smoked himself to death. Recap remembered him working at a health food store and what a great advocate he was of the organically grown and such. He wouldn't eat tomatoes, "nightshade family" he'd say, then light up another cigarette.

It was in the Magpie that Jim F would sit around after hours after his night's gig and strum his guitar, make up lyrics on the spot. It would start off delightfully and Recap, remembering, thought about Attali's book *Noise* and about music's strange transformations through history, its impulsive roots and then its various diversions and captivities. How the technology of instruments affected musical forms, the piano the sonata for instance. How the politics and sociology of it affected an audience's relation to or participation in it. In the electronic twentieth century how recording, originally intended to record historic moments, merely stumbled into the record business and then onto the airwaves.

How the phenomenon of stockpiling was the norm. And when you thought about it, it was very disconcerting, like the overkill of nuclear arsenals. You could hardly get around to playing it all. And this was most dramatized when you had visitors, and given you were possessed by your arsenal. You could hardly pick what you'd throw at them. Whatever you put on you had the urge to take off and put something else on, somehow have World War Three then and there, a big bang of consumption. More than likely you fell away and the excellent recordings mouldered and you caught music as you could and on passing radio. Or you started going to concerts.

Of course a farmer in his modern tractor cab can take a lot of music. But then "everything palls" and à la R. Murray Schafer, Glenn Gould and John Cage you found environmental music, in all senses. There was the conductor in the radio interview who said he otherwise never listened to music, would rather sit down at the seaside where he lived in the eastern States, let the sound of the sea wash over him. On the farm the hum and drone and still telling modulations from the ground up through all the mediation of machine and tractor were the necessary music of the farmer as he insinuated himself into his seeding.

But then the impulse to lift or raise up to conscious or complete enjoyment is the impulse that ends in demarcated musics, CDs etc. And so the movie about the threatened coal miners who were also a brass band makes perfect alienated sense. Music in its capture and ordering of noise and in its flirtation with return to it, intra the piece and extra, the chaos of pieces, in its extracted and abstracted articulated states, is simply life by other means, in its thunder of lately collapses, a "new key" as Langer says of the language of emotion, which psychologists, philosophers and anthropologists say is unnatural and key to the cognitive.

Jim F's attention would go around the table letting his song pick up each of the remaining, usually drunken patrons, friends of the owners, and one or two waitresses, say a bit about some special trait and then move on to the next person who would turn red and smile. He could get them singing along with a catchy chorus. Once he got Sue to help him write a song about his shoe. "Come on little doggy and bite the toe of my shoe". They sang like it was the very strings of their hearts. This was music about as unpretentious and inclusive as you could get and everyone laughed at their inclusion.

Of course as the night progressed Jim F would spit out the things that were often thought but never said, and went overboard from there. People usually went home at this point. In fairness people did ask much of him and could suck him dry and this was sometimes his revenge. He might show up drunk for a gig and everything would go fine or it could be a disaster. One night he came out wearing a dress over his jeans and cowboy boots. He had lipstick on and a cowboy hat, sat on his stool, played a few bars and then refused to go on. Sometimes he would harangue the audience.

One time he went around a big table of rugby players and told them all to fuck off. Recap was there watching the guys decide who would get to punch him out. Recap went over and picked him up, threw him over his shoulder and then carried him out through the kitchen and into the parking lot, over to the trees and grass on the other side. Recap could hear him sighing, as he cussed, like a kettle unplugged, but like the pot, calling *him* a "crackpot". When he set him down Jim F started pissing at him and Recap had to run to escape the tremendous arcing stream coming on from the halting and staggering source, night of the living deadeye.

The day after the musician cum mush you would see him walk in with purpose, polite to the point of anti-social. But O would you ever hear the tightest, meanest blues when he picked up the harp and especially when someone good sat in with him on guitar. A kind of revenge was parsed and parcelled out at high energy while his eyes looked nowhere and the contorted Hyde face lay hidden somewhere under a smooth impassivity.

Jon in the Underworld

Recap spotted Jon on the Fenland where "silence danced in the spaces of that place". Jon moved on ahead. "Silence moves with dragon flies". But this was the "deep wonder and winter". No odours of the "squirrel middens". "You like that word 'middens'" Recap said. "Your sort of word. I remember you using it often". "'All poets deal with garbage' said McLuhan". And in those heady meta-message days Recap would have also said "the garb age". And having nailed it implied a "still point" in the "widening gyre" and therefore have TS'ed a Yea.

And then he would have gone through the new archeologies with Foucault, but Jon would recognize only the pendulum one, and before Eco's book was on the scene. Recap had tried to trap him by a deft intertwining, arguing that M. Foucault was somehow made way for by the phenomenon of the semiotic world and that the greater semiotician than de Saussure was Peirce who had, wouldn't you know, made what living he was able to, in great measure, measuring pendulums for the US Coast Survey. Then came Blodgett's lovely *Arche/elegies*.

Jon took an hour to do the trail and went counter-clockwise to see how many were on the trail that day, capturing the deeper silence in the equinoctial light and, "curiously" he said, apprehended only a couple of locals. At this time, panned back to the prairies, Recap might have stopped his swather to stretch his leaden legs and piss into the pungent turnip smells of a canola field. He would have looked at the grey mouldering leaves on the ground shed weeks earlier and would be somehow pleased with the fade to earth of these ephemeral factory plants. And would have looked grandly but quickly at the vast evening horizon where the mountains were merely a low serrated edge to it all. The ford six would be firing away and would call him back into the cab to push ahead with the hydrostatic drive. Monocultural rime to the monotheistic condition.

Jon argued in the piece on Indian beadwork that the plains people were given to geometric forms, partly because the women were not allowed to represent objects and thus, say, disturb the magic between a hunter and the animals, but partly because of the condition of horizon and sky in the prairie. That geometric form was the expression of a prairie monotheism. Mountain landscape is broken and local and so the beadwork, and before that, quillwork, was full of flower content. All complicated with inter-influence and ironies involving natural geometries.

Recap thought about how he and Jon would define one another's sensibilities and would imply that each was in need of, as it turned out, the other's position without each himself feeling the need to move. Recap would have said Jon was, in Isaiah Berlin's famous terms, a fox in need of the hedgehog's one big idea. And at this point the knowledge must have crept in an increment or two that he, as hedgehog, needed the world of increment or Tolstoy's poignant details.

Recap reconsidered this interchange and recognized that of course neither position could exist purely, that a human sensibility one or the other position could not add up to. And if "add up to" is the symptom of how the sensibility is always already whole and therefore better characterized as the "one big idea" position then one equally has to recognize that the immediate task at hand for this presumptuous idea is its handing itself over, as if it had any choice, to the variegated phenomenon of the earth-world.

Recap considered the rule of elegance here, in itself, and as key to capturing Jon. This "capturing" of course made him hesitant, tentative and made him laugh. It reminded him of the time Bart Robinson had come down and spent a couple of days on the farm, getting into the spirit of radio communication between truck and tractor by parodying trucker CB radio talk. The radios were not CB but Recap laughed at the airwave names Bart came up with and thought of the way they had all become radio hams.

Bart had talked with and taped Recap and his mother on the patio in town and he had wandered around by himself and talked with the townspeople. When his article came out in *Equinox* Jon read it and annouced that Bart hadn't "captured the essence of FoxHog [not to be confused with Vauxhall]". Jon of course had never been to FoxHog. Later he and Pam came down and he sat on a little plastic tractor in the garden and Pam took his picture. He also got the kitchen mobilized and made a very good hollandaise sauce for the brussel sprouts, and also whipped up a fancy dessert. Once after reading a reference to elm trees in a Recap poem he declared that "you don't have elm trees in FoxHog", that again before he'd been there, where Recap's yard was full of them.

"Capturing the essence" is of course a clue to the problematics of elegance and of the ironies in trying to capture Jon. Elegance must rise out of both the natural world and out of the interpreted world, if the two can be separated. It must capture them even as it escapes them. Jon was aware of elegance, in fact thematized it many a time. He was aware of it in science and math and in writing.

But isn't elegance a bit of the big idea or its incarnation? It can be simply reincarnated and not do justice to the new life it finds itself in. For one who had no time for philosophy and who liked the empirical or literal side of things, Jon was awfully elegant. And of course one can see the dangers of elegance dramatized in some of his "chronicles", ironically. Perhaps what one sees more are the pitfalls of having to meet a weekly deadline. Some of the chronicles were not of course, were the coming up with something. Up too far, into the realms of lazy elegance.

Recap had been reading Jon's *Indians in the Rockies* and had pored over the sentences and had been drawn into the argument, the history and prehistory, and the scenes of the rodeo and horse races, the "slow race" Jon thought Lewis Carroll would have appreciated. But Recap still managed to stop and smell the sentences, the words, "quadrifolium" from geometry, "tarn" from geography, and "Hanjumbo" from the Stoney. Surely Jon came into his own, with the elegant, in this book. Walking the line that threads in and out of itself and in and out of a world, a possible world but *definitely*, that word and rendering work of the logos, tracked, as he points out, for over ten thousand years in this valley.

He was a great one for propping up the status of the artist and yet around the time he would have been writing *Indians in the Rockies* he was saying in the *Crag* that Indians didn't have art, they had culture, which they lived. Recap thought about this and how it was also alluded to and illustrated in the argument in the book. Jon had begun to lament the days of the Indians and question the re-presentation of Western art. His huge foray into Kelsey's world, the fore rays into a pristine world of first things had triggered a great longing, for his childhood, for a deeper participation.

He had apologized for a Wordsworthian slip of a poem he thought he'd written as part of the *Fells of Brightness* and Recap had had to step up and defend the two of them. He was thinking of Sheila Watson's lectures on the *Prelude* and the decided pull out of a mere pretty and peripheral romanticism, of that wrestling with the Germans Coleridge and Wordsworth too had done. Shlegel and Kant were tough angels.

The Germans were pulling out of that first blush of Romanticism too as can be seen in Goethe's career after *The Sorrows of Young Werther*. He caught the bug of science. Coleridge, for all his crawling in the Quantocks and traumatic carrying of his time as a child, caught forever, or for the rest of his mortal days at least he thought at the time, in a chimney of some cliff, and so composing his swan song, attended all the science lectures he could and befriended Humphrey Davey before he was a Sir. So Jon needn't have been ashamed of his Wordsworth trailing barometers of Coleridge, and could have his dearly beloved science to boot.

Perhaps it was his Blake kick, through Frye, another kick equally leaving behind its stamp (or archetype), that created this slight crisis that was otherwise elegantly solved with his devotion to elegance. That time in the Cascade bar Jon was talking about the William Blake society he wanted Recap and others to form, even ordering copies of the collected works for everyone, and some guy at the next table said he'd just come from Williams Lake. Jon was the first to laugh.

Surely this longing that had been long coming, as in his "born in Banff 1941, reborn in Banff 1968", had its moment of sentimentality as symptom of and antidote to a one-sided hook into science, especially potentially distorting in such a literary man. But the antidote of sentiment was not good enough, though he once, in an explanation of a special sense of sentiment he attributed to Coleridge, and had said was a quality Recap possessed, distinguished between sentimentality and true sentiment. His solution to the hole left by his neglect of philosophy, and for the FoxHog problem, and for the pitiful quality of cloying sentiment was his elegance, the embodiment of an evolving form that endlessly, but for the dignity of occasion, worried *over* the facts.

All this elegiac longing for a culture, not of services, but of involvement, brings along more ironies. But the ironies within ironies are nothing a deft dialectic can't handle. And he touched on it in meditating about the beadwork, in thinking about costume as necessity out in the elements and about decoration as one of the elements, of culture that is. The empiricist who thrived on variety, on the many spirits, recognized the oneness of a participatory culture that fully employed art.

And another irony, that put him in Hegel's great striving and, alas too, longing. Art, Hegel maintained, had lost its identity in an idealized Greek past. In the Western world we live in the non-identity of Art. He meant Art doesn't know itself and that it was involved in no vital equation or even relation. But then, having recognized the alienations of history, he devised strategies for surviving them, for carrying the recognitions of the non-identities as defence against the false gods or equations, or dominances in disguise, and for spiralling the world up just enough that it might come back on/as its own ghost of possibilities so to re-gauge and re-engage itself.

Monotheism, as the now truism goes, paved the way for science, consolidated the spirits into one and engendered a uniformity that heralded the laws. But then science slingshots back from some Archimedean point in space, spreads back into the manifold of empirical fact, thus riming the spirits above, if you neglect the invisible disposition point of your subtended participation. Jon had his cake and ate it too, therefore Recap, untimely in March, zoomed back and continued his stroll with him in the silences of equinoctial light. He told him how he saw again Jon's film, his Stanford Master's thesis on Jimmy Simpson, and now after reading Ted's book needed to see the film again.

Recap: how different it was from his memory of it. He had forgotten how much was shot of the natural landscape. He had remembered only a static angle on Jimmy talking at length. But the shifts and juxtapositions of talk and image were wonderful and the purely visual segues masterful. The footage of the lodge exterior was funny and entertaining and of the essence in regard to Jon's taste for the actual happenstance and makeshift of the world. The lodge reminded Recap of those houses he'd seen in New Denver, with that afterthought add-on and as-the-spirit-moves-the-builders look.

In Ted's book, he told Jon now, how interesting he found that part about how Jimmy, the snowshoer, "Nashan-esen" ("wolverine-go-quick"), would develop and get into a rhythm and once in, would compose music and plays as he went about the arduous task of checking his trapline. If something interrupted him he would lose the music or the play until he got his rhythm back. And how Murray Schafer would have loved his concerts out in the middle of nowhere, of everywhere, well at his cabin at Bow Lake.

On a cold night he would play the harmonica, even operatic things, improvising to get the half notes, just so his dog would start howling and the sound would travel the whole length of the valley and would get every coyote in the area going and the place came alive with this wilderness chorale, quite capturing itself! That time two prospective clients were negotiating and Jimmy offhandedly sculpted a plasticine mountain sheep and then a buffalo and then returned them to a ball in his hand. The two hunters were amazed and appalled when the animals disappeared before they could get their hands on them.

A little allegory for art as lifted out of things and as a remaining, but as not getting out of hand. Not completely satisfying allegory though because there are the remains, the middens, and there is the over and above, the left over energy as Keats dwelled on. And one thinks of Jimmy's partner that time after the winter supply of booze, one bottle of whiskey, was drunk. Nothing left to do but read the one book they'd brought, but he almost took it out and shot it, as he threatened to do to his snowshoes once when they had failed him. He had got so involved and biased in a depicted battle he was somehow there. The endearing immersion has a moment, but the absurdity calls us up again and asks us what we are capable of, asks if we can live without grasping for the removal of our removal, which, after all, makes it all possible.

Dr Rock in Store

Recap turned down the canned goods aisle in Keller's and saw Rock in a daze, or staring at the pasta across from the canned goods shelves which were truncated by the diagonal counter of the delicatessen. As he approached, Rock dug out his list and then saw Recap. He'd just been talking to Tom and told Recap now about the book he was reading on the Irish. He laughed first before he actually told him anything. Then he said that the author said Freud said that the Irish were the only people impervious to psychoanalysis. He had another good laugh and went into the next item. Apparently St Brigid was a woman who helped nuns with unwanted pregnancies. "A Catholic saint was an abortionist!" and he laughed louder.• Recap brought him up to date on some gossip and then Rock gave him some casual advice and they went about their shopping.

Recap met Tom the poet for a coffee. He'd quit drinking and seemed to Recap to be stepping out of a certain position and course, not to deny a past or necessarily change directions, but just to stop and reflect on the possibilities

---

• Rock would have to wait another day and need to be seated to hear Don Domanski's news of John Synder, former worker for the US National Rifle Association, leading a campaign to make the gun-toting St. Gabriel Possenti the patron saint of handgun owners.

of steering or managing his sensibility. He was doing a bit of journalism just for the discipline but ultimately remained true to the poem as starting from scratch and aiming as high as possible, with no cheating, that is not abandoning being abandoned in the middle of his "thrown-ness."* He said he started from the remembered images of places, wondered and wandered in memory about them, back in Ireland, in and around Limerick. What depth charge was impounded in the image, what was in the delayed shock wave that rippled through from events that still lived in some background of time?

He talked about Irish speech and distinguished it from accent and then talked about the "professional ethnic". Had no time for being an Irish stereotype even though he knew his drinking in the past and the pieces of his mind he'd given to fools he couldn't suffer nevertheless had lent him this very confusion. Recap thought about the long time Tom had been giving sober second thought to things, and watched him soaking up new ideas and impressions of the literary scene in Vancouver, Toronto and as it landed at the Banff Centre. He would have his son visit, sometimes bringing a friend, and he would step back and figure out what kind of a guy his son was growing to be, what kind of talent he had. Recap watched them go by the cabin on a new day's outing or tired and returning. Finally one day he caught the unmistakable resemblance between father

---

* The way Heidegger would have us finding ourselves inhabiting impossibly our own Archimedean point. Akin to Ortega's shipwreck we, so shored up against the endless sea, or against the shore itself, don't always realize.

and son and then couldn't decide whether it was a feature or a manner.

One night Recap and a woman from the Centre retreat program and Tom were sitting in the Sally Borden and the woman challenged Tom on his lack of eye contact during the conversation. Recap was thinking of the sparks that would have flown had Tom been drinking. Instead he watched him redden and saw the energy rise but heard him explain how the respect he'd learned growing up precluded that kind of eye contact upon a first meeting. Finally Recap saw a bit of a smile in the corner of his mouth.

Recap reminded them that they were sitting on the same couch and that therefore the logistics militated against an easy eye contact. The neuroscientists talked about head turning for different states of mind, different brainwaves and he laughed to himself wondering what brainwave Tom was having, what wormhole from the past was not just turning his eyes away but turning them inward.

In the coffee bar they talked about blood pressure. Recap had had a dizzy spell and some nausea in the middle of the night when he got up to go to the bathroom. He mentioned he'd had a fair amount of wine. Tom's blood pressure had been high and now it was almost too low. Tom said that it was a sign of low blood pressure and that wine had that effect. Then it could have been just some locked up gas. Soon they were onto health food people and the distortions involved in the foregrounding of physical well-being. Recap told him how an old girlfriend had phoned to try to sell him vitamins.

She told how her sister, who had so much energy anyway, tried them and noticed the difference immediately.

Recap said that the sister must be getting dangerous. Then as the spiel went on he suggested a reductively analogous test to the Turing one, namely that he would play the devil's advocate and thus they would debate, the last "man" standing would obviously have had and have the most energy and if he were the man no vitamins need be sent or sold.

Then he said that as the vitamins diffused through the population the energy would get so high that people would start getting on one another's nerves and all the bottom up health would be cancelled by all the top down stress. He was telling Tom how he asked her if she wanted to know what he'd just had about an hour earlier. He told Tom all he had to say was the name, "Chocolate Eruption". Tom laughed at how this must have horrified her. "No, no, she said you could eat anything you wanted on these vitamins!"

That got Tom back on Irish speech, as he was reminded of when he first came to Canada and was working construction. He'd gone into a Burger King, which they didn't then have in Ireland, and couldn't bring himself to ask for a "Whopper". He'd had problems when he asked for it "take away". He and the woman had trouble with "garnish" and "relish". Then she shouted over to him asking what he wanted on it. In a low voice he said "lettuce and tomato" but she couldn't hear so he repeated it but changed the "a" from a short to a long, then she asked him to repeat it again and he raised his voice in his mind but not in actuality and also changed the long back to a short "a". Recap told him about Jimmy and how he would say "duck egg" instead of "goose egg" for a zero, and "hen-toed" instead of our "pigeon-toed".

Later they got talking about poetry again and about Don McKay and how Don said that he was a metaphor freak and that he was in eternal conflict with analytic language. Tom pointed out how strongly conclusive the poems they'd heard weeks earlier had ended. Recap said yes that they certainly weren't mixed or tacked-on metaphors, very integral. Rebecca had told Recap on their floating walk around Tunnel Mountain on the closed road how much she liked McKay and in question period at the reading had wondered about how he managed to be so surprising. Recap and Tom agreed, "that would be your metaphor, Rebecca". But as they thought about those strong and tidy endings Recap came to the conclusion that those muscular metaphors were not all that unakin to propositions, say "speculative propositions". Tom didn't know whether he was happy with the proposition strain of poem. Recap thought he didn't mind the poem as special proposition.

He reconsidered Tom's poems and what he said about their genesis, that pinch of place and then the definitely indefinite or inconclusive moods and atmospheres and how the moods would pinch too, or fold and then spread again and the place would be mysteriously waived but then a wave of it was somehow there too.

He thought to himself how often Tom saw the failure of a poem to be in its being only journalism. This twist of him writing journalism now, of course alongside and different from his poetry, but it was interesting and what was he trying differently in his poems? Recap was beginning to see him as the perfectionist who of necessity therefore refused anything correct, political or otherwise, self-reliance in the unreliable. And he'd said he'd been reading

Emerson and was much moved. Recap said so had Nietzsche been.

Recap: when Jimmy died, a few months before Jon, some clerk from the provincial court had phoned him to say that a box was to go to him. It was a box of Jimmy's poetry. What a gap between his poetry and his life. His life had been a constant oscillation between triumph and defeat, hope and fear. "The fear of not fearing" had been his favourite announcement, either roared or said almost under his breath. His mother had once told him never to sit and brood. And he did and didn't.

He talked about how Crowly, a doctor, had come to Canada but couldn't hack it. He'd laugh and talk about how he was "smart, oh he was smart", about how diminutive and then he'd put his hand up to his chin and gesture down an extension and say he had a "long horse face" and laugh kindly. Jimmy had known a lot of doctors and used to drink with them and also get drugs from them. One time something he'd taken almost took him. He was waiting for a bus when his legs went numb so had to grab a telephone pole to hold himself up. When he was on a stretcher bed somebody asked him what religion he was and he replied "Mohammed".

Jimmy never looked back in his poetry and hadn't really given himself a chance, was reinventing the wheel and didn't take advantage by reading what was being done today or even seriously what had been done before. There was a gap between his poetry and his life but there was a gap between his life and his life. Recap would type things up for him at times and was told to fix whatever was necessary but of course the substance and the simply fixable weren't always easy to sort out. Recap sent them off to magazines for him but they'd had no luck.

And yet that gap closed and he would write poems with increasing intricacies and playful language games. However one stood on games, there was an increasing confidence and competence in the writing. But always there was a crucial line or two that just didn't seem right and somehow like a bad apple vitiated the prospective absorption in all the good lines. The good lines were there and he didn't seem to know how to get rid of the bad ones or to decide whether they needed to be replaced. He would just go on to new poems.

With all the booze over the years he began to hear voices and knew there were people using his brain for mathematical theories and books of all sorts. Of course he grew to love these voices. As the years went by he became at times resentful toward Recap but would show it only for moments. He would hang up on him but the next time be happy to hear from him or see him when Recap came to Calgary.

Recap: Tain used to cook supper every night in the mid seventies for the two of them, or at least supper would get cooked on Tain's hot plate. One night after Jimmy finished his potatoes, hamburger and peas he went right to the can down the hall. When he came back he declared "Jeesz Tain, those peas went right through". Tain replied that they'd had peas every night that week and that the peas in question were at least a day old.

Jimmy didn't like the change in their drinking habits when it became obvious that Tain's girlfriend was going to be around for a while. One night she and Jimmy left a party before Tain and when Tain got home he was immediately informed that Jimmy had "done something". Tain didn't know how to react because he knew it was not a simple matter of lust but some move to discredit the girlfriend.

Tain worked himself up to some harsh words and started moving Jimmy out of the room. As he went by the hot plate Jimmy grabbed a sprig of cold, leftover broccoli and stuck it in his mouth. Out in the hallway he grinned defiantly at Tain. Their chests were inches apart and they stared in each other's eyes. The broccoli stuck out of Jimmy's mouth and almost brushed Tain's chin. He kept a straight face and Jimmy finally turned and left.

Recap: phoning Jimmy in Calgary from FoxHog he remembered Jimmy'd been in the Colonel Belcher Hospital earlier for some minor ailment. When Jimmy answered, Recap said "hello, this is Colonel Belcher". He could almost hear Jimmy's heels click as he said "yes Colonel" with a gasp of deference. Recap wished he'd not kidded him and when he cut through the spoof as quickly as he could Jimmy grumbled at him. It was a time when he'd been hallucinating and had even swallowed a bottle of pills, to no effect. Recap never knew anymore whether he'd be all theatre of the absurd and joking himself or down in a pit of despair.

There was that picture of him from the sixties when he'd been a hot walker in Vancouver. He looked as though he was starving and he was apparently, had huge pus bags under his arms. In the picture his eyelids were half closed and it surely wasn't blinking. It looked a sickness unto death. He'd walked out of town on the railway track and then went off into the woods. He lay down and buried himself in leaves, then a bird hopped on his chest.

He took it as a sign and got up again and continued down the track and then found a case of beer, which he took, again as a sign, as well as a beverage, though he said it was one time when it was better as a sign. Drink was an object of much meditation and distinctions. What was and wasn't alcoholism. Drinking was often the occasion of its very disparagement, almost like his story of the Kerryman who came to a raging river. He said aloud "God is good, and the devil ain't bad either" and when he got across in a little boat he said "fuck the both of ya!".

The Determination of Rebecca

Rebecca, whose lovely smile could simply radiate or go abstract when she talked and reflected, stood for that power of overcoming early mother loss, and losses and pains indeterminate. She lived in and outside of the family and thought about the relevant norms and ideals. She suffered the heart-rending longings of dogs, laughed with the laughter of children, could sympathize with and not laugh at the desires of an old man. She sought the support of and supported other women. In short she was, as we say, open and vulnerable. Yet she didn't suffer to be fooled, had no sympathy for hypocrisy. She took the trouble to go places and learn things. But in the end she was determined to write the world as it came to her, both in the inspired sense and in the way that it failed to live up past the tragedies of the past.

Recap: Jon and Pam and Rebecca and Recap went up to the old Roubakine room in Donald Cameron Hall to hear Alberto Manguel give a talk. This was years before he was appointed to the Arts Journalism chair. He talked about his first time in Canada in Toronto and how the bus driver on the bus he was taking went out of his way to help people make their connections, or figure out how to get where they wanted to go. This apparently did not conform to his experience in Argentina or Europe, or in the States. Jon was greatly amused by this kinder and gentler bus driver.

But then Manguel went on to be more critical, particularly of the multicultural fairs that he said were token gestures and superficial other-cultural engagement. Rebecca remembered them from childhood and had been much fascinated by them and in question period told Manguel as much. Recap was knee-jerk sensitive to the political incorrectness. But he admired her sticking to her remembered engagement.

And he now thought about how none of us have figured out this great clash of cultures and the problematics of New World Order dominances. Perhaps at some levels these wars were already finished. But of the self-conscious advocacy and reclamations of threatened cultures in the face of dominant ones, or the One, no one has figured out where the bridges will go, what new third positions must be synthesized to effect real mutual recognitions. Something was over and something was not over. We walk on an electronic bog, ie we walk *on* into unknown convergences instead of sinking, to divert Peirce on the progress of science, dramatizing both its uncertainty and its dynamism.

At the end of the lecture they all stood up and stretched and looked around at the others. Way up in the back in the corner still sat Mike McIvor the environmental activist. They all smiled and nodded to him. His beard in long strands down from his chin, and his relative altitude, put Recap in mind of a dark and lordly mountain goat.

Years later Rebecca worked as cook on a trail crew for the summer and met other women who worked in the back country. Then another year cooked at the Mt Assiniboine Lodge. Recap sitting in the Cake Company reading the paper heard people at the next table raving about her cooking. Later still she met other women writers and they continued to meet, read and critique one another's work. Six of them gave monologues at the Margaret Greenham. They were all powerful and full of wit and hard won truths.

Recap listened from the back and remembered the first years of a writing group when the men seemed to dominate, an old story. Rebecca's monologue told of her nursing her mother when she was dying of cancer and then of a more deliberate choice to work with AIDS patients in their last weeks. Jane Newman gave a funny survey of trends and fashions, sexual and political over a couple of decades.

The group went on to do more monologues and poetry readings. Rebecca writing a quick and darting, densely textured and catalogued phenomenology of erotic tenderness in the wilderness. Jane took herself seriously enough to add to her art and poetry participation, political responsibilities, that is got herself elected to the town council on a no-more-development platform.

Recap: he'd phoned from the farm for Rebecca at the Whyte Museum early one Saturday morning and got Jon. Recap was caught off guard but asked Jon if he knew where she was living now. Jon with much mischief said "she's living in the Boys' [for Boyce] house." This got Recap going for a minute till Jon explained. Recap remembered her fondness for Dorothy Boyce and how bright Dorothy was in her nineties. She had studied chemistry at the University of Toronto when it was a rare thing for a woman.

Many educated and independent women lived or had lived in the valley. The coming out to the wilderness and living with the rugged outdoorsmen did not always work out. Jon wrote about the character Ike Mills with fondness but he also wrote about his wife Alma and her thwarted musical career. Recap had listened to the poem about her on a short-lived Sunday afternoon CBC arts program. It had been interspersed with cello playing and invoked her lonely practicing as a consolation and slow withdrawal.

Recap's father had asked about Eileen Harmon when Recap moved to Banff and Jon had introduced him to her. She seemed a no-nonsense type and was an avid hiker-nature lover, into and behind all those postcards her father produced, but warmed to Recap despite his self-perceived both decadence and naïveté. He had his father written all over him, she'd said, thinking back to the U of A in the '20s.

Mel had told him how he spent extra time, beyond being a tenant, with Eleanor Luxton who he said was very aware of current, out of past, town politics in her old age.

She would talk about her father, the museum he founded, but also about her time as an engineer in a man's world long before she began writing her/histories.

Recap-decap: he sat down in the new dining room at the Banff Centre and ate a nice meal with a bit of dessert too for free on Rebecca's ticket. He told her he was reading Harold Innis, about the effects on civilizations of alphabets and different kinds of writing. She thought of Manguel's new book on the history of reading and saw a conspiracy, well a little one that militated against her interests in living the content outside and on the ground of all the histories. Recap knew the right responses to this, or did he?

He let it rest or go and didn't say anything as he recognized the rightness of the primacy of life in the folded now, yet couldn't help but think the rightness too of the corrections of these other historian outsiders, ie to the primacy of life. Not that all the corrections were right but that these arresting messages from the mediums of unaging intellects, "post cardiac", were inevitable re-sources for the source, so to speak.

Tain gets out of Banff

Rory and Laurie were from California, and Rory had been tarred with "moral turpitude" by the customs officers for some white lie he'd been caught in. No it was not for saying that the Canadian male had been castrated by the defeat of Team Canada at the hands of the Russians. He was quite a Freudian back then and a hell of a guitar player. Laurie played the flute and the two of them had a gig at the Grizzly House for a week. Tain had known Rory in the mid-seventies for a couple of years. His hockey remark really got the manager of the Grizzly House going, even though the guy was a literary intellectual, living at the time with a now famous TV personality in Quebec.

Tain had been upstairs from his own basement suite at a party in their main floor, much larger suite and seen the nude self-portrait of the "castrated male". He also remembered overhearing a heated argument once as it drifted down to his suite through the vent. When the voices got further away he allowed himself to move a little closer to the vent so he could keep up with the progress of the tiff. He later forgot what was said or what the issue was.

Rory had worked as a studio musician for Santana and others. He did a lot of Crosby, Stills and Nash, and maybe Young. Laurie had been a schoolteacher but was picking music up fast. Tain remembered her talking about *The Magic Mountain* and *The Man Without Qualities*, that older edition without the part Musil withdrew and without the notes for an even longer book.

Tain had told them about James Joyce laughing at his own puns and jokes as he wrote and as Nora would hear him from the other room. Tain's girlfriend told them independent of this, when Tain was there and had to laugh in nervous embarrassment, how Tain had been laughing at his own funny poems that day as he wrote them. Tain pleaded a morphogenesis with a slight time ripple or a separate recapitulation, trans-individual or -Atlantic, pleaded with an erasing laugh that he tried in turn to wipe off his face with this masking hand.

Rory and Laurie prodded Tain into coming on a four-day hike starting from Lake O'Hara and ending forty winding, climbing miles at Marble Canyon. Tain could lift his girlfriend over his head with one hand. He would have to grab her by the fly of her jeans at the waist, get her to his shoulder and then with a punch extend his arm. He would do this too often. His girlfriend was reminded of a mutual friend that would lift his girlfriends in the classic over the threshold postion and dance around at parties like some wild Cossack.

Tain's trick was a little more blunt and stunt but she indulged him and made sure she didn't have gas. It was almost the only time Jimmy seemed to enjoy the girlfriend, as if she might be hoisted on her own petard, as it were. Tain could also do a strict bicep curl of over a hundred pounds with one hand. Thus it was decided that he would carry the iron frying pan and some other heavy items. He also stuffed a good supply of books into his pack so that he could read around the fire each night they set up camp.

Nobody had counted on the fact that Tain might otherwise not be in very good shape, that his cardiovascular system might not be up to it or that his legs might be a little unused in all that time in the bar. It soon became apparent that it was going to be nip and tuck for Tain. The first night he was so tired he couldn't even help make supper or put up the tent. In fact he could hardly eat and by some cruel irony couldn't sleep either. And the first leg that day was probably the easiest once the climb from Lake O'Hara was completed.

To add insult to injury and insomnia Rory and Laurie would every night, as true Californians, make love*, with just a hint of smugness and leftover sixties-in-the-seventies hippyness, O people of the Volkswagon van. At dawn they would go at it again in the little tent where the three of them, until the doubling up, were shoulder to shoulder. Tain was still doing his own tossing and turning on the hard ground, convinced he'd not slept a wink. The other two had been snoring all night long.

The second day was worse, a long rough trail in the morning and then a big climb in the afternoon. Another indication of Tain's withering pride was his constant jingling of a pop can as he was, like the horse, mortally afraid of the Grizzly, which he'd been lead to believe resided in the area. He was paying for the toponymy of his blithe night haunt, that is the Grizzly House. Adieu fondue and steak. Sure enough, they stepped over bear shit on the climb.

Somehow the effort of climbing dispelled his fear, though he continued to jingle. That night brought them to a locked up warden's cabin he had again, in another, further elaboration, been led to believe were not off bounds for hikers. As long as you left everything as you found it, it was supposedly okay. They had to pry the windows open though. Recap: at his second unpropitious meeting with

---

* Rory would say "fuck" and try to roll it into the pavement of off-handedness even as he would want to achieve the bump† the self-consciousness now was and at the same time referred to.

† The self-conscious bump is nicely illustrated in the movie "Shampoo" by the older character (Jack Warden), trying to be hip, when he and a host accidentally surprise a coupling couple in the summerhouse. Before he can see that the woman (Julie Christie) is his own mistress he gushes "now that's what I call fuckin'!"

Sid Marty he'd mentioned this and Sid was not amused. Tain upped the ante at Sid's rebuke and told him "you think you're big, I heard Blodgett was a way bigger than you". Sid grumbled that there was always somebody bigger.

Later they became friends, especially when Tain would take him around to the watering holes Sid, as a married man, wasn't familiar with. At Tain's favourite, the Buffalo Paddock, they arrived to find a long line-up one night. As they came up the stairs Tain yelled "get out of my way or I'll knock ya all down like dominoes". Of course they got in because Tain was a regular. Later Tain did something similar to get them into a party, which similarly tickled Sid's wicked sense of humour, and might have gone too far for Sid's tastes when, upon finding they were out of booze, he opened the cupboard and then drank, proverbially, the vanilla extract on hand.

Again, even on a mattress, Tain couldn't sleep. At least in the morning they waited till he left the cabin before they started screwing, to cast an inuring turn of phrase upon them. When he figured he'd given them enough time he returned to the window, their makeshift door, and there was Rory with a bucket of water washing his balls as if he was some prize bull. So Tain went back and got some water boiling on the fire he'd built, then went deep into the woods for his morning call of nature and felt nice and natural squatting there. When he came back around the corner of the cabin Laurie was standing a few yards from the cabin with her coverall jeans and panties around her ankles and was wiping her voluptuous behind, which was on the far side from Tain, it must be said, making for a plus and a minus on the voyeur scale, direct revelation and yet intimation too, with no tricky clothing, just skin and normal perspectivalism.

When Tain had first looked out the cabin window he saw a porcupine crossing the tree over the stream that they too would eventually cross on. After they'd gotten back to Banff Tain told Jon at the old Book and Art Den that they'd camped at Porcupine Crossing. Jon looked at him and then from side to side like someone on that TV show *Candid Camera*, then nodded that he understood, or pretended to understand, where they'd camped. Actually the cabin was by Helmet Creek down from spectacular Helmet Falls at the end of the massive Rockwall.

As soon as they made it over the creek they started up the switchbacks of a steep mountainside and when they got to the top there was still an up gradient till finally they came to a headwaters, and a confluence of streams in a high pass. When they crossed the shallow water and got their feet and pant legs wet they started up a long slow climb heading south in the pass. Tain was getting farther and farther behind. He would stop, like a beast of burden, completely exhausted, hang his head and curse. Then begin again.

Rory and Laurie would wait finally, look at him with grim smiles and then head out again. They reached a snowfield and sat down in it far above Tain. It was his carrot and he trudged on. When he finally made it to them he saw they were mixing snow and Tang and offered him some. He took it greedily but his thirst was beyond slaking even as his belly ached with all the cold ice and water. Towards evening they began to descend, but they had to bushwhack since they couldn't figure out where the trail picked up again.

Rory had the map and was sure this would get them to the path again. The way down had its own treacheries and Tain often slid on his side or back and got scratched with branches. Once below they realized they had to get over another stream, much more dangerous. What would David Thompson have called it, a "rivulet", according to his declension of navigability? Again they got across on a fallen tree.

Finally down the path a ways they stopped to camp for the night. Tain plopped down on the path crosswise, bejesusly crucified. He awoke slightly at the sound of voices, Rory and Laurie talking to another couple of hikers who'd come from where they were going, but he couldn't get up, fell back to sleep, not before he realized they were stepping over him. Totally bereft of pride he slept like a baby. Later he got into the tent and willed the two lovers to let her rip and they did and he slept a little more but still tossed and turned eventually and then just lay there till the sun came up.

The hike the next day was easier, mostly down hill and when they were close to the end they went into the shallow wide stream and had a water fight. Tain was rejuvenated at the thought of getting back to Banff and when they did in their separate cars he forgot his humiliations, got a shower, went to the bar and basked in his alighted body. But he licked a few wounds with pensive tongue, and capped gently with his left hand his right lowered, womb-punching fist — the trick with the girlfriend, over his head.

Horny John

Tain watched Horny John as he approached Tain and his girlfriend. She grabbed his arm and laughing asked him to protect her. Sure enough Horny rubbed his hands and shouted with glee when he saw her. He threw his arms around her and hugged and kissed her and then rubbed and slapped her upper arms as he laughed lustily. Tain just watched but wished he'd desist. Horny finally let them get on their way.

Horny John arrived in Banff by jumping off a moving freight train. He had the scars on his forehead to prove it. He told Tain that someone had tried to hang him in Vancouver, in fact did but let him down before any real damage had been done. He played guitar in the streets. Some cooks in Banff threw him into a garbage dumpster behind a restaurant where he worked as the dishwasher. Probably his best job was on the garbage crew in Banff when it was still under the jurisdiction of the Parks. He met a wonderful young American woman from the Mid west on his daily rounds.

She'd regularly seen him take the garbage and one day she left a rose with a note to him on the top of the plastic bags. Horny didn't need encouragement at the best of times and no doubt eagerly spoke to her after that. For all the opprobrium he lived under, including his dire nickname, he was quite the man of words. Well-read and up on the pop music scene, he wrote a column in the *Crag* on the local music that was available. His nice/pen name, "the lounge lizard", threatened to eclipse even as it would preserve his other nickname.

Well into his careering careers in Banff he became convinced his name had been holding him back. He'd become friends with several Indians from Morley and one day he told Tain that they'd given him a new name, "Katoonda", that meant "the wind". One night Tain espied Katoonda and a few friends shuffling across the Texaco station lot, where Wild Bill's is now, making carousing sounds but bearing down with drunken purpose towards the King Eddy. Tain was drunk without purpose heading home or to some last stop. He yelled across the street loud enough to stop the commotion-with-feet, "hey, Horny Katoonda!" Katoonda got a fix on him and then threw his head back and howled a crazy laugh.

Horny had made his own leather clothes and sometimes carried a leather satchel which was often full of songs he'd written and sometimes contained a novel he was working on, set in Montreal, Toronto and Vancouver. He'd run into lots of the name literati from the east. He was opinionated and often criticized various writers as not getting it or as too that or too this. In his local music columns he wrote elegantly and was very fair and elaborately descriptive. Probably he was even a little over-praising but it was a small town and he was willing to compromise just a bit, especially for the odd free beer.

He lived with the woman from the States for over a year. Their cabin was wall-to-wall mattresses. It was the happiest Tain had ever seen him. The government job paid well and he would see them in Safeway with a huge cart of groceries. But after that ended, both job and relationship, and as the years went by he became increasingly bitter and full of rage. He went back to Vancouver and Tain dreamt that he had died. Tain had also dreamt that another friend from the coast had died, that a big locomotive had run him down, signifying more the fatefulness than the actual nature of the fatality. This other friend was a larger personality than Horny and could speak Latin and Greek but was also involved with motorcycle gangs and some mean heroin worlds. He was eventually killed but had done it himself "on purpose", so to ironize, driving his motorcycle into a bridge abutment at about a hundred miles an hour.

Horny wrote Tain a few long letters and then showed up again but lived mostly in Canmore, working in Banff from time to time. He took to sleeping behind the furnace in Tain's house when he went to the bar after work. Tain had seen him in the King Eddy dancing by himself, a sort of dark inversion of the kind of elaborate ballet of joy that Jon Whyte would perform on special occasions or just some night at the Grizzly House when things were seeming a little too pedestrian for him.

Horny wore a long scarf and flung it around the dance floor in cold gestures reminiscent of some kind of Spanish dancer or even stylized bull fighter, but full of rage and a sense of death more the terror of Goya than the *duende* of Lorca. Once Tain had been sitting in the Magpie and Stump with Horny and Jim H, a dangerous combination that he should have been more attuned to. But he was getting tired of their arguing and so left.

By this time Horny had been sleeping by the furnace every night and some of the other tenants complained about him being there when they had to do their laundry and especially when they had their kids with them. One night Tain had heard water running in a way that wasn't indicative of the normal plumbing of the place. He jumped up from his mattresses and went out into the hall and behind the furnace. There was Horny in an incipient lake still half asleep and drunk, struggling to sort out dream from stream, not of consciousness.

He'd been in the dark literally until Tain had straddled him and then snapped on the light behind the furnace. Water was gushing out of the hot water heater. He'd somehow inadvertently turned the tap on at the bottom of the tank. His leather coat was soaking wet. Tain brought him in to his room where he slept on the rug. The room filled with the smell of the roofing tar Horny had on his clothes and boots from working on the addition to the Banff Springs Hotel. Later they threw his coat in the dryer. The landlord came down one day and asked about Horny sleeping there and between the two of them they decided Tain would pay a month's rent for Horny for a room upstairs. He gave him the hot plate that he wasn't using now that he had a stove.

Tain must have known deep down something was going to happen between Jim H and Horny because the next morning he went upstairs and knocked on Horny's door with a sense of foreboding. He heard a rustle and then feet on the floor and then the door opened. Horny with a face covered in dried blood, almost black. Apparently Horny had put up a pretty good fight and of course would never back down. He was skinny but hard as could be, the bounce of a punk but the posture of an egghead, which in a slightly demonic sense he was.

With his long stringy hair and long guitar-playing finger nails, and that wild look in his eye — one says "eye" instead of "eyes" to mean the uniformity of intensity — there was a touch of Rasputin in him. When he was with the young American woman, who was tall and beautiful and wore a peasant dress and whose parents were of course rich, he was happy picking up garbage and composing songs.

Jim H was not much bigger than Horny just more muscled and better fed. Horny had hardly been eating. Tain started inviting him down for breakfast after that. He had no doubt got Jim H's goat. The two of them had wicked tongues. When the police broke it up Horny was still not subdued, fighting on pure psychic energy. Jim H, not normally a bully, in fact usually fighting above his weight class, had everything to lose, Horny nothing.

It was Truman who phoned one night to tell him that Horny had been hit by the train at Canmore. Tain then heard stories of a fight in the bar earlier in that fateful night, that he might have been dead before the train hit him. Everyone who knew him saw the sad symmetry in the valley, of his life in the mountains bound by the train that had delivered him and then had taken him away.

When there was excitement a few years back about American artists wrapping whole islands and fencing with plastic huge land tracts, Horny used to crow about the sea unto sea Canadian railway. Katoonda died by the real weight of the biggest numbing down symbol in the land. In *Wolf Willow* Wallace Stegner talks about paths that homesteaders made on the land, to and from their few buildings and fields, and implied how this evidence of their lives was only just a notch above, as well as a notch in, the land, in nature, a necessary tattoo and mirror but in a balance with the balance of nature which is an opacity that calls back to as well as tempts the mirror, and mere, user.

Who has seen Katoonda, wiped out in the total art of the embedded mirror? W O on the radio said "the point is there's no vanishing point", talking about his novel and of his experience on the Morley reserve. However much the Morleys here converge. However much, according to Tony Hall, U of L native studies professor, "the corruption", the dispossession intra Indian on the Stoney reserve converges with, nay is swallowed up by, as it was created by, a narrow elite in the general populace who exercized and, on the other side of the mirror with some irony, exorcized the possession, province-wide, and did it with their narrow arrow vanished behind the scenes — self-administered virtual poison pill, some kind of holy burden of investment that would argue the unthinkable cost to all of reversing this self-vanishing base of the economy.

Recap: in his cabin on the other side of the mirror, so to speak, he mused about Horny, then went blank, and then his vision diverged again onto the plains of the late 1850s, onto the Palliser Triangle, onto the foothills, the Rockies and the passes through to the Kootenay Plains, and then it ranged down the Columbia River. He thought of Palliser, Hector, Sullivan and Blakiston. Their slogging journey to Red River, thirsty on the Saskatchewan plains, swimming, fording and rafting across dangerous rivers, breaking trail with snowshoes for the dogs and covering two or three miles only in a day, slipping with the dogs on windswept lakes and then out of Fort Edmonton uniquely finding and slaughtering a small buffalo herd, feckless on a frozen lake.

They encountered all this as openly as possible, carrying and getting carried away by their own open, but oddly closed and closing, "civilization", even as we now, Recap thought, buried it and were in turn buried in it all. And the all included the voyageurs who carried 200 pound portage packs, forehead-rigged, and who carried these explorers of course in the canoes. And it included the Cree who carried the supplies and who carried them in the sense of eventual outcome on a kind of credit in the greater and greater circles of protracted transactions. As did the religious Stoneys, and, more hesitantly, the frightening Blackfeet, and Kootenays, offering their splendid horses they otherwise kept, as in cared for.

He thought of the capped off food supply in the late twentieth century, layered, embedded and regulated into daily portions in supermarkets and fridges. He encountered his memory, trying to think the wholly, and terribly holy, raw, think it through memory, inveterate cook. Reactively and actively he remembered the desperate diets of the explorers, at times holding out on supplies, rations, but mostly hunting their daily food. Buffalo of course, rabbits, ducks, geese, fishes, including salmon in the upper Columbia in the mountains, tree grouse, after the Stoneys showed them the snare on a stick trick, moose, deer, elk, black and grizzly bears, "panthers" even, and mountain goats that were uselessly lean in winter.*

The Stoney women cooked moose for them, skimmed the fat off, and the resultant meat for their energy-burning

---

* A lot of these meats have become the "Canadian" haute cuisine of the high-end Banff restaurant, The Pines.

drive (intra and extra) was about as good as starving. Someone even skillfully shot and cooked up a tasty skunk once. Days slogging through dense forests always clogged with fallen timber in the mountains they almost did starve. Over Howse Pass looking for a way from the three branches of the North Saskatchewan headwaters over to the Columbia the rain soaked the pemmican so that most of it rotted. In many areas the horses, going without feed, were pushed on and on.

And the last winter Palliser had his men shoot his own horse, Carlo, after heading south between chains of mountains, on the Kootenay river. Carlo had been the best of the lot Simpson had provided for them at Red River back in the spring of '58. Poor fellow was exhausted. They tried to force him onto a grassy spot where they thought they could leave him with some hope but he couldn't make it and so rather than leave him to starve Palliser asked them to shoot him, unable to do it himself.

Recap thought of Bourgeau, "the brick", the botanist from the Alps, recording the flora, Hector studying the geology, Blakiston the earth's magnetic field, here as already more and less than here, all of them looking for new passes through to the Columbia and the Fraser and so to the coast. They zeroed in on and met the Boundary Commission "nailing down" the 49th parallel in the southern ranges, and all their wandering, shocks of land and weather, the quick thresholds to the habits and the innards of the animals, in the air, on the ground and in the water, contracted to a railroad whose trains to this day blindly and blindingly spill the guts into a rawness, an unrelated rawness. Sometimes on the track into the heart of steel, death has an impounded ear for what still is, lost.

O wolf, and the soft paths in *Wolf Willow*.

Pretty Lights and Uncanny Vistas

Recap looked up from his book and out through the condensation-beguiled window, down the alley past the Presbyterian Church and across the street over the high school playing field to the traffic lights at the corner where the heritage Esso service station building used to stand with its painted bricks and its tiny, forsaken gable window. He watched the cycle of green-orange-red a number of times and laughed to himself as he had to consciously break the spell.

He thought of windows and other spells that benignly haunted his past, like small candies, even as he almost synaesthetically tasted the green-orange-red. Life savers or screen savers, he savoured the thought and rethought the colours of the otherwise vortex whose suck he could command at will until his will ran out, that is escaped him but also used him, somehow, up. He remembered as a child in their second house, how he would visually sidestep the Christmas tree, look up and out a small rectangular window above the mantle. The window was mostly black in the winter night but it transported him to a Christmas beyond Christmas.

Recap could reinsert himself into these quaint albeit higher little moods, or spells, if not interruptions. But he also felt relatively omniscient to them or that he existed now through the windows, looking back and enveloping these not quite primal scenes, living in the lifted and therefore under-the-table beyond (thank-you [fog] very much) as it of course continued to both dirty and laundry itself in confusion.

In the old high school gym, however much he was more than usually rooted in rooting for the home basketball teams, girls and boys, there were always those moments when he drifted up to the top of the tall windows whose bottom ledges were seven or eight feet high, windows you didn't readily look out of, windows in fact that looked in on one, however manifoldly and indiscriminately. And yet they drew you, that is they sucked you over a few treetops and left you in the sky by day and lost in time by night, such as into and beyond the lateness of the boys' game you were lucky if you could stay for.

He could capture something of the same as he used to walk up on St Julian Road to the films at the Eric Harvey Theatre. Either lights from the intriguing houses or the passing car lights that washed up on the tall fir trees made him revisit that mode of mood-lifting, and of course in the mountains at night if there were stars, or heaven forbid, a moon, one went wholesale "tourist to ecstasy". But it was on black snowy nights through the street lamps and past the light-frosted trees that one's flight, paradoxically, was complete, that is complete flight but completed too, alighted in the free fall up, till up is over and orientation is dissolved.

Hogwash one thinks as quickly and the whole is in the particular scenic intimation, a hole in the whole to the whole in the hole. One sees oneself embedded, down if you like, in the past and one sees oneself ensconced in the scheduled future, or contained in another city in the present where the ur-world of an innocent advertizing cedes itself to itself, but it is the present in place that clears your name[s], unframes you, that is, makes you both shy and aggressive, too big and too small and robustly unfit.

Recap: the log house on Beaver Street across from the old bus depot where Jon lived, that is, in the log house in the early seventies and the depot where Jon hung out years earlier when he was a much younger tour guide. Al Purdy had come over to the house after his reading at the Whyte. Naturally the beer was flowing and Al was teasing a young woman who had recounted as a girl what the skating rink was like in Banff, the music and the lights in the trees.

Al wanted to hear "lights on the snow flakes" and then questioned her on this, and then questioned her on everything she said, "and was there little lights on it [them]", until she quit talking and her friend consoled her and together they made a pact to hate Al Purdy and thus it was that Al Purdy came under a spell. He liked Tain because he was digging a basement in the side of Tunnel Mountain with a jackhammer. They figured he should start writing poems with this godawful sounding hammer. Tain told Purdy that he'd got *North of Summer* for Christmas but had ripped the dust jacket in his haste to open the present. Jon thought this was a sweet enthusiasm.

Recap again looked at the traffic lights, distant through the condensation. As he looked he became uncertain he was even seeing the red and the green. When the amber came on it erupted with a flash like a super nova in another galaxy. He thought the brightness of transition. He closed his book and put on his coat and headed for the nine o'clock movie at the new Lux.

Approaching Banff Avenue he looked at the candied, regulated skyline, and as a farmer so often in an outer space of only points of lights, however clustered, though nothing like the medieval dark of European peasants in the winter say, he couldn't help like the coloured effects of this satellite city, transparent even to the rubber-necking rubes who otherwise carried their part displacements only as far as they could be rest assured. Recap sat down in the theatre, slouched a bit and when the lights went down, switched brain waves to enter Tain.

Recap: Up on the screen Tain was dressed as a cowboy and was the designated bouncer at the Magpie and Stump Halloween party. It seemed like just a formality till an Egyptian mummy started arguing with a woman at the table set up for the punch bowl. The mummy was pretty big and had hold of the woman's hands, bending them back as if it were a contest of strength, and no contest. A bunch of other guys swarmed in but they couldn't get the mummy away from the woman. The knot of people was itself getting reckless and started to bump into tables.

Tain pushed in and got a good grip on the mummy, then slowly but decisively lifted and pushed it back toward the band, Kenny and Shane, and then to the door. The band kept playing and the mummy kept shouting in its muffled way "it's me Tain, Randy". Tain couldn't remember a Randy and just kept pushing till he was out the door. He held him up against the barn board wall. Randy's arms were pinned up high but he could flap his forearms and rap his knuckles on Tain's forehead.

Finally Tain warned him that he would have to hit him back if he didn't stop rapping Tain's head. Tain had been in quite a few fights but had never actually hit anyone. The knuckle rapping continued so he let go his right hand from Randy and jabbed him on the jaw from about six inches. The mummy slid down and sat on the outside floorboards. Tain began to unravel the bandages from Randy's head in order to see who this mummy was. When he got close to the mouth the blood starting showing through so he quickly bandaged him up again. Someone had phoned the cops and then Randy started fighting with them.

Next day Tain was walking back from the post office and was turning on to Banff Avenue when he spotted Randy, whom he'd finally been helped to remember by one of the cooks, riding in the passenger side of a turning car. He looked glum with his preserved pout now. Tain felt a wave of wretchedness seeing this mummy with a fat lip even as on the sidewalk he couldn't help crookedly grin around the corner.

Clarence Under the Scaffolding

Recap headed up from the Groceteria with his paper and started under the scaffolding on the building which housed the hardware store that was closed now during the new vertical addition. Clarence greeted him with a "how ya doing there young fella" and Recap returned a "not too bad there old fella" even though they couldn't be too different in age. Clarence leaned on a broom and asked what he was up to and Recap shrugged "the usual, actually writing these days, writing about Jon a bit." Recap had kept walking before this exchange till he got to the end of the scaffolding and back on the sidewalk where he leaned on the metal crossbar below the first level of planks above their heads. The sun was then at his back and shone over his shoulders into Clarence's squinting eyes.

Clarence said Jon was a smart man, that he thought he'd been a university professor once. Recap said that he had just begun to write a history of Banff when he died, and thought how Jon had told him he was dividing it up into decades and was trying to find a single dominant event for each decade on which he could hang things, and that he was building up his files, a folder for each decade.

Clarence said that someone should talk to old man Henry from Henry's Electric before he died. He was in his late eighties or nineties now and had said "they" hadn't got it right, talking about Pat Brewster's little history. Clarence said that the recent article in the *Crag*, part of a series on old timers, about Bruce Beatty stealing the train from Banff to get a case of beer in Canmore was not quite right either. Clarence himself said he remembered he had a lawyer, that the defense to the effect that he hadn't taken the train off CPR property wasn't just Bruce's after all. Recap recited there was always a clash of stories.

Clarence said that Ken Jones, the warden, was another guy that should be written about. Before, he used to hike and fish with his dog in the back country. He was at Mt Assiniboine camping when Ken happened upon him and declared "ya know Clarence, they're doing things differently now, no dogs allowed out here off the leash". Clarence didn't say anything for a while and then pulled out his brandy and poured a healthy portion into each of their coffees and they sat and drank and changed the subject. When Ken got up to go he said "don't worry about that dog Clarence".

Recap: that first fall season in Banff, sitting along the wall on the bench seat under the murals on the side where the mountie was single-handedly holding off, with a rifle held crosswise, the rebellious railway construction workers depicted as Caucasians. Clarence had overheard Recap's group talking about poetry and leaned in passionately to talk about Walt Whitman's *Leaves of Grass*. While they could get worked up about poetry alright in their own good time, they were taken aback by this sudden expression of passion and conviction. Clarence seemed to think their lack of response was disapproval but it was more a dumbfoundedness and sense of inadequacy that they felt, sitting in their heretofore comfortable distractions.

Clarence was usually jovial but Recap knew he was a hard worker, contracting carpentry and construction jobs around Banff for years. He remembered walking out past the graveyard toward the Bow Falls and seeing a lone figure on top of a half-built car port for one of those beautiful homes just above the river, with the even more beautiful view across to Sulphur and down the valley. Clarence stopped hammering for a second to give him a wave.

Recap would get intimations of Classical Greek architecture at the oddest times. Rows of huge dead or leafless poplar trees on the prairie would do it. Not that this was supposed to be doing justice to the prairie. It was just a pleasing estranging effect. Along the road above the river the fir trees were single and powerfully spare in their sentinel positions and with the rocky banks and exposure to wind from off the river and valley. Although there was an invasion of Group of Seven northern Ontario here too, he was again hit with that Greek intimation. Clarence on top of the low pitch skeletal roof mounted on poles rimed this useless possession of Parthenon that kept crossing Recap's path.

Now again in the sun Clarence tilted his head so the beak of his cap shut out the sun. Recap watched a spill of water from the planks above splash down on the cap. His parka was open and his raw red skin was exposed to the mild March air. In his deep but thinned out voice, huskier than husky in its hushed rasp, he said he wouldn't have a dog again, though "good companions", because of the way they tied you down. Then he said he better let him go and Recap said good-bye and continued on to the Fine Grind while Clarence* started to sweep the sidewalk, in an unapprehended solecism and textual eruption, under the scaffolding again.

Banff: The Hole Jon Left

In 1976 June 16 Jon lamented the burning down of Temple Lodge in his column in the *Crag***. It had been the perfect scale, not too small, not too large. It had magic. It was a "hearth surrounded by warmth". It was the seed of its own end. He recounted how Cyril Paris said what it felt like watching their first lodge on Norquay burn. They were down in the town and there was no way to get up there.

---

* About a year later Clarence was found dead in the morning from a heart attack in the new Brewster hotel where he worked maintenance at night, really his first inside job, after he'd done the "outside" construction of the building.

** Letter writers might refer to the grammatical slip here and laugh at the consignment of the eternal flame to such inadvertent ether.

They simply stared at the drop of sun as if in a magnification of grass.

Jon in the months before he died expressed his bitterness about the amount, O etymon, O "mountain" root, of development in Banff, about the balance of visitation to the town and park, the loss of the "shoulder seasons". Recap thought about his thought that were Jon to come back to life after a few months, or just a month — a day(?), his thought was in a downward spiral — there would be an infinite gulf, a hole that could not be filled, that Recap would not be able to fill him in on the things that had happened! He thought this alongside what everybody who knew and loved Jon said, that he had "left a hole that couldn't be filled". But on second thought he realized how right the latter cliché was even as the loss-of-news hole was backwards, superficial, a tain regularly contained.

The proof was in the experience of phantom dialogue with Jon on all sorts of new art entries, movies or just things that had happened in the town or general cultural scene. One could hear Jon's response and if it weren't specific or you couldn't quite make it out, you knew that he would be up to it, could quick-study it, have an opinion, in the strong Kantian sense. Of course one thinks of people growing old and losing touch with what is happening in their still remaining lives. But we're talking about being at the height of one's powers, however much there is a necessary relaxation phase or restoring to one's potential, ironically here, unfocused.

If philosophy was a hole in Jon's life that was finessed with an elegance, in the way that Eliot talked about Henry James' sensibility, from which a few derived sentences could sustain Pound indefinitely, so that a whole Jamesian novel needn't be read, let alone lesser, non-Jamesian ones, then Jon's death was an elegance, special to the general elegance of all deaths however they might be buried or overshadowed by meanness or tragedy in particular cases.

Recap: walking down from the Centre with Bruce Ferguson, Sandy Nairn from the Tate Gallery in London, and Jon. As they passed by the graveyard where Jon's ashes are now buried under his own words inscribed in stone, his concrete poem epitaph, that is the word "earth" printed four times in a circle with the letters continuous and continuously forming multiple words, "art", "hear", "ear", "heart", "hearth", the circle squared as in the four corners of the earth, Recap gestured to the huge lawnmower on grounds just inside the wire fence. And then said "the great mower" with the scythe of relief in his fey voice. And then said "the great no more".

Recap continued to mull over his earlier superficial thought and affirmed the wobbly vortex of a real personality once achieved, once lived and then continued in its inhabitation of the others still living, was stronger than the stream of news events and was even up to the reportable new histories of similarly, still current, wormholed personalities. There is this gravity of thought holes that warps the events around them into questionable generalities, but unquestionably generalities, however in debt to the cowed and contented facts already chewing themselves over and above simple singularities.

Recap flipped to the time a few of them, drunk and maybe a bit drugged, had been sitting around the staff table at the Magpie and Stump. Dave had accidentally knocked over one of the many glasses on the table and then in a sweeping gesture deliberately knocked the rest of them over. Recap in the pause before the already coming laughter was able to float "ah now you're generalizing", which remark got swept up into the laughter even as it put yeast into it.

A completed life leaves a hole, in this case not in the history, which rises regardless out of the other saving living holes, and not just in the historian, who remains himself a hole, but in and for Jon, the nothing that is there, in contrast to, as he quoted from Stevens in relation to his *longue durée* stroll around the Fenland and contemplation of the silences, the nothing that is not there. That is, the hole the death leaves is fraternal to the hole a live mind is and which a complete personality creates so that it speaks into and warps the future with its variable continuity, anachronizes the news of the day by the riming rim of its own incompleteness, reborn with the crunch-of-death or deaths-in-life (spun positive) completion, and emits imaginary numbers: "let them count the ways" of possibility and let them weigh the possibilities.

Recap blew his cover and paused with the light that couldn't escape *this* distended time, thought about part of a title of a book of poetry, namely "Warphistory". There were those of course who would insist you couldn't ignore getting "warf-istory" out of the word, and would laugh gently but mockingly at the unintended slippage. Recap thought about a master(!) l=a=n=g=u=a=g=e poet Steve McCaffery and his elegant blurb with *The Cheat of Words*, how the reader "must negotiate . . . an insistent slippage of meaning". It is "writing to disturb all drives toward centrality, and stability", a "neo-baroque festiveness within its [this poetry's] regulatory skepticism".

Recap thought about that "regulatory" Kantian cap and then about Michael Kosok's essay that argues that Hegel's system is just a generalization, and incidentally an anticipation, of Gödel's incompleteness theorem. He thought about how the blurb managed and finessed the slippages itself, cogently to argue and cap-ture the meaning of the "insistent slippage of meaning".

He thought about McCaffery's interview in *The Power To Bend Spoons*. "Yet a perspectival readjustment allows the reader to write these multitudes of slippages and losses; to recover them to non-paragrammatic writings that inevitably contain new ones." He thought about that ironic "contain" and whether the sentence containing it can be considered to be true or not and thought of something like Russel's paradox or the liar's paradox. He thought how Deleuzian* rhizomes or the rhizomic movements though apart from, play off the arboreal (hierarchy), almost a "look mom, no hands", where the mom has to hand it to it (the rhizome), are in fact recapitulated by the relentlessly renormalizing, nay prophetic "reterritorializing" arboreal, whose metaphoric base itself slips away to simply a sense of

---

* Recap liked to read in the coffee bar in the early evening but when reading Gilles Deleuze's stimulating and deranging-re-arranging *What Is Philosophy?* (printed in big bold letters on the cover) he got a little self-conscious. The question of him not knowing what philosophy was (an honourable, in a special way, ignorance), was even weightier than the earnest pretentiousness of such reading material displayed in a public place. So with scotch tape he covered the cover with a patch of lined notebook paper. Of course the question of philosophy was so bold, though muted to some degree, it showed through the blank disguise. And when friends came over to talk he would second the transparency with a confession of his ployful considerations.

an uncanny always already orientation. Only a conservative, albeit curving, register can place its own displacement as it measures and becomes impressed by the new and different, say Deleuzian "concept creations".

The Joyce/Gell-Mann quark floats free when close to the hot origin (big bang), is captured coolly later. But coolly later the quark is lost in thick matter. It is captured then in its freedom! The only way out of Russel's paradox and Kant's antinomies and, empirically beyond the big bang or prior quantum foam, is through "Prince" Spinoza's whole-to-part infinity of infinities, or so says Leslie Armour.

Then he thought about Wyndham Lewis's attacks on Joyce and Stein and their regulating their systems of non-systematic language use. But that "regulatory" is an elegance on the order of the Möbius strip, inside and outside the system at once, and so the hedge is a hedge is a hedge. And it works wonderfully and pleasurably. And the incarnated proof, from Kantian taste, was bp nichol's love of both Stein and Lewis.

The moral is that if you want to girdle your Gödel, do it with a möbius one. Recap sighed and thought "okay, I'll take 'Whorf-istory'", his "separate languages, separate universes". But he knew he couldn't do that, knew the girdles were bridges and that language bases constantly moved as they generated completenesses or, on the other hand, clarities. Hegel's endless labours of the negative kept cleaning out the field of presence as it birthed into the past and was distinctly beheld. These labours set up shop in the noise outside the perfect past.

So where was the noisy Joyce in all this and for that matter where was Lewis? By the logic of bp's taste they must both be right, or at least all right, and if that ain't ironic. Joyce, waking the dead in that circle of his, must be said to be complete, but as a world of inconsistency. And Lewis, the great scourge against time, with his endless spatialized distinctions and expressivist clarities and clarifications, stands outside, always in incompleteness, no matter how big those books are.

Recap thought of new portraits of the artists and how the artists would have you not capture them. The poststructuralists and language poets are too much for words, ironically, and, ironically, the traditionalists traditionally acknowledge or build into their words an outside to words. After Putnam Recap insinuated the ethical into the equations, or that should be, relations, if the non-identities of Hegel and Gödel's girdles are in play, that is, he recognized the element of choice inhabiting re-presentation that goes on interminably in the inmost fold of the human condition and, as Hegel implies, almost with a life of its own, even as that problematizes the action of the will implied here.

He insinuated and let the insinuations come to term. He thought about the question of his honesty, basically, and how the question reached to the political horizon. How one could get away with clouding and how one couldn't get away from clouding or confusing the reason and goodness. In theory, completeness and consistency be not damned, one could tell all, but in practice one muddled and fumbled, through weakness in both reason and will. But even if one did tell all, that is tell a tall tale that through consistency, from the ground up, found just the right height for itself, that is, just a head (full of history) taller than history, there would always be, however plateaued, or geo-plate-toed (not Plato-ed in this lower limit), the history to come.

And Hegel, for all his absolute spiritedness, said we can't jump over our shadows, however much all our post-isms might lead us to believe (a curiously mocking and ironizing expression). All of which reminds us that our biggest hopes, though bigger than Normal Mailer's hope to be perhaps good enough to be a Balzacian character, can be no more than to be characters for the relatively omniscient novelists of the future.

Of course there is always the moment we give too much credit and also, the clichéd and embarrassing moment, embarrassing too at the second level, ie for the novelists' willing passivity, the characters tell the novelists where to go in the novelists' own words. That is, despite our overcoming at the hands of the future we may yet warp and worm it, not to discredit it we should hope but to offer a mutual rescue, or at least a cue, or then just an eternally tain-ted res. And of course into any human future that chances us and our past, can anyone doubt that Homer, Plato, Shakespeare et al will continue to shoot holes.

Recap thought *fragment*, that Walter Benjamin idea, coalescing a symptom with selfsame antidote, and he thought of the intellectual wars over universality in the background both/and foreground of the real wars. He recited to himself that fragment was a general idea that gets taken for granted, forgotten even, as reason assumes its new position outside the new, already old frame. He'd been up at the Banff Centre listening to Michael Ignatieff talk about art and culture and universality. Ignatieff was slamming the deconstructionist reign in the cultural field and argued the universality of art. He touted the magic of the work of art, meaning not some black art, but just the metaphor, in Hegel's terms, only a *representational* charm, pertaining to a transcendent quality that was desecrated by deconstruction. (Charm being peripheral and not integral to the beautiful for Kant.)

Recap talked to him later and said that minimally the deconstruction was the necessary, double-hooked price any artist paid for his/her constructions. In order to intervene in the culture as an artist one had to go to the smithy of the soul where glory and despair neutralize any magic effects, but then as a construction takes shape the spell dispelled comes in the back door, and again the artist is outside his work, smaller than it and is inclined to rid the magic again in order to put his/her hand on the power where it is prior to any effects, not because those effects can always be Frankenstein effects, but because for the artist's presumption to know and create to come into effect, the artist must find that place in the centre of the flower Shakespeare talks about in his sonnet where the flower to itself is not a flower.

It is here Recap thought the real importance of the fragment, not the romance of it, lay. The beautiful [Kantian] truth of art is only as good as its last interpreter who is only as good as his/her *in time* distended presentation, à la St. Augustine, of a re-presentation. One only holds so much in a presented time, hence the fragment,* the fragment that is not only the romance of the shard or the immediate chaos of the rotated or horizontal sublime, but the unit, little strutting general, in lieu of an arching unity, that can be held in the hand, grasped, and that can produce the arches over time that always escape us or mock us till some little general makes pieces with it again.

But that military metaphor is unfortunate, if playfully undermined. He thought of Pound, not uncontaminated with military senses, but at the end in the recanting cantos, celebrating "not destroyers". Pound disagreed with everything Lewis said but praised his "live mind". Lewis chose literal blindness rather than risk the loss of that live mind and its insights.

Recap read Myrna Kostash's critical review of Ignatieff's *The Warrior's Honour* and was moved by the wrestling, with the wrangling over the truth and meaning of the so-called ethnic nationalisms. He was worried about, not her empathy with the struggle of people struggling with their own new powers, after generations of oppression, as well as with the new world order powers, the new powers that be, but with her unnecessary alliance with certain postmodernist uncertainties. In other words the attacks on universality ultimately appeal, and rightly so, to new tendered universalities.

Just as Charles Taylor argues that the recognition asked for by the marginalized or cultural minorities appeals to and presupposes mutual transcendences that converge to new third positions, for as sheer other they transcend one

---

* Recalling Kant's meditation on the relation of the beautiful and the sublime.

another with bad prejudice, as opposed to the good pre-judgements, as Gadamer would say, constituting their respective traditions. Taylor of course points out the asymmetry now of the mutual relations and of the consequent responsibilities.

Recap went back to that mathematical logician and one time Maoist, and now still logician who works a wider Wittgensteinian field and thinks about his Jewish religious tradition, that is Hilary Putnam who wrote:

Philosophers who lose sight of the immanence of reason, of the fact that reason is always relative to context and institutions, become lost in characteristic philosophical fantasies. "The ideal language," "inductive logic," "the empiricist criterion of significance" — these are the fantasies of the positivist, who would replace the vast complexity of human reason with a kind of intellectual Walden II. "The absolute idea": this is the fantasy of Hegel, who, without ignoring that complexity, would have us (or, rather, "spirit") reach an endstage at which we (it) could comprehend it all. Philosophers [on the other hand] who lose sight of the transcendence of reason become cultural (or historical) relativists.

Recap looked up and wanted to defend the Hegel who seemed to know one must hold to one's circumstances. One could scrutinize the past for clues to how freedom might work but to pretend in history to hold the absolute idea absolutely was not possible for the Hegel he knew. As far as the war on universals went he was the first to recognize the false universals or the abstract or one-sided universals, but that for anyone to advance their cause they would only do so by way of participating in new speculative propositions rooted in, not the particular nor the universal, but in the individual as the mediation of the two, sort of halfway to the universal, as opposed to cut-off formal propositions. Reason in Hegel's dialectical sense or Peirce's melodically recurring and developing sense, is flexible, not in the sense of arbitrary but in the sense of self-correcting as it responds to the contingencies and to other individuals' reason it recognizes. Putnam had it when he said reason is both immanent (to a culture) and transcendent of it. Again he wrote:

Consider now the position of the cultural relativist who says, "When I say something is true, *I mean that it is correct according to the norms of my culture." If he adds, "When a member of a different culture says that something is* true, *what he means (whether he knows it or not) is that it is in conformity with the norms of his culture," then he is in exactly the same plight as the methodological solipsist.*

To spell this out, suppose [Richard Rorty], a cultural relativist, says

When Karl says "Schnee ist weiss," what Karl means (whether he knows it or not) is that snow is white as determined by the norms of Karl's culture

(which we take to be German culture)

Now the sentence "Snow is white as determined by the norms of German culture" is itself one that R.R. has to use, not just mention, to say what Karl says. On his own account, what R.R. means by this *sentence is*

"Snow is white as determined by the norms of German culture" is true by the norms of R.R.'s culture

(which we take to be American culture)

Substituting this back into the first displayed utterance (and changing to indirect quotation) yields

When Karl says "Schnee ist weiss," what he means (whether he knows it or not) is that it is true as determined by the norms of American culture that it is true as determined by the norms of German culture that snow is white.

Recap thought of Myrna's eulogy for Jon, how she evoked that lean dancer's body with its beatnik walk, gliding hips ahead, and how she said she "loved that man" and then he thought the sadness that Jon had loved that woman, not meaning that they both hadn't loved or didn't love others or thus to say whether it was a transcendent and/or immanent love — all of which he recognized to be getting ridiculous as a speculation. They were friends and fond, with prejudice, of one another.

Recap looked out his window at Cascade Mountain, the "false front mountain" Jon had said because of the amphitheatre on the other side. On this side he didn't take his mountains so seriously that he couldn't be greatly amused by Dennis Burton's claim that for himself and a group of other artists the mountain was full of faces, in fact the pink panther was up there, apparently formed in the snow patches in the central gully "smiling gleefully at Inglismaldie".

Recap would drive through the park gates coming back to Banff from the farm and he would be seeing Cascade and not be seeing or thinking of any faces but he would catch himself suffering the loss of Jon, even as his presence would haunt the valley. He missed terribly the wit and the outrageous caprice of Jon, of "beyond exceptional pass", who could chuckle warmly at Pat Askren's painting of block letters sitting crookedly on the mountains spelling "moutain", "complete" with the missing "n". And this made him think of the card he had sent Recap, five rows of five letters, big block letters filling the front of the card, in fact the alphabet but one; there was "no 'L'!" and so it became, presto, a Christmas card. He missed Jon, the serious artist who would stand up to the big names who came to *his* mountains. And yet he became friends of everyone from Aaron Copland to John Cage and especially to Murray Schafer, even as he celebrated Jim Deegan's *Timberline Tales* and the life of Lizzie Rummel.

Recap thought of Jon entertaining the Four Horseman (of the apocryphal lips) in the Magpie and Stump and how earlier in the Whyte Museum, McCaffery, the theorist, was cracking practically everyone up with his lip service to words. Recap thought about the "neo-baroque festiveness" of his poetry and then thought there is a human nature for the language guys after all, and already their own historians (Bob Perleman) are putting its promises in perspective and noting what they failed to deliver, that this neo-baroque was where what broke was the "news that stays news" and was what wasn't to be fixed, though endlessly fixable. Ludic human nature out looking for its fix and so doubling up at being in one.

And what to do when utopia arrives? Con-template two dancing dialectical derivatives of *fix*, what is predestined against constant[?] reflexive correction. What is predestined is the stubborn anti-logos, ie the indefinite, temporal and surviving — both template and con job. Fat chance utopia will arrive. Its job or Job is its absence and rimes the ambiguous asylums of history. The absence in history is unbearably tensed, in time, in the poise that peeks and peaks at the poison that would satisfy. The angels in utopia get on one another's nerves and ride off to the bodies of nobodies and what on earth you think you are up to, that is, so splits the expression, both your fallen past as persistent mischief, and your hopeful future.

Recap: Jon's encyclopaedic knowledge and how it must have put more than one famous visitor off, especially as he would have read up in their field and could easily toss off a few insider remarks. On the other hand these remarks were just the opening for them to feel at home, for quick and magnificent friendships that lasted long past the visit. The first off-putting, if the he or she were to come back or stay any length, was usually followed by a warming up. The man grew on you over time.

Recap had actually, like an electron, taken both routes at once, as Jon would bombard him with his more extensive knowledge and then as the generous bard induct Recap into the community of poetry and give himself over to Recap's work with a close appreciative read. Both routes reappeared one prolific year in which Recap had produced another manuscript every time Jon would turn around, three one-hundred page plus manuscripts in one winter, the progressive polish only outdone by the increasing rate of wearying repetition. Recap: Jon sat down at the oak table in Bruce's house on Bow Avenue across from The North Landing, took the lid off the latest box of budding Recap's poems.

Jimmy sat nervously at the table and he and Recap watched the critic at work. Only a few minutes went by and Jon pushed the box away. "Awfully Latinate" he said of the diction. Two or three poems and that was it. Jimmy was more furious than Recap who was caught off guard and unknowing in a risky logopoeia, the Poundian caveated category Jon would later, in a generous-meaning spirit, assign him. Neither Jimmy nor Recap could see that Jon, in the role of the diction cop, might be checking Recap's blind enthusiasm in order to help him step out for a moment so he could smell the musty and unintended self-parodies daily accruing. Their perceived revenge came later when Wilfred Watson accepted about ten pages of the manuscript for the *White Pelican* (Watson seeing only one of the manuscripts at this point was later to observe a repetition element in the later [not enough later] manuscripts).

Wilfred, whom Jon greatly respected, phoned him from Edmonton to get hold of Recap. Jon parcelled out the news cryptically and slowly as he paused and shaved some in the log house on Beaver where Recap finally found him after hearing from Terry Brennan, the folksinger and famous Bob Dylan fan, that Jon had some kind of news. "I told him" he said and then continued to shave. "I told him . . . [pause] . . . you were . . . [pause] . . . very perspicacious". He continued to shave while Recap accepted the Latinism, still wondering to whom he'd been described and why.

But there was the famous night almost two decades later Jon introduced Al Purdy at the Whyte, possibly Al's third appearance there, when Jon calculated his praise even as he worked it up. First Al was the best poet in the Americas, now that Robert Penn Warren was dead. Then he stopped and reconsidered. No Octavio Paz was the best, Al was second best. Al piped up "Jon, I didn't know you read Spanish". Recap would hoot at Jon as he arranged the pantheon. Then the very next night up at the Centre in Sid and Myrna's suite after the CKUA live concert which separately included Sid singing, W O reading, and Karl Roth playing jazz violin, and with the audience getting its applause cued and conducted, Jon held Recap and Pam and Sid and Myrna and some others rapt with his stories, and when not rapt, had them cracking up with his jokes.*

After the healing of one major rift, a result of Jon's bravado in the literary world and Recap's naïve and romantic stinginess, they settled into an unavoidable friendship, complete with inside jokes and their peculiar outside references, the intertwining biographies as the tradition-like entity that these jokes presupposed, the coming to agreements on the pulse and points of departure of the culture, give or take a few philosophers. A friendship whose potential in death Recap was only *growing* to understand, ie in relation to the depth of Jon's knowledge and care for the Banff area. At one tain time Jon's description of Recap to John O. Thompson was simply "a bar regular". Now that Recap had pretty well closed the bar era and was beginning to smell the flora and turning to the history of the place, he smelled the parking lots and was overwhelmed by the Joni-on-Jon effect, ie "not knowing what you've got till its gone".

Recap: Tain walked into the old Book and Art Den with the uneven floor that creaked, in the winter of '72 when Jon was the manager. Jon would stand behind the counter and dare customers to bring a book up for his inspection and to his standards, when they just wanted to buy the damn thing. He interrupted a conversation with a film

---

* Cary Grant had been sent a telegram by some fact-scratching journalist. "How old Cary Grant?" Grant replied "Old Cary Grant fine."

maker from Edmonton and introduced him to Tain but insisted on calling Tain "Recap" and added, with his weighty less-is-more emphasis, that Recap had a good memory.*

He then turned to Recap and said I want to do a book of yours.** Turning back to the filmmaker he said that Recap was a poet of wit, and getting polemical, that wit was what the CanLit scene needed now. Tain was shy, gun shy of this Recap swept up in the polemic, but then pressing in on his memory was the encounter the day before with a woman painter. She'd related how much a fan Jon was of Recap's poetry.

Years later, after Jon's death, this same woman told him she'd heard Jon on the CBC tag Recap's little sequence of poems a minor classic. Recap doubted his judgement here, but he did remember his own sin of omission when he could have or should have defended Jon against a mean-spirited attack rooted in simple resentment of Jon's dominating energy. And Recap had seen one of his grand schemes as perhaps "unCanadian", now that he thought about it, rather than necessary disturbance required to found anything, a literary history of Banff, in this instance, to challenge any otherwise neurotic literati to take thence new directions (with a nod here to the south, west coast style, re our own possibilities, not "murkin" ones for Jon).

---

* Recap had once in an interview tried to explore how memory worked, by talking about how its patterns and construction were rooted in levels of intention and even crooked little purposes as these trickled back down to affect immediate vectors of action fated for accidents that would become significant memories.

** Jon was an editor with a local publisher.

Jon's only religion he said was "to capitalize EARTH". But he wrote about Paley, the mathematician with the theosophical connection, and, though *Skeptical Inquirer* subscriber to the end, continued to flirt with his own sentiments and the possibilities of ghosts, the result usually being mock literary device to invoke the imagination as understood through Blake and *Sartor Resartus* (once correcting Sheila Watson in this connection on the difference between a battery and a cell) and *The Tempest*, and the imagination as something Jung, for all his one time literary appeal and reading of Kant,* had neglected.

This imagination could of course lift off the EARTH for Jon just fine and become Clarke's and Kubrick's technological vista to the stars. It was bigger than poets and scientists and included gods and animals and other and ancient cultures, but stopped at God. He would gesture to the strange goings on at Skoki, "a lost ski", and Brandy, his dachshund who got lost one night but returned, happy as could be, the next day with some new skiers, all governed by Paley of beyond the pale, after his fatal skiing accident years ago. And then it paled as he said "I make nothing of these events, I just report the facts". The irony of tone undermining the statement as such was intended, but not believed.

He would stop Recap in the street and hush his voice to tell him that so and so world-renowned writer had died that day. Recap would say yes he'd heard or no he hadn't

---

* Recap had heard a recording on the radio in which Jung had boasted how he had read Kant, unlike Freud. And those archetypes do rime with those Kantian categories. Freud must have been reading his Nietzsche or getting him subconsciously, albeit resentfully, through their shared love object, Ms Salomé.

and then look down, and depleted. When Cyril Paris died he devoted his column to a wonderful celebration. When Norman the female golden-mantled ground squirrel, of the cute variety, who had famously inhabited the Luxton museum, died, he wrote a eulogy and recapped her history with the fumigation episode again and mixed in Malraux's "museum without walls".

That May in '91 Jon looked ashen at the Writers' Guild banquet when he almost precipitated a bun fight by provoking the Minister of Culture into slagging Mel Hurtig upon reminding the Minister that the *Canadian Encyclopaedia* would read better without the cellophane wrapper, he drove back with Sid, Richard and Recap, and he talked about Henry Kreisel's death, how quick it was. It was liver cancer, the same as with Jon, then six months from his death. Two weeks later in June Recap and Jon drove down in the bus after the Guild executive meeting and he talked about being at the Saskatchewan Writers' Guild conference, "Lorna and Patrick", and said that he heard Brenda Riches, Recap's once editor, had cancer.

Then he talked about bp nichol's love of Pogo. Recap was about to leave him at the Calgary bus terminal and then something made him stay and have supper. Jon said he had to buy a vacuum cleaner. And then Recap asked him how the conference with Marvin Minsky and the musicians had gone. He heard later from Marie Morgan that Jon had been a riot, a welcome change. They drank their coffee and that's when Jon told about overhearing the Reform party members in the faculty lounge. He told his conference about it, adding the one-liner "speaking of artificial intelligence".

Recap drove home to the farm one spring and thought about Jon's love of that little dachshund and, to noses even closer to the ground, his loving talk of squirrels and marmots, how he joked in a column that marmots would make good pets since you could just let them into the back yard when you went away in September and they would dig down into the rock garden. Even upon returning you wouldn't have to worry about them till the end of June when they'd emerge again.

His hoard of knowledge that checked the flights of the ignorant, and then his sensibility that flew up after the fact, in both senses, ie he acknowledged the flight as such and acknowledged that the facts never settled down. He got them into his poems and columns and non-fiction but he needed more time and that drastic chance Eric Auerbach was given when the war cut him off from his books, when he simply sat down and wrote *Mimesis, the Representation of Reality in Western Literature*. Jon died into his friends and his possibilities were suddenly dramatized, his potential tragically and ironically realized, that is the smothered great potential was recognized at the heart, and now it drifts and diffuses through the museum without walls.

He was working out the "flowing together of two streams" as he observed of the Kootenay and Stoney beadwork. "Animal; plants and flowers; stylized mountains vying with curves, squares and geometric representation". "Their beadwork . . . reflects the diversity of all the tribes they came into contact with, as well as the complicated aspects of their lives as horsemen, fishermen, and agriculturally-based peoples, and the divers environments in which they live: the mountains, the river environs, and the arid Tobacco Plains". "The Blackfoot geometries, their own boreal background . . . the melding of different traditions". Jon wore his beaded buckskin jacket on special occasions, "rich in woodsmoke odours", and he was thinking about the place of art, about its growth, its accommodations, "without walls", about the local broken mountain visions and about how this suited his broken-open sensibility.

Recap was tensed between what Jon had accomplished and what was lost promise now; together these "imagined" the pantheistic dialogue for the surviving others to stitch together these now set adrift knowledges and elegances into something they could wear as "the skin of culture" and yet "allow much surface for individual expression". Recap thought this in carrying on with the trickster vacuum cleaner, in the spirit of his quoting, from Paz Jon thought but couldn't pin it down, "poets are a creation of language designed to sustain itself". What Recap really missed was that leathery face, the face that could be haughty but that you were challenged to crack into hilarity with genuine wit (or maybe just sheer goofiness). A face that with the glasses intimated owl, or rimed his dachshund he would carry in the crook of his arm, a face at times ridiculous with its inattention to itself and then elegant with reassuring authority. Recap missed having coffee with him and wondering what marmot of his mind would pop up next.

Seeing Stars

Anna told Recap about the time she was twelve and had been sent to vacuum her room. She closed the door and just turned the vacuum cleaner on and let it stand there running while she lay on the bed reading. It was a saucy and endearing story and for some reason Recap told her that it would have been about the time his father died. If he were another poet or a former self he said he might write about this trans-Atlantic correspondence.

Maybe he would have made part one of the poem Dr Rock's get well card screaming inside the garbage dumpster. But he would never write such a poem now, except as maybe embedded in a story about how he had refused the poem, and in a way write it anyway, preserving it by letting it out of the preserving jar, probably not Plath's bell jar, more likely Stevens' jar in Tennessee, there for its absence, well there for cleaning up the mess of everything and for leaving as it was, garbage in and garbage out, but twisted into new life, nay, a living, the living out of a life, moving on openly, yet living out a fate too.

Recap had gone into the Lizzie Rummel room at the Whyte to check out the new summer lunch menu and that's how he met Anna, young Dutch woman from Amsterdam. She sat at one of the dark antique tables taken from Joshua's in the stone Brewster building that had housed the A&W when he first came to town and now was Sergeant Preston's gift shop incorporated into a much larger Brewster building, hotel, pub and shops.

She had dark reddish brown hair tied back in a loose pony tail and looked like a ballerina with her build and in the way they are so at ease and casual in their bodies. Her smile and laugh were most engaging. Open and full of good humour, she was chatting with Richard who sat drinking tea at the next table. She had books and pages of a letter she was writing spread over the table.

They were making one another laugh about tourists who wanted food with no this and no that in it. Anna had served somebody from California who wanted everything no salt, no fat, low cholesterol, decaffed, no sugar etc. Richard was comparing a similar story of his own but then they took it a few steps further and Recap helped them. They were getting a little too giddy by the time they were imagining steak with no meat and subsided into vague smiles and then slid into a new subject.

Of course there was some irony in turning to slagging the latest Hollywood movie for being full of the cultural equivalents of high fat, cholesterol etc. Anna had just seen *Tin Cup* and thought it pretty low rent. Recap of course agreed but decided for argument's sake to defend it as full of interesting allegorical symptoms, with Costner's cronies adding up to a retrieval of the melting pot and the US Open golf tournament as metaphor of the power in America being open to the grass roots, and with Costner's wildness standing for the vitality that the "corporate" golfers of the pro circuit lacked and institutionally shut out. In fact Recap now thought about Costner's allegories and utopias/dystopias as an interesting phenomenon in the film industry and of course not without precedent and even tradition.

The two doting old toms tried to suggest Canadian novels for her to read. Like the video you might pick up for an evening, they couldn't quite pinpoint just the right one for her to rush out and buy or to find at the library. Recap began a list of western Dutch Canadian writers, Van Herk and Vanderhaeghe, otherwise so different, and then was reminded of the story Jon had told him of a Dutch bookseller telling someone compiling a bestseller list that *The Wars* was the top seller at her store. But her thick accent made for some mischief and of course Jon had it that *Divorce* was being touted as the book to read.

Both of them were completely enamoured with Anna, whose middle name was derived from a Greek goddess which seemed to be just if you allowed for that easy manner, quick wit and utter approachability. Recap couldn't tell whether she was twenty or thirty and thought that this must be because of her European worldliness but then he figured she must be closer to thirty as he took into account what she'd said she'd done and where she'd travelled. She knew about five languages and had worked in Rome for a year or two. She liked to read and wrote regular letters to friends back home but skied and also taught aerobics. And she loved a good laugh, drank coffee and was big on wine and the odd glass or two of vodka.

Recap would run into Richard that summer more often than usual as their habit of tea and sweet-taking at the Rummel room settled into the habit that was not mere habit but the base for their "real obvious" real obsession. They kind of fudged the age difference issue and Recap at least could shut out the knowledge of her boyfriend since he'd never met or even seen him. With all the conditionality of the channelled prospects the rivalry was kept within gentlemanly bounds and carried off with mutual innocuous denial and for good measure, danced over and around with exchanges of information about her and updates on the various inside jokes developing among the three of them.

Anna went back to Amsterdam and began working for the U of A exchange program and was sending them cards from Sweden and Spain with news of even further travel. She sent Recap a book on the Netherlands called *The Low Sky, Understanding the Dutch*. Recap had of course finally met her boyfriend and tried not to like him too much but it was hard because he was bright and "nice" and obviously cared for her, and he was tall, tall, tall. Recap had read in *The Globe and Mail* that the Dutch were the tallest people in the world. Recap was a hair under the average Dutchman who was something like 173 centimetres, about the same height as Anna who though said she was the same hair under.

Recap made many joke references to this till it began to pall. But revived the mock height issue for his letter back thanking her for the book, surmising that the low sky was what had enticed the Dutch so upward. On occasion the height thing had driven Anna to give awkward and humourous assurances that made Recap want to make assurances back that there were no Freudian depths here and what we had here was just a bit of Zen on its way to tall tale city which was only there for the beyond, ie of the measure principle. But he said nothing back and simply let the issue drift and remain the one hair forward and two hairs back ambiguity, with the pun[s] in "ambiguity" at the centre of a tiny, barely detectable confession of love.

Richard and Recap had both been on the phone overseas to her and then Richard decided to take her up on her invitations to Amsterdam. Recap met him on the street and Richard told him the news of his decision and that he was bored and had been writing all summer and all winter and needed to do something. In fact he told him he had 1400 hundred poems now, "good ones that is". Recap smiled at the unintended other meaning and then wondered if maybe it was intended and smiled some more. Recap had met him for the first time at Bruce's down on Bow Avenue. Richard sat on the floor in the bare breakfast room and in his deep voice talked about cadences and Robert Browning and Plato.

He had been published in good literary magazines but wasn't sending much out these days as far as Recap knew. He would publish small, stapled books every few years. Recap would buy them at the bookstore and read them with care. The poems would put you powerfully into nature and an ecstasy "besides". They were carefully constructed and full of right rhythms, great heart that made the intelligence more intelligent. If you were only familiar with the poems and then were to meet him you would be surprised at the fussiness of the man and very particularness but also by the wicked wit and fondness for some sheer silliness. Recap heard him read some doggerel for the local poetry group one year and he had everybody in stitches.

The joke was that he worked with the public and hated people. On more than one occasion Recap walked into the tea room and he would be telling Anna about the day's stupid questions he'd had to answer at the Information Building. For all that and the fact that his family was long rooted in Banff, his brother a warden, he was not especially, or at an ideological level say, protective of the Banff Park. The deep woods were simply in his blood and imagination and he just happened to hate people, well some of the people some of the time. Or let's say he didn't like being bothered at the information building while he worked out the cadences of his latest poems in his head. Other people's poetry often put him to sleep.

Recap had angled out of the parking lot and down the lower steps of the Information Building to the sidewalk one time as Richard was standing on the stoop of the top steps happily giving directions to a couple of women, gesturing with a raised hand. Recap interjected "are you preaching then?" Richard laughed and took up the theme and pointed to St Paul's beside the Information Building on the corner of Wolf St and Banff Avenue, indicating his competition. Recap threw this preacher Richard into his letter to Anna and then apologized obscurely for how we benignly Frankenstein one another.

Recap had been invited by Anna to ski the trail from the Canmore Spray Lakes down to Banff at the back of Rundle at midnight under the full moon in January. Dr Rock reminded him of his age and how fit the people were and possibly, on the other hand, how green they were too. Recap took it as a challenge but as Rock listed all the things he should take and all the things that could go wrong he did have to start fighting off a creeping anxiety too. It had been quite a few years since he'd skied the back country and he wondered if he'd be able to keep up to these Netherlands-to-Canada cross-country-ers. He managed even to infect Playcefire with the anxiety to the extent Playcefire drove by the golf course below the Banff Springs in the late afternoon on the day of the event to check if they had arrived.

Full moon day was too cold and stormy so, Dr Rock heeded beyond their control, they postponed the adventure till the weather was nice and then did it during the day. Only four of them went, Anna and her boyfriend and his friend who was their age and a super fit cyclist and skier, and Recap, the afterthought. The boyfriend's friend was about a hundred and forty or fifty pounds and wore maybe two or three ounces of clothing, tight-fitting spandex pants and little jacket top, carried on his back one small bottle of water that had a tube running over his shoulder so he could drink at will on the go. He raced ahead and set the pace. Anna was in terrific shape, had won road races, ie running, but was new to cross country skiing so she fell back and her boyfriend stayed back with her. He'd skated in that grueling Dutch marathon race they have every year if the weather cooperates and gives them ice.

Recap skied between the leader and the Dutch connection. De-tained in the back of his mind was the embarrassment of the forty-mile trek in the summer many years ago with Rory and Laurie. But his regular running and leg workouts served him well and he settled into a pace he could handle and feel he still had reserve with. They stopped about halfway, at Goat Creek, where the curve of the path down the steep grade onto the narrow bridge over the open and fast flowing water gave them each pause as they made the approach.

The boyfriend was irked at the racer for racing and spoiling the leisurely ski and nature appreciation and made a patronizing remark about ignoring the other man's woman, how the racer wouldn't have done this had his wife been along. Recap was able not to ignore the other man's woman, and when the boyfriend asked if he would stay behind with Anna when they were about to leave from the picnic table at the end of the Spray loop, he assured him he didn't mind a bit. He and Anna skied side by side until they got to the steep places and then went one at a time.

On one hill Anna got one ski on the inside track of the left and one ski on the inside track of the right tracked pair. As the two pairs diverged she began to ski in an increasingly splits position and started to shriek and laugh at the same time. Recap waited at the bottom and laughed as he watched. He was getting thirstier all the time and they stopped to drink as well as look at the views, and they talked about things unrelated to the outing. He was trying to imagine what it must be like to enjoy the huge Canadian outdoors as compared to the Netherlands, as they in fact talked about this, counterpointed to his thinking and then talking about the distortion and futility of jock absorption, even as he had tried to keep the pace, and as his aching shoulders with their years of bench-pressing put the lie to his anti-jock talk.

Recap: Anna telling him about her friendship with an award-winning Dutch author, anonymity-minded enough and friend enough that she ended up going to accept the award for him. She and Recap were sitting in the Fine Grind and she told him she never knew whether this guy just wanted to talk to her or whether he wanted "to take me out". One day he invited her into his bedroom, turned off the lights and asked her to lie flat on her back on the bed. She started to blush and laugh as she related this and then said that on the ceiling were glued all these phosphorescent stars that glowed beautifully in the dark.

Recap laughed and alluded to the kind of faith in which she'd carried out this experiment. Then he laughed again and blushed himself when he thought about and told her of the stars on the ceiling of his own bedroom. The first night he saw them he couldn't figure it out. He'd turn the lights on and couldn't see anything on the ceiling and so turned them off and there they were again. He thought at first they were tiny holes, dumbly rehearsing a pre-scientific belief about the stars and the sky. He asked if she wanted to see his stars letting a jokey tone cloud the inviting one.

It had been lucky the racer had raced because, although they had done the nineteen K in just over three hours as against Rock's prediction of five hours, they'd started after two and it was getting pretty hard to see by the time he and Anna skied down the steep winding trail into the golf course.

Recap showered and then, tired but with that afterglow from hard exercise, walked over to the restaurant to meet Anna and the boyfriend for the victory celebration. As he was going up the stairs he realized his fly was down. When he got to the table he told them of this near further and actual retroactive embarrassment. They didn't know the term "fly" and Recap got awkward in explaining and also lost any appropriate note of humour with which he could have excused the inconsequential information. Their blank looks made him squirm a little and he realized he'd blown and then blown up this fly-down story into a psychological fly-down story, not for being risqué as such but for the residue that petered out into banality that hung in the air unremarked but not veiled either. This was the end of the road and the height of the nether regions.

Rock and the Fenland

Recap: Dr Rock would read big fat Chinese novels, Recap's own unread copy of a Celine biography and once a book on forensic medicine. He had put the book in a special jacket or plastic binder and had his nose in it on a bus in Toronto and felt he was getting some funny looks. Later he claimed his cousin told him these special jackets were what women put Harlequin Temptation or Harper Torch novels into so they could have their way with them on buses etc.

He knew about special tools, knives that explorers had used, and would find someone who still made them and then order one. He would mend his car muffler with tin cans and could tell you the history of and a whole lot of particular anecdotes about the French Foreign Legion, including the time he tried to join it and didn't get past first base, actually a dingy little office in Paris, upon a summary refusal even to consider him. He once told Recap about some intestinal cure he'd performed on himself that involved cotton batting and charcoal and a few other things, maybe oil. And from working once as a paramedic on the 401 could talk about goings-on in the chest cavity, hiatus hernias, the vagus nerve, the Valsalva reflex, about how you had to regulate relieving a patient's bladder with a catheter to avoid them going into shock.

He read the Koran as evidence against a blanket them (Iranian fundamentalists, the Taliban?) and drew Recap out on the issue, but Recap, trying to avoid conflict[!?] and lamely fudge agreement, related a half-remembered Hegelian explanation of fanaticism from the *Philosophy of History*. No doubt it involved a lack of mediation, with Hegel of course having a bias for Christian evolution when he wasn't seeing the day philosophy would swallow religion whole, in the sense of necessary historical gullibility and also of its overcoming.

Rock would eat caffeine pills before a walk up Sulphur and then reward himself with a couple of shots of tequila after. He would bundle up in the summer to a degree that Glenn Gould never dreamed of and then ride a stationary bike for an hour. He would go for months doing no physical activity while he nursed a sore shoulder, sore knee and a sore hand.

He would lie on the sofa and read for hours and then get up with a crippling crook in his neck and he would quote Lord Chesterfield on sex: something like a moment of pleasure in the most ridiculous position all for a consequent life of misery. Recap aside wondered about the difference between how an eighteenth-century audience would take this and how a late nineteenth and twentieth-century audience, post-Darwin, would take it.

Yet there seemed to be something in the evolution paradigm that rimed with the Christian one, and then there was the thought that there existed a perverse commonsensical wisdom that existed below the paradigms and straightforwardly supported the wit. Rock was always behind the scenes, talking to the manager of the coffee bar about getting boxes, talking to the butcher at Keller Foods to procure fat, otherwise discarded, for the bird feeder, talking about higher education with the East Indian woman cook at Evelyn's coffee and lunch bar who had graduated from Oxford.

And probably it is safe to say that Rock was a great lover of the "I told you so" position. He got no little glee from being able to tell a house buyer, who had already bought a certain house and who was now going to fix it up and then flip it for a tidy profit, that the zoning laws forbade it and that there were all sorts of structural flaws, including foundation problems that would make any renovations extremely difficult and costly. This was retroactive "I told you so" ("I could have told you so") and seemingly sweeter in the subjunctive zone.

And yet the man was divided. There seemed to be a moment in the winter after Recap completed the Canmore-to-Banff ski trip wherein Rock was sorry nothing had happened to vindicate his various warnings. But there was something deeply human in the man, alongside the perhaps inevitable cruelty in humour that possessed him as he surveyed the endless parade of human folly, a harvest for him. He seemed to be glad that Recap had survived and that they could continue to wrangle and try to persuade one another to listen to their respective spiels, or even just to share the casual gossip that cropped up.

One day in the summer he listened to a couple of young American climbers planning their next ascent as they sipped their lattes. He saw them poring over maps and then turned to Recap, shaking his head in unsympathetic despair over these dead men walking, at least as far and as quickly as he could judge. Recap figured that one couldn't really tell from this little bit to go on, whether they knew what they were doing or not. Rock had of course read *Into*

Thin Air and was seeing double here, but of course Rock was not unfamiliar with the Rockies either and his hit rate for predicting human fiasco should not be underestimated Recap thought.

In any case in the time being there could be no hit until the climbers actually attempted the climb and maybe no news when they did, whatever the story. A death or serious injury was not required for a hit, there were plenty of delicious moderations to outright disaster. With the element of luck, or a few "almosts", the story could take on even more power, as threat seemed to tease and bide its time even as it waxed its ubiquity.

Recap to Rock (in light of this waiting for Godot's eager brothers, whose arrivals nevertheless needed peaceful, not points or peaks, but bases, of departure): just into the loop on the Fenland trail a giggling and dripping wet elderly American male. He still had his life jacket on and hurried by, presumably back to the canoe rental place just up from The North Landing on the Bow River, but not before he related that he'd tipped and sunk his canoe in the creek.

Recap had wound around through the trees to the foot bridge and encountered an elderly American woman, bedraggled and equally soaking wet but not at all laughing, yet not cursing, just looking worried. Later that night Recap went to Giorgio's for supper and was reading as he waited for his meal. He heard voices behind him urgently discussing the day's events. He heard "I would never have let you drown, dear" and turned slightly to get a look. It was the comical and not so comical canoeists.

He remembered his Labrador, Kelpie, giving their wet clothes a good sniff each and he retrieved the fact that a kelpie was a water sprite that either saved you or drowned you. His mother had read about Robbie Burns being so distraught over a woman he'd just escorted home that he walked back the wrong way, in the rain, and ended up back in town. When he went into the pub the bartender told him he looked like a drowned kelpie.

Recap had looked at the colourful canoe, seemingly bloated with water by the refraction, tied up but resting at the bottom of the creek. Kelpie jumped in further up and swam out toward a Japanese couple with a small child in a canoe and Recap called sternly and bow, ie bow-wowly, to her, and the child laughed and the father gauged her vectoring as he turned tail and tried to paddle away. Or did the father laugh and the child recoil? Rock laughed when he heard about the water disaster and had a good laugh at the marital discord in the replay, and Recap thought that this minor baptism for Rock's irreligion would do in lieu of something more arch, like a founding or archetypal error amounting to Mount Ararat, even now generating a new race to the bottom.

Stable of Identity*

He once met a young woman who became his lover. It took him some unfolding of time before he could unravel just how quickly he'd been suckered. First it was her assistant at work (a hotel where her stint as TV reporter helped to land a good job), who was constantly alluded to and

---

* Recalling Northrop Frye's *Fables of...* in which, incidentally, he talks about Wallace Stevens' high modernist eschewing of the ironies of incident, the news that doesn't stay news.

praised, a shy man yet with whom she reported she shared graphic sexual references. What she was regularly about, going on and updating him, was mock covered up by a curious shift away from the pure devil to the detail.* When he was on holiday the temporary replacement took on this extracurricular role, moved into the territory of humour to compete with her good cop attribution of funny man to Recap.

Ignoring the script, Recap also liked the young substitute, prodded by her to retail jokes that were as puerile as they were prurient (smelling pussy etc), jokes whose punch lines Recap could smell a mile away. It was reported the young man liked older women, that is, of the age of Recap's young lover. Oh she was thorough. And the substitutes ranged far and wide Recap realized when he awakened to this suckering, with a wealth motif often too, one guy was worth such and such ("a lot of coin!" she ejaculated and underwrote), another on whose photography ("perfect** in every way") she tacked the throwaway "I don't know why someone doesn't give him a million dollars" — all gold-bullyin', at bottom. She had parroted a quivering

---

* Recap had told how, when at the track running and he went by the bleachers in which there were a few rugby fans, he would run like a gazelle (the "yeah sure" included by implication at his own expense), and then once past would revert to his lumbering style. A week later she told him how she and her assistant took a break and went running, how "he runs like a gazelle but slowed down for me, gosh it was awfully kind and generous of him." Recap took to calling him, whom he liked very much as it happened, Mother Teresa, just to heighten the incongruity so worked by her for purposes of additional praise and simultaneous mock diversion.

** At the category mistake Recap rolled his eyes, proxy for imperative Kant, too polite and subtle in his grave.

groupie-like awe of the anthropologist Wade Davis, a celebrated speaker at the Banff Mountain Book Festival, but of course when Recap tried to talk about an ambiguity in an essay whose main point he had to agree with, her reflex was to deny deny, ie when asked, said what Recap had argued didn't make any sense to her.* She outlined no position since she had claimed to see no argument and of course had never read any of Davis' books.

But what got to Recap was the strange subterranean action triggered by the slow build-up of the arsenal or pantheon of boyfriends, built by obsessive (sexual cv) references to houses driven by, to juicy scraps of escapades and journeys made, by micro-opportunistic ambushings of Recap's casual queries, if not questions she'd laid out for him to ask, and by certain allusions combined, from across the table in a restaurant, with that wistful look away at intimate memories so naturally presented to Recap whose history of this moment was supposed to so delicately register the innocence of it all.

---

* Davis had said that no culture is absolute, that first world Western culture is just another culture alongside the others, analogous to how all the plant species are equally of wonder, ie the ethnosphere is parallel to the biosphere. Recap pointed out that Western culture, with its cultural appropriations and multi-cultural policies and de facto practices (however inadequate), its deep historical and historiographical reflections, its technological progress-cum-constant-obsolescing, its disciplines such as anthropology that produced a Wade Davis who (rightly) negates and transcends his own culture in opening to others, is, in short, not just another culture alongside them but a destroyer of cultures, is a self-destructive culture even as it is retro appropriating itself while already, as the academics say, historically imbricated. It is, with its ambiguous science stances and relentless critiques, an anti-culture that both destroys and, on the other hand through a recognition of this, produces a measure of conscience and sometimes even commendable action, however rear guard. It transcends itself, *fait accompli*, with a double hook.

The reflex of deny deny (any real conversation) and the constant positioning for power precluded any spontaneity. Recap was bored but didn't know it in the mask of making love (which was often and of marathon duration) until the mask finally fell away and a new set of more literal masks insinuated themselves upon his *realization* of the pantheon of old lovers, ie when he inscribed them into his various positions, literal and figurative. He needed to become them as he hovered over her in order to keep, among other things, his interest up. Such was the desperate irony, fulfillment of her always bragging how she "put out". James Joyce would have understood. But partial Recap was not the *moi*, or any, Emma and couldn't, once out of the tain of sexual anonymity, flow to Marian Engel's *Bear*, nor could he be Mollified as a Pan-elope of lovers in the wings or by the nom de plume, something de Koch, embedded in Doublin', many times over.*

Playcefire As Alley Cat

As he walked across the alley entrance Captain Recap realized he had become transparent to Playcefire, who was getting out of his car and said "Oh, hi" in a most put upon

---

* Recap had had high expectations when he first went for coffee with the treacherous young damsel. After coffee when it was obvious they'd had a hard time grinding out a conversation† he was very deflated and wished he had not committed to a concert date. At the concert hall he was immediately struck by the tight sweater and jeans she was wearing. And so there hangs the self-suckering tale: the anti-Don, ie the Donkey Oaty.

† Weeks later Recap would look off slightly to try to start a conversation. Turning back he would catch a fallen and inattentive face until she realized he was looking at her whereupon she would give him that look-at-me flashy smile, freshly [w]run[g] from some telling untold sadness, not knowing, itself, itself, at times hiding, at others, put to good use, ie as a card played.

way and then quickly explained he had a lot on his mind. He had once related to Recap how a couple of women he knew played the most juvenile of games with one another as they would have one of their regular spats. Recap felt at the time the judgement was a little too knowing and a little too self-exempting, meaning that the game syndrome was pretty universal, and felt now they were living it out. Playcefire seemed to choose to reveal transparency in the way he performed, à la Brecht, the explanation of his mind's "lot", allowing his true, chosen true, no longer "true", regard to slip out.

Recap surmised he must seem transparent to Playcefire in the sense of false but a kind of false that no one could put a finger on, not even Playcefire, even though the quality would have been as present as the air. Or worse, in terms of elusiveness, as it was more a falsity of omission. It was certainly not written on his face. It was a transparency that seemed to back out of the black mark of deceit, more like a Nabokovian transparency. His not being there for Playcefire had regressed to his simply not being there. His sin in Playcefire's eyes would be the sin of not honouring a man even with ill will, as Nietzsche had explored so thoroughly.

Of course this was not possible, for as bound up in such knowledge the ill will just re-routed itself, and the sickness just exercized itself further into the skull in the ice cube mirror, a twist of health split on the glass. And yet this duty, to honour with hate, was not really one Recap couldn't shirk. It was like the duty to love, it gave him claustrophobia and then a tertiary disgust, close to the brain like the nose and the no accounting for taste. But it was the last, reflexive, purely abstract trace of a once positive situation.

They stood in the alley, the one Peter Whyte painted fifty or sixty years earlier and that was still, with the grill vents, power poles and garbage cans, the underground route to any Alberta town or small city. The sun shone over Playcefire's shoulders and into Recap's face and they exchanged their rhetorical talk and rhetorical listening while they nodded to people they knew walking briskly by in the lunch hour.

In the coffee bar Recap thought about his Nabokovian transparency and realized its validity, that is its applying to him, and its base validity as a station of inevitability. He also entertained the possibility that he exercized an extreme egocentricity, not in judging the drama of Playcefire's untrue, true-colour *untrue*, although a potential regress suggested finally that the acting must be inspired by the truth however much the presentation was smoke and mirrors. He was accurate enough in his judgement, but very self-important in attributing anything more than a bit part to Playcefire's role here, or a consuming passion for it in its moment. Recap wondered how this bit of bad news for their friendship figured in Playcefire's taste for disaster in the news.

Bad news, the temptation for us all, and then Recap wondered whether Gramsci's "pessimism of the intellect/optimism of the will" computed any differently at the personal level or whether the will and the intellect could actually be separated, or for that matter could personal optimism, whatever its springs (to question-beg), be separated from the larger life around.* Then there was the Hegelian raising of the stakes of Heinrich Blucher's lowering and levelling "pessimists are cowards, optimists are fools", a brave but desolate contraction, in contrast to his more famous wife, Hannah Arendt, saying that love was a promise, a stretch to the future, and a forgiveness, a stretch to the past.

The more important question remaining, if it weren't just a personal stake again, how to be a greater humanitarian, beyond the realm of one's personal acquaintances, in light of Nietzsche's demolition, at the motivational level, of this self coming over, or say of the Dickens character who neglects her children for the greater good in distant lands, that is in light of these two unblinking investigators into human misery?

Recap thought that if the Nabokovian transparency was a kind of death, it was perhaps a kind of birth too, out of one fold and into another which was the arrival at a kind of empty freedom that comes after the achievement of selfish worldly goals, or comes after the achieved freedom from oppression, with its distortions to the will that both cranks up and sets back hope, or simply comes after a good marriage or the death of one's parents.

An empty freedom that comes as a developmental stage, or at the realization that, after so many times around the

---

* Adam Phillips' resolution to the pleasure principle vs the reality principle is simply to keep them both in a vital tension. Recap looking at impressionism and then expressionism in the Van Gogh Museum decided the tendency of impressionism, while beginning the move to expressionism, tended toward the reality principle as opposed to the tendency of expressionism toward the pleasure principle, the ego's all-out generative illusion.

block, one is in orbit and the gravity is different and that the levers one has on one's redundant energy are of a different proportion, that the fold one lifted out of did not exist until one escaped it as a predication of same, that is the fold was created by the folding back on what one was and once was in. An empty freedom, if the only thought were to turn back and as if nothing had changed and one had simply to juice all the old pleasures, or to get the old kite of happiness flying impossibly above one again, flying where one now floated and lived, posthumously à la Keats, a redundancy of a different order, of form, if you will, instead of content.

The logic of positions reversed was not completely clear. One floated, orbited in a slow reconsideration that yet, in having bit into a general other potentiality, was essentially light-speed ranging, as if the orbits were gigantic oar-bits (circle sectors), ie a leveraging from pivotal pasts to the fiction of quick change artistry, or parallel lives in the wide sky, where "or" is spelled out as full "other". If one rests all fixed up in the floating, restitutional light of all lives, then what was previously anchor, the drag of *ressentiment*, *becomes* now, becomes subjunctive over the (whose?) dead body, as if. Becomes field potential for what might have been, what could have been, what should have been.

The fictional attention to the confined first person subjective experience, as it moves or floats to the subjunctive or to a range of others, is not simply the other as better self but a complex crisscross, à la Paul Ricoeur, to the self as another and then the slide to other people, and presto, not perhaps a budding humanitarian, but at least the jettisoning of a heavier self for a self that is suffixed *less*! A thin self, already spread. Recap thought the old thought that if friends become enemies what hope was there. He reopened the case of Playcefire and considered the bottled up selves.

This coming back to life as fiction, or as subjunctive, served well as a mode of understanding Playcefire, self-made man. That description fits in the conventional sense, with all the highs and lows and, after Arendt, not without a certain amount of creative violence that is one with all foundings. At first there wasn't, and then on the time continuum, there was, his various businesses. But behind that meaning there was the ur one of "self-made", a sense that comes tragically with the gap between blood parents and adoptive ones, and that also comes, with pain and celebration, in the gap between adolescence and adulthood where one escapes one's parents.

It was the gap in which the movie *The Last Detail* was made, where the duty of details, a physical fight, a deflowering and a drunk-unto-sickness (Kierkegaard minus one) are performed, where the detail flips into the redundancy of form, after all that energy. The kid is allowed these singular details of awful freedom and then taken to the military prison, the uniform, prison cliché come to life clanging ideally, upping the ant[i]. Gertrude Stein would understand.

Playcefire knew the tragedy of love in that gap between the maker and the self made. That unacknowledged gap was the gift of his making, the source of his understanding the game of positions and positioning. It was also probably the source of his sense of formality, of loyalty and, ironically, his sense of the imperative of the normal. He would talk about someone's behaviour and pronounce "now that's not normal". He was good at training horses and dogs, and he could see through mushy thinking about actions, behaviours and job performances, that is he was all for the training of people to be their various roles, or at least perform their various duties.

It was privileged kids with too much time on their hands who talked about revolution or changing the world. This of course sounded funny at the beginning of the nineties, before the sophisticated organized resistance to corporate world rule. The small sixties revival, in its smallness and its being caught in "second time farce", in itself, but in the age's general sense of farce too, became even more vulnerable to his attack. Recap would beg to differ in the rich/poor gap of a service industry world and Playcefire would acknowledge some validity to Recap's arguments but basically remained unconvinced.

Recap: Playcefire's perverse taste for the bad news story but then his quick responses in life to accidents, dangers and potential tragedies, his experiences around horses and bad situations, riders thrown and hooked in a stirrup say, and how he and a trainer would move strategically to corner a horse in a corral. He knew how to steady a spooked horse and how to give a rider confidence again.

Recap connected the "self-madeness" to duty, the upside to the gap between self and love, and the problems thereto. Recap: Playcefire happened upon a crowd scene along a bridge at the side of the highway on his way back from a taxi fare to the Columbia Icefields. In no time he could see that a teenaged girl was being swept down a fast flowing, high stream and that nobody seemed to be doing anything.

Not cowardice the psychologists say but a kind of natural stupidity where people just can't believe someone else isn't already doing something about the situation. But it was also a matter of bravery, for the stream was dangerous. Playcefire ran down alongside of the stream and shouted encouragement and instructions to the girl and then eventually got ahead and out into a negotiable position in the water and was able to grab her, pull her to shore. It was that kind of reduction to disaster that saved Recap from reducing Playcefire's world. The self-made man who knew how to go for the main chance was the man who could cut through the paralysis of a crowd and do what to him was obvious. That gap in the world was his glory and his despair.*

The despair side he filled with the consumption of bad news, or with the performance of duty in the outside world, now crowded out even more by the numbing and dumbing of the irreal world. Recap knew that "life's tragedies" themselves had an afterlife as simply characters in a new play, and though not forgotten, were undone by "new ancestors", new relations.

Again he considered the necessary fiction as a developmental stage, subject to the correction of others' fiction and subject to the general opacity of otherness which, although endlessly min[e]d into fiction, was stubbornly resistant to exhaustion and remained just plain constant reminder and, at the darnedest times, stitched the fiction

---

* Playcefire was split, like anyone. There was with some prejudice the pleasure-principle Playcefire where the made self sequed to the made world. This was the Rosy Recap knew who had travelled east to FoxHog where on the farm on night shift he rounded up the dawn.

to the crowded-in-ness of black hole actuality, a nice symmetry to the ever checking-out (perceiving-as-cancelling-as leaving) of God, the Son, and now the phallus, always unDante'd comedian, infinite ghost to Jacob's ladder self, from unknowable tain to post knowable transparency and as if something noble were the third, hidden terminal completing the transistor.

So, crowded out by the mystic camp of Frankenstein-in-stitches and crowded in by actuality itself, the original fiction or subjunctive sliding has its work cut out, smearing time to fish possibility out of actuality without denying their wormhole convergence, and on top of that, as fiction, competing with the capping effects of media-facing. The strong fictive option was there though and downgraded the tragedy into an open and normal problematic, flush with the rest of the crowd at the stream of human voices as they flow into a rosy drowning out.*

As Recap considered his being *fixed up* in a floating potential, and how the anchor became his kite, he sipped his orange juice in the coffee place. Suddenly he cleared his throat even as he choked on embarrassment, saw himself in Playcefire's eyes as someone squeezed out of the intriguing shadows, out of the tain of the mirror, out of the wombs of the world, to euphemize and idealize the proposition. Someone who no longer scared anything up. Caught between Auden's "divine bore and the boring

---

*Again the *raised voice* (see page 11) borne over its own cultural ontogeny. "Robert Hilles" waived and lightly cryptographed to Rob-art† Hills.

† Art thief lifts the thief of time upon its folded once.

world" he looked at the superimposition of bodies in the salient-in windows and lip-sync'd a possible, anxious, staccato whistling. With these measures of breath he shifted his weight and felt a small chiropractic adjustment in his lower back. He read his spine as he read the news and then cut to beyond his impalement.

He read Salutin on the Kinsella-Lau affair, his making it a point of departure on how writers' lives are essentially empty and not interesting compared to say the variety of lives in the movie *The Full Monty*. Recap considered the actors playing actors on the stage and couldn't help see the undressing as the progress to the reflection and reflexivity of the writer, and didn't know whether he was making or unmaking Salutin's case. The full Monty of course was empty, or capped, not there, except once in the covering eyes of the entertained ladies.

We the movie audience at the *once* were behind the entertainment, each a phallus, thing-in-itself, looking at the ladies looking, full tains diametric to the *empty* reflections,• the workers reduced to a fixed phylogeny. And he did detect a condescension up in Salutin's case. Roman Jakobson thinking about the so-called ordinary person said she was as metalinguistic as the writer. One had simply to consider a quarreling couple in the bar and how they interrogated one another's word usage. Is it possible that whatever is at stake in "life", put in quotation

---

• McLuhan at a topless club in San Francisco checked out the waitress, then pronounced "she's wearing us."†

  † John O. Thompson's "at last a bareness truly bare / lewd lascivious naked air."

marks as a loading of the argument but as protection too for the supposed innocence, is coincident with the writerly attitude, its smear campaign to spin untimely experience out of the nothing innocence? The experiment, out of experience, that attempts to get things under control by opening itself to the worst, over and over again.

The actual writer is not discontinuous with an actual person. How could the gap ever be bridged if that were the case? They are both however discontinuous with life or their own creations (writerly and readerly-proto-writerly), that is life is always over for both, one and the same, over and again. The deaths are the seeds of actual death but also the gaps for recapitulative writerly and *righterly** diversion, that is the chances for change, as well as the mere turning to distraction.

The writer is simply collapsing the wave function, as if Jimmy Simpson were to have kept his plasticine sculptures instead of squeezing them back to potentiality. It would be a trap to say that if he were to have written down the dramas he composed in his head as he snow-shoed between traps, that that would have been a trap. Once you open your trap you introduce the writer and all the activity becomes potentially, more rightly, writer retro-activity**.

---

* See Hegel's *The Philosophy of Right* for a tracking of Right's wayward† path.

   † The pun to redundancy suggests the detour is right and that right will out, at least recapitulatively.

** Paul Ricoeur recurred to Recap: From Aristotle's *muthos* and Augustine's meditation on time Ricoeur said we live pre-narrative lives. Present distention, clearing house for retention and protention, is also, over and above, the rise and shine of explanation†, which in turn turns in, ie is put to bed in narrative.

   † Explanation: *planus*: clear.

Recap said to himself "Don't Look Now", roguing the weeds of the present, citing the movie and telling whomever to wait for it.

Brunt at the Town Party

Recap felt each year a little more out of it, not drunk but that too, at the annual winter festival in late January. But perhaps he'd reached his limit, not drunk but that too, and was coming back with no expectations, so took the dance in the new convention centre at the Springs as a pleasant spectacle. He watched another old "her" (not *the* [even older] Her), many years his junior, take to the floor with a friend or new beau at the first waltz number, whirl around in small epicycles and simultaneously in big ballroom dance circles. They were the only ones up and danced beautifully, she in red velour pants, tall in heels and he taller, returning her radiance. Recap sighed at this Ptolemaic universe in motion.

He was surprised to see Brunt at the party even though he worked at the Springs. He'd ever only seen him in gym gear except that time a few years earlier at the same festival party when he wore chef clothes and wouldn't at first serve Recap roast beef because Recap had lost his ticket stub. Now he wore a cowboy shirt and jeans and smiled resplendently and laughed at Recap with his scotch in one hand and beer in the other. Everything Recap said had to be funny it seemed, else there wasn't anything to talk about. And the humour was founded on Recap's indulgences.

He could raise Brunt's eyebrows in the gym with just mentioning a dessert he'd eaten or a brandy. Here with beer chaser and all he was caught red-handed, and yet

Brunt seemed to think it right that Recap play the fallen clown. Recap started jabbering like a fool prisoner to a silent cop and the jabber loomed worse than bibulousness even as they intertwined. Nevertheless or because of it, the more he jabbered the more Brunt seemed to radiate a religiosity, rising out of his flush phylogeny from time to time to a guffaw that hiccupped to a high pitch at the end. The irony for Recap was that he felt his drinking was pretty slight and that he himself had become puritanical in contrast to the Tain of yore.

Recap began to squirm at becoming part of the spectacle instead of its observer. One year he would end up dancing the whole night practically and the next year he would just mingle, drink and watch, then go home in the usually freezing early hours of the morning. The whole affair was like a school reunion and cast a bit of a spell on him. Most of the people were young and new to Banff and to Recap but sometimes he would see an old face from the past and there were always a few groups of old faces from the present too. Recap and Brunt started to talk shop, that is weight lifting and what the past had cast began to dissipate.

Recap thought it funny that in the shop they didn't talk shop. Recap was set in his ways as far as working out went and Brunt was so professional there was nothing to say, except give a bit of advice if Recap sustained a small injury or a shoulder was giving him trouble or unless Brunt were giving a lesson to a paying beginner and then of course he talked back to and up from square one. Usually they discussed everything but lifting and Brunt was full of observations and as much bullshit as Recap and often ruined a set because he was laughing too hard.

Recap made him laugh one more time as he declared he needed more liquor and then left him in his pure redundancy. Recap drifted into the crowd and remembered his own awkwardness as he lined up for another booze ticket. The slight spell did return though and offset his out-of-placeness. He re-entered the hall by a different doorway and then sidled into the shadows. He thought back to the days, for only one year really, that Tain downhill skied. He had a tri-area pass and came to feel a slave to the expenditure. He knew it was decadent and so were the times.

Recap: the "UI ski team" had tried to enter a float in the Calgary Stampede parade and were turned down of course. People would knock at Tain's door early in the morning and he would groan and then get up. It was like going to work. One morning Clarissa knocked and tried to drag him out of bed but he wouldn't be budged so she unzipped her ski pants and pulled back the covers, then hunkered down on him and he skied right in even as he pretended to sleep. It was zipless and quick. She laughed as she closed the door and ran off to catch her ride to the slopes. Tain fell back to sleep and dreamt of an essence on a slippery slope skiing.

He was heavy and strong in the upper body back then but his legs were pretty shaky and so he skied with a wide stance. The bartenders he skied with called him "wide track Pontiac". He remembered big Hughie who liked to see his bigness reflected back from the world around him. He owned a Newfoundland dog and would sport him down Banff Avenue.

One time for the Super Bowl Hughie invited to his house, Rick, the one time California college wrestling champ, Bruce Gainer (even his name was right), who had played in the CFL and in Banff drove a retired hearse and who had a jaw that went with the piling on call Tain had seen him get on TV but who was very bright and bighearted, though terribly shy outside of football (he once hiked halfway back up Ptarmigan at Lake Louise just to help Tain with some stubborn bindings), Tain, who had played football at university, and Jimmy, who made up in guts for what he lacked in his now diminished size.

Jimmy didn't care much for football but he liked to drink and he liked to be around physical types for the possibility of danger and just for the reminder of his own wild jock days. Though he also liked, with his age and injured back, to be excused from the proving grounds, to lead an otherwise ascetic life, if you could discount the booze, which he did. Mostly he liked a quiet proto- *and* real writerly life. He did his various dishwashing jobs and then in some small room with a little tape recorder playing music he'd taped, tapped away at an old typewriter Tain had given him.

Tain came into his own room once and started unpacking groceries, creating some crackling thunder noises with the paper bags, when he noticed that Jimmy was taping Beethoven, holding the microphone up to one of the speakers. Jimmy was trying not to laugh and held one finger up to his lips. When Beethoven started to thunder himself Jimmy reached over and turned the volume down on the old stereo that Tain had inherited from his sister, and which would take a stack of seven records. When Beethoven waned he reached up to turn him louder.

Once he told Tain that he wished he had Tain's strength and Tain said "what would you do then?" Jimmy said "enjoy me strength" and then lifted his beer glass with hardened bits of potato on the rim and bits of tobacco floating in the beer. He sat across from Tain on the other side of the room against the wall, like when he would say "isn't life strange?" and Tain would say "compared to what?"

Jimmy wouldn't bother answering, would just sip some more. In a poetry group Tain tried to make this into a significance, deriving meaning from the mean that comparison establishes and then, since there is nothing to compare with life, he said it was therefore meaningless, which you can celebrate or mourn. But the dialectical twist was that Jimmy's rhetorical question was legitimate in that life allowed itself, through a strange fold, to get a strange comparative advantage, or vantage point, on itself.

At Hughie's place they sat around the TV, "enjoying" themselves. Their own little town party. The Newfoundland slept and Jimmy interrupted the action with inane questions that either made Hughie laugh, or irritated him, depending on the progress of the game. Sitting there acting the macho men of the hour, only Hughie and Jimmy seemed to be really enjoying themselves, and for different reasons. Tain was in a small way honoured to be among the elect but felt quite the imposter, even though he'd beat in arm wrestling both Rick and Hughie, who was the biggest in pure volume and weight. And Rick had once beaten an Oakland Raider.

Rick and Bruce were in the best all around condition. Tain's forte was barroom arm wrestling where it was all bicep and forearm, hooking it was called and was just brute strength, no technique, no psyching, no quick off the mark like organized arm wrestling where the bicep was rarely used and where the size of hand and the grip strength was much more important. Barroom arm wrestling ruined your arm after a few contests or after one good one. Tain had also, in an inadvertent contest before he knew him, once out bench-pressed Bruce in university, who was then called "Hercules" by the fans.

Once just as he was leaving Tain arm wrestled a guy in a Lethbridge bar. Without warming up, as usual in these contests, they just went at it. Tain felt like he was taking him and then suddenly his elbow popped and he backed off. Everybody heard the noise and Tain assumed he had done some damage but he was able to hold the guy quite easily and decided just to leave it at that.

It turned out he had done no damage. It also turned out that the other guy was a champion power lifter, winning a major international competition in Seattle. In later years Tain came to know that he had lifted hundreds of pounds more in the squat, bench and dead lift than Tain ever could when he took up that kind of lifting, and that the bicep was quite insignificant for the big lifts in power lifting.

Rick was a canoeist and wilderness man and didn't really care much for football. Bruce had escaped from football and wasn't really interested in being reminded of the hyped-up slavery. Tain didn't really enjoy drinking in the middle of the day and especially in these stag conditions. But Jimmy was happy and Hughie was determined to enjoy, swilling down the Blue faster than Jimmy, who was not a guzzler but very steady. Tain liked the company fine but began thinking of excuses to leave. The game got really one-sided and became an intrinsic insult to the dedicated fan. Hughie was obliged to lose and did genuinely lose interest.

Tain took up this note and, finding immediate sympathy from Rick and Bruce, was able to get things, the backfield say, in motion for adjournment into the end zone, as it were. All sheepish in the grip of Hughie's heavy-handed usage, the reciprocally reflecting meat metaphor bunch arose and went home. As they walked Jimmy told Tain that the game was pretty bad. Tain couldn't tell if he'd even noticed it, what with his constant teasing and interrupting Hughie. Hughie had interrupted nothing in particular at one point to say that Marty, as in Sid, should have been there, "he's a big boy".

Recap interrupted everything in general to say to himself that, apart from some feminist critique and subsequent defensive appeal to irony, folded forearms Frank Lentrichia was a big boy too according to an aged Kenneth Burke, the brilliant structuralist Jon admired, who never missed a Marxist "resource term" aporia in the thirties but also never let it prevent him from a social activism either.

Burke's "dramatistic day" had you born in the morning into a conversation of which you could make neither heads nor tails. By noon you might catch a bit of the sense, and by four o'clock you could maybe say something yourself. "Honey I just got back from Mars, I mean *Red Mars* by Kim Stanley Robinson, and I'm twenty years younger, the earthworld was credibly recapitulated into even more of a dystopia in four or five hundred pages, and hey I shrunk Aristotle".

Recap, thirty pounds lighter than Tain, thought of the Rungius painting that hung in the Whyte house, the one of the magnificent moose looking out from the rich autumn colours of a mountain valley. Jon had said the wild animals of the Rockies were the real heroes. Recap thought that certain definitions were ignored here but with a biocentric bend and bow, as in "out", there was a heartening, and disheartening, truth to the claim. If the tragic Machiavellian lion was the metaphoric hero, as opposed to the fox, then the tragic animals, fox included in this new ratio, were the heroes over Nietzsche's last men.

They were much to be admired, even if they were impossible role models, pace some radical, in the root sense, therapists, or what was it Recap was trying to remember? Might it have been a question of animals in their subtle and variegated adaptations as models for scientific invention? But that was a horse of a different colour. That was the animals' pre-Frankenstein science, their phylogenetic science, a preclusion to the idea of hero, its aspect of self-possession, both good and bad, but then it's the definition again, and the idea suggests too, precisely belonging to others, a rising to the state of, not genius, but genus.

Heroes in their *special* fates and in their "inherent melancholia" that presumably Lewis would claim was not a pathetic fallacy but just the opposite, the unencumbered emotional legacy to humans, whether a legacy by which to define, or one itself to be re-defined or refined, or to be overcome.

Another thing about animals as heroes, and in their dwindling parallel universe, pace a certain proportion of recognition of and curiosity by them about humans, was that there was no threat of a backfire effect, or of the question of what to do with the hero in times of peace, or if not a war hero, then in times of Luther's "ordinary life". The no threat• was part of their pathetic charm and the essence of their tragedy. The biocentricity says we can half say "our" [tragedy] and half not.

After the town party Recap took off his thinking cap and if Rock were present he would, he half thought, just for the hell of it, give him a small kick and say, after the other good Doctor, "thus I refute — myself", that is if Rock were half the rock Recap half thought he was, and Berkley were considered through Peirce's critique and Peirce's category of secondness were given its unforgiving correctness, the way everything and everyone you bump into corrects, by definition, your course.

He jostled the people in the lobby where the various portable bars were, and all the statistical bumps kept him stable if not, with the amplified rock music now, and with the pressure of his thumped-up alcoholic blood, slightly concussed and cancelled, cushioned only by the arrested development of the spell which was the dispelling of *this* particular time. He developed an edge in the crowd, either because of one too many bumps or of the long wait for a drink, or because of the implosion of actuality, and then he bumped himself just as he was already hanging over. Ah the energy when the night cap wears off and the rising sun's raw empiricism is drunker than anything.

• Of course cougars, bears and wolves, say, on their "own" ground and terms can be of considerable threat, notwithstanding whispers of a peaceable kingdom.

The Kite and the Anchor

Recap was getting ready to leave his cabin when he saw Andy Winfield leaning on the railing of the second floor balcony of the Information Building overlooking the parking lot. He remembered Andy when he was editor of the *Crag and Canyon* and you'd see him walking around Banff with his camera. Recap called him Scoop. You would see him sitting in the Cascade Café with Cliff Wheatfield, the both of them smoking and drinking cups of coffee. Andy read novels when he was there alone and Cliff did the crossword in the *New Yorker* or investigated the paper.

One year Andy devoured dozens of books on Mexican history. Whenever Recap got into conversation it quickly came to feel like a mild argument but Recap could never figure out about what. He would just put his two bits worth in whenever he could and listen to Andy and his amazing stream of knowledge. Cliff on the other hand was not forthcoming in conversation, but Recap always felt he was in a mild argument with him too. Cliff went for the small imprecisions of your speech and corrected the word usages of the columnists in the *Crag*, including at times Jon. He also edited some of the books that came out of Banff but decided to shelve his literary talent for a career in jewelry making, usually in silver or gold.

Recap would stop in at his shop in the Cascade Hotel and get to know him better. They no longer seemed to be arguing and it soon became obvious that Cliff wanted to get out of Banff. He would show Recap pictures of some land in the BC interior where he'd like to go and live. He started asking Recap about agricultural matters. And the two of them tried to translate what he had replied into the appropriate scale for Cliff on a few acres of non-prairie. He wanted to know about grinding his own flour and Recap couldn't help him at all.

For a year or two he would haul out the photographs, often new ones, for he visited the place whenever he could and he liked to drive so the many hours on the road didn't bother him. Then all of a sudden it all came together and he just left town. Recap's friend Mel dropped in and surprised him a few times and told Recap he seemed happy and as ever Cliff, that his sister and family who lived nearby were the nicest of people and that they and Cliff had made him feel a much welcomed guest. Recap hadn't seen him since he left town but heard for the first years at least he was still doing silver work.

Andy once borrowed Tain's Country Joe and the Fish albums and maybe a Coltrane and for many years kept reminding Tain. Now, by way of recognizing Recap, he didn't mention the albums anymore. Andy used to work with Horny John and his lounge lizard column and played steel guitar himself around town from time to time. He once rolled a huge wagon wheel down the street from the Magpie and Stump where he had got it. Tain, in the spirit of the caper, intercepted him and took it back. Scoop in a later editorial said that Tain had carried it over his head with one hand. It had been with two hands Tain corrected him, but not in the letters forum.

Tain vaguely thought he should have his albums back but the feeling began to fade and so did Tain. Recap figured Andy deserved them since he was the musician and the music historian. And maybe Andy figured the huge wagon wheel Tain had retrieved made up for the missing smaller discs. Recap went into the Barbary Coast, a sports and blues bar, one night and there on stage after all these years was Andy with a band.

The blues they played was terrific! For a moment Recap saw Andy as the Judge in Greg Hollingshead's "favourite" novel *Blood Meridian*, only quite a bit smaller and not as hairless. There was a look of happy shrewdness to his face, eyes narrowed with concentration and knowingness as he delivered the blues. As he played the harp his fingers held a cigarette. He looked very healthy and who would have guessed these many years later, with others gone, and with Andy's ever present cigarettes and probably not a few beers.

At a party at Andy's once, Tain was sitting drinking, then suddenly bit into his glass and started nonchalantly chewing up the broken chunks. The whole room looked at him, including Jon and Andy, with consternation. Andy's wife convinced him to come into the kitchen and spit it out, and he did. A few minutes later, with cheese in his mouth this time, Tain did it again, and again broke up the conversation and then spat it all out again after fake swallowing it.

The evening progressed and Tain came out of the kitchen to the living room to find Jimmy and some young woman writhing down on the rug to the music. It looked liked they'd been dancing and had just fallen over. Undeterred they just kept dancing. Tain left and went to the bar, quite a few bars, and then to another party. He had promised to come back and the promise never left his mind, so some time in the middle of the night he made it back to Andy's. He either tripped going up the Rundle rock steps at the gate or simply got sick at that point.

He remembered wheeling around with one hand on the railing post and he thought he might remember smacking his face on either a horizontal or a vertical Rundle rock. He woke up under a fir tree in the early light, a way too soon for a hangover, and went into the house through the back door. He had to step over a couple in a sleeping bag, a couple he was surprised to see a couple, and in the kitchen met Andy's wife Donna who was getting breakfast. He asked if the party was over and Donna looked aghast at him, not for his time lapse but, he realized later, for the state of his dress.

He slunk home and as he crossed Banff Avenue a huge carload of Indians turned around him. They were all laughing at him. Tain said "what are you laughing at, your muffler's dragging". In his own room he examined his clothes and noticed all the pine cones sticking to them and hadn't realized pine cones were like burrs. But on closer inspection he realized the sticking agent was as much his own vomit. The pine, often after all, at least in name, a commercial deodorizer, had done a nice natural job of camouflaging or least mitigating his true abject state, notwithstanding Donna's worried disapproval and the Indians' laughter.

Recap now thought to himself "attenuated Tain", the agent of a deaf distant outpost and he thought of the muffled laughter, and thought again of Tain chewing glass to attenuated laughter and then thought the man in pine cone drag, his Copernican turning around the Indians and their muted oral tradition, was finally himself perhaps a stand-in for Muffler-About-To-Fall-Off.*

Recap hooked up the dog and started down the alley and waved at Andy finishing his cigarette, squinting into the sun lowering in the valley. As he approached Wolf St behind St Paul's he saw Ruth on the sidewalk and they stopped to chat.

The paintings in her latest show, called "From My Window" had frames within frames and frames on the frames. When he remembered some cute thing his dog had done she laughed and patted her, and then told him she'd calculated her cat would last her well into her sixties. With respective "mummy" and "daddy" labels she turned them into old shoes and Recap protested mildly, blinking at the arithmetic projection, at the fate and resignation to it.

It reminded him of his mother calculating that this dog would last her to the end of her life, and then some. He thought of the stunted lifetimes, chronologically speaking, over against the intense uninhibited emotions, and thought the animals' temporality was large enough to turn back and through itself, to languish and to race, in short to add up to enough of a chunk of a human lifetime that it became unbearable to think of their deaths, in one's real implication with them, and in relation to their metaphoric comment on and even mockery of one's own life *time*.

When they parted he thought of Ruth's journals she'd kept for decades and how she constantly reviewed them and sourced them for her art, including especially in her

---

* Recalling, with a twist, Kroetsch's *The Words of My Roaring*, not to mention *Gone Indian*.

direct retrospective performance art. Her latest journals reflected back on the reflections in her art of the documentation of her life. The new Jewish material, retrieving too her time in Israel on a kibbutz, now floating into the mountain landscapes.

Recap: the Jon of *Gallimaufry*, and Jon the historian of mountain Indian "cultural" art, with its history of inter-"national" influence, would probably find the layering right, in the lifted, in the dangerously creative and even dialectical sense, tradition. The strategies of "overdetermination", both symptom and provisional guerrilla antidote, of a radical poetics that by definition works through, but away from, popular culture, works as time capsule resource. The "inter-'national'" would not correspond to the current order of "International", and, significantly, orally differentiated by the long and short, first "a", denoting of course the First Nations.

The uncertainty inherent in prehistory was parlayed in history. The artist was responsible and yet could never escape being some ratio of symptom and antidote, and in varying ways was always useful to the culture even just as symptom, including the action of neo-imitative magic. Already Ruth's work, with its multiple frames, bespoke sensitivity to conscious and unconscious superimpositions. He thought of her chattering away with the best of them and then he thought about her silences and those eyes, sometimes lost, soulful, and sometimes ironically smiling, sometimes smouldering.

She might not know the latest poetics strategies in their own terms but she knew the "disgust" they were tuned by. Recap: she told him she had to choose to attend an anti-development meeting over his poetry launch. Tom had said that Ruth "had it", that serious artistic possession. Behind the constant quotidian worrying was that charged world she entered every day, split between the objective and her subjective preoccupations, and then bridged with the "mirroring wheel", and then thrown open again, split and then bridged over and over through the documented decades.

Recap could hear her affirm "I'm an artist!" and could hear the ironic doubt, but it was the healthy doubt one finds back at the well where the signature is prohibitive and is shed, where the well is ground zero one might almost say, but that's too lifted already. It was on the level, the ordinary, the off-centre, or from "her window". That was the well, scary not for romantic depths but for the banality, in its moment, beyond good and evil.

Recap as captive audience: Jane Fonda accepting the academy award for her father after he had just died. She arrived on the stage breathless and for an unendurable period just looked out as her lungs heaved. The audience squirmed and her first tentative words just made it worse. Then she got a few more words out and still the audience was so with her it was turning away. Then more words and then she went on and on and the audience came to squirming from the other, bored and used up, side. The actor won out, dominated and buried the life, not uncoincidentally. And would we have wanted to be the otherwise ghouls?

The thing was though that one saw the actor descend to the well, more out of a vampiric desperation for new necessary blood than anything, and actually open herself to the raw un-actor, which was there and no doubt real, and open herself to the raw squirming of the audience of a lifetime, to an unbearable madness of energy below the method. At the point of destruction she was restored, and who wouldn't hope for the "self-construction that comes out of self-shattering". The professional actor wanted her pivotal match, got it, and went vampire with extreme prejudice.

Recap thought yes, that such drama of death, the ordinary death, was not the ordinary, was perhaps even the ordinary's other and always interface. It was the ordinary's ordinary consideration that was the ambiguous well. A sudden dust swirl from Wolf St beside St Paul's had him squinting and he reconsidered the well as the pre-Rhino party, the one that can't afford the price of admission anymore, that is, can't afford to go to its own party.

He looked into the ordinary and heard the rumble of rhinos, nothing fantastic, nothing Bamphibilous, just the coming of the uninscribed black ball, with the lumberjack light riding its rolls and whose finger holds whirled into the invisible hand, the ordinary ball he knew he was set up for, both more and less than the Fondas, especially the one selling her own sweat you can implant in your own boob tube (fractal implication intended) and once wrapped up in an actor, but then buried in a media empire vampire.

He crossed Banff Avenue and headed past the Shell station and caught Herb just before he got into his cab. Herb asked about the dog and Recap gave a long account of her lesioned back. As he left him and continued on past the Banff Park Lodge and the new Mineral Springs Hospital he thought "Herb, now there's recap". Talk about a daddy. Recap and Alice remarked on how devoted he was to his son, in fact seemed to shut down the rest of his life for him. Voracious reader and sixties guru, he'd seemingly exchanged his philosophy of spiritual progress, with thoughts of reincarnation and higher and higher knowledge, for the simple starting over of his son.

They were not critical of this, in fact they were touched, and speculated that perhaps there was no irony after all, perhaps even a relative solution to the problem of unthinkable omniscience. That this mutual education and re-education was the real grounding that he used to talk about and more appropriate, by leaps and bounds, than the engineering he went back to university for and took two years of.

Recap angled through the woods across from the Bow View Lodge toward the river and thought back, so as not to put too fine a point on it and not to invoke Josef Skvorecky's *The Engineer of Human Souls*, that Herb was the real "dad" Ruth spoke of, not buried in his son's life and certainly not your bourgeois family man.

He was more like the "migrant intellectual", albeit rooted for generations in Banff, that Kroker, with whom he argued in the Clive Bell Theatre, speaks of, and somehow too the revolving reversed sun, caught in the strange, that is in the preserved pre-Copernican perspective, gravity of son. Recap: Herb wanted Zarathustra to come and jostle in the streets and Kroker wanted to kick him back up the mountain everytime he came down into the town. Recap headed into the Fenland with his little "daughter", and noted without gravity his earlier, accidentally sexist pun in a mess of astronomical conjunction.

Mountain Painter in the Prairies

Recap packed up, and with dog barking wildly in the back, drove down the alley to Wolf St heading for FoxHog. Heading for home, the other home, and he wondered which was the kite and which the anchor as he slunk down Wolf and turned left down Beaver avoiding the lights and traffic on Banff Avenue. Somehow he felt guilty if he stayed in Banff any longer than three weeks. It used to be connected to his mother, home alone in FoxHog and her less than subtle hints about how long it had been.

Since she had been dead for over two years he wondered if it might be more than just the phantom phenomenon, something to do with the privilege of being in Banff. And then he wondered if it might be something to do with his prairie psyche. Surely all the time cooped up reading in the Rockies was only made possible by all the time in the big sky and wide open space on the farm.

As he slunk, something to do with not really telling anyone he was leaving, and just a plain slinking feeling in his new vehicle while his dog whooped it up, he thought of the commutativity of the kite and the anchor and he thought, rather ridiculously, of the action of a slinky, to catch the anchor cum kite. The spiral construction would work for a gradual dialectical action incorporated into the more dramatic flips that need not be considered merely back and forth, and that, by just considering temporality.

For the slinky model to hold you had to consider time as descending, in a Darwinian or cosmological sense, then "down time", or Derksen's *Downtime*, breakdown or respite, the eternal spring, the suspension of time, all these confusions and linkages if you consider the very Hegelian

Joycean (Viconian?) idea of the mind as a mirror that *becomes*, through spiral interchange with what it mirrors, a wheel, which then doesn't proceed straightforwardly, but with involutions, re-routings and ridiculous epiphanic recapitulations. Adding in new and evolving relationships you break out above Plato's futile swinging between abstinence and indulgence, and yet Recap had sunk to that undynamic too, another reason for the slinking feeling, as the way to FoxHog was a coming out of indulgence.

Sir James Jeans the physicist made the simple observation that we all think everybody else is unfree but that we, ourselves, are free. The commutativity of Plato's futility and the commutativity implicit in the first person plural suggests something different, and the Sur Real physicist's thought is a thinking that is thought out completely, that is outside of the model of the truth he states, a truth which nevertheless undoubtedly strikes *you* in the *I*.

As he turned down Beaver Recap saw Phil stopped at the stop sign waving at him. Wild mountain man Phil, once a climber and now a horseman and still a wonderful painter. Recap had bought two of his paintings the year before. He painted the mountains and he painted the North and he painted the prairies, the foothills. He did a black and white of boys playing shinny on a street, looking down from above, very life-like. When you looked closer it was all thumb prints.

He would do a series that would start out a realist landscape then go minimal and then abstract. All those paintings looking west at the foothills, sometimes the mountains in the background, and always that small fence, well not always small and not always foreground. Sometimes barely perceptible. Walter, historian of the treaty-making in the west, and art collector, analyst of the colonial art and architecture, was struck by those fences. Recap was supposed to find out for Walter the price of a painting of the Morley hills and did but then bought it himself. Walter forgave him.

Recap thought of the two paintings in the dining room in his house in FoxHog and saw himself sitting at the table with his back to them in the evening. The morning light showed them off the best even though they were on an east wall above the dark wainscoting. He thought of his mother's periodic bouts as a painter. The painting she worked on the most was the one reminiscent of Phil's prairie storm, looking west. He'd never thought which direction you were looking in his mother's. Phil's of course was way more accomplished.

He saw himself looking west with his back to Phil's painting in which one looked west but which hung on the east wall. He thought of all the shedding of tears he learned to do in his mother's last month. He reflected that weeping's nature was of the broad brush stroke. And he thought how you caught emotion and were measured by it in the traps of multi-directional and reflected space, something like a physicist's experiment to observe electrons and photons and/or waves. You didn't and didn't want to appreciate the fullness of emotion in the immediacy of the imminence of a loved one's death. He had learned that crying was a bodily process that saved you from unbearable empathy.

The harvest had been late and riddled with snowfalls. The crop was tremendous that year and she worried about them getting it off. Most of it went feed but prices for feed were twice as high and then some as the price of number one in the worst of the eighties. They eventually got it off. They had taken turns visiting, morning or evening, on days they could work, otherwise they could visit her any time and together when the crops were too wet. He would let the tears stream down his face as he swathed.

He could predict the short and long circuiting of the emotions, and then how there would be a long time delay. A thought experiment for elemental emotion. The point was that the emotion increased in poignancy but rounded out before it reached a singularity. The tears would cloud more than the vision, would wash away the unconsummated sharp bluntness of it.

There was a moment of super poignancy as the tears fed on themselves, and as the narcissism factored in, it became like a child crying falsely for that lost true crying. The original empathy was long buried in this progress of the crying game. And empathy, as opposed to being at a loss with oneself after, is the most mature aspect and the hardest, presupposing that one has a life of freedom to live and perhaps only to find at the death of the last parent, notwithstanding the immaturity, ie a life to live, inhabiting the above maturity.

The living empathy, by definition, dies when the parent dies, and there is relief from thinking their thinking their death. The afterlife empathy and after all personal loss hit, as we say, with time, and strange traps. Decap-recap: being too close to a powerful blast. To withstand it you would, perforce, not get it. Light years away you could take its measure, and by the logic of the sun-as-star or the star-as-sun you could take and get away with an actual blast.

But it was the little traps that would get him Recap had predicted, even in that month of bodily emotion and crying. To get through the funeral and reception he had capped the well, capped it till its afterlife came, where the poignancy would be bearable even as its strength would only then be fully realized in the astronomical distances.

Months after her death the first clever trap was sprung just after he had come into the house after running with the dog. She used to say how the dog came directly into the den, while he took off his running shoes, to tell her that they were back. This time he watched her trot through the kitchen and he followed and got to the end of the dining room. There was a slight pause as she sniffed the chair and then trotted back where he held the corner of the buffet, half hunkered down as his body convulsed and the tears flowed over the running sweat. The dog sniffed and wagged at him and he let the colour of crying brush over him and then fade from one "blunt" to the other.

He drove along the Trans-Canada toward Calgary. Recap: the annual summer holidays to Banff when he and his brother and sister were kids. They stayed in cabins with fireplaces, the Pinewoods and then Becker's Bungalows. It was hard to decide which was best, the anticipation, the old "just around the next corner" (on the old highway), the arrival and realization in the smell of the cabins or the *let's do something*, swim, fish, picnic after the quick cabin fever, or the quick recapture of its warmth in the smaller commutation within Banff, itself within the FoxHog to Banff macro slinky.

Recap: the time after his father had had his stroke and was told to take up a hobby, like golf or fishing. His arm was never the same and his other arm he'd thrown out in a baseball distance-throwing contest he'd won, so his golf swing, though vicious, was not supple enough to be effective. And fishing was a family disaster. Spinning reels would all get wound up in themselves or end hanging in the trees.

His sister hooked her own arm and then again hooked his brother just above the eye. His father had to cut the hook out of her arm. That sort of thing didn't bother him a bit. Recap had told this story to Paul Quarrington the first and only brief time he'd met him, and whose baseball novel his mother had read, and Paul told the story of a friend who was asked to cut a hook out of someone's arm and was so bothered by it he averted his eyes, and put a slash in the arm alright but nowhere near the hook, let alone getting it out.

No one ever caught a fish, well one they didn't have to throw back. That was always on the north side of Johnson Lake. But one time they went to the other side, just for the heck of it, not from anyone expecting anything really and not on someone else's advice. It was difficult to walk in the much more heavily wooded shore, let alone cast. They stopped at one little baylet and within fifteen minutes Recap caught two trout, about a foot long each.

He felt that proverbial almost sexual thrill at the bite and then pull and then went through the equivalence of a post-coital depression when they netted and had to kill them. The mysterious other recognition flip-flopped into an ugly recognition, but he was able to push it away as they decided to quit while they were ahead. They hiked back to the car, slinking and going head over heels with fish in the creel.

The new recognition at a flip of the lid worked to the good somehow, over the drying, smelly and unsavoury dead bodies. They simply closed the lid again and the blind weight worked wonders as they argued over who got to carry them. Once the fish were eaten they were transubstantiated into a parable you couldn't, for the symmetry say, simply swallow, hook, line and sinker. Unable to mount it on a mantel, or to wear it, you were beside yourself with the parable and just told it over and over again, till you killed it and then of course you got religion, *ligare*, tied to a disappeared death nowhere between anchor and kite, nor earth and sky.

Late in September after his father's stroke and after Recap and his brother and sister spent the summer and two weeks of school in Drumheller while their mother and father spent time in Vancouver, they went to Banff for ten days. Banff was cold and rainy and empty of tourists. They stayed in a large bungalow at Becker's and the fire they maintained was essential, not just a luxury. On a dark and stormy night they played the fire and rehearsed "on a dark and stormy night", and also played Monopoly, which recapitulated the typical history of development: level playing field, equal chance, and then gradual separation and widening gaps.

The promise of everything ahead, the young fire and then the impossible odds. They ended squabbling and ruined, flipping the board over and scattering the useless money. But the disquotational stormy night took the cliché back to the well. All ten days the sky was overcast and it continued to rain. And the cabin camped up a home for a time aping itself dramatistically. They may have even done some homework. Their father slept a lot and they played Monopoly again but kept their cool in light of the quick temper and frustration he was now prone to. The other side was his easy, too easy tears. Back home by the end of every *Father Knows Best* program his face was streaming, and his breath noisy as it caught. Recap would grip his chair and lock on the TV.

Recap came into the hospital room in the morning and his mother beckoned him to her chair where she sat by the window, looking healthy and happy. She put her arms up and they held one another and let the tears well up. She said "I think we need this" and they just held for a few minutes. Then she spoke comfortingly to Recap, giving him a way to speak again himself. She had been so many things in the last month. She went over her practical affairs, she would have days of reminiscing, "remembering the good things". She told funny stories and talked about her dad and mum.

She was very proud of her father, the fiery labour politician whose biting tongue even his fellow travellers feared, especially after they mispronounced the words he put into their speeches. Once on the telephone he berated a reporter who had misquoted him. He pounded the wall and bellowed "I'll come over there and beat you to a bloody pulp". His wife's voice from the other room floated sweetly in, "dear, why don't you use the telephone".

His wife sewed and scraped together the meals in the hard times when he'd been defeated in the Social Credit landslide. And she knew how to handle him. He just read and read and then got back into local politics. When he first came over to Canada from Scotland his employer in Nanton told him he was repairing the machinery too well. He was at Regina, didn't sign the manifesto but was committed to their social idealism. He criticized the communists and disagreed with some of the big unionists. When he was dying she said he pushed the intravenous away saying "I don't want any of this crap".

Recap: his mother's acting career after the drama she took at Normal School in Edmonton. She and his father belonged to a drama club and travelled around the small Alberta towns doing plays. She later continued to write and do monologues. She practised on him and his brother and sister. One time she frightened them, not by the content of the drama but by becoming someone else. They stood there in the basement playroom cowering against the wall as she did a monologue, wondering if their mother would come back.

Once she did one at school about a woman who, with a child, very reluctantly went to the boxing match in which the woman's nephew was fighting. She started off disgusted and pacifist. Slowly the fist emerged, she got drawn in and by the end she was yelling "kill him George, kill him!" Recap could not stand being in the auditorium so he went out into the hall and then as she began, he listened from the doorway at the back. She'd captured the audience and Recap too in no time and he moved right back in and found a chair and was laughing and agog like everyone else. In later years still, after his father had died, she would write plays for the reading club she belonged to.

That first fateful day in her hospital room they stood around waiting for the Doctor to bring in the news of all the results. He had been good in his manner but nothing can mitigate that news. The biopsy was positive and the X-rays had shown something. She broke the tension with "I knew those little buggers were up to no good", referring to all the black marks on the X-ray slide.

Recap had talked with the young minister, how a sweetness had risen out of her in that last month. Both of them were reminded, somewhat ironically for the minister, of "Phaedo" in the Platonic dialogues. His mother was not Socrates and had not chosen to die like he had, and yet it was as if she had, too. He had taught his friends how to die. And Recap thought his mother had done the same and not just passively, but with a cool theatricality that did justice to her *being there*, and, at the core, beyond good and evil, and beyond the slide to a one-sided dominance à la Fonda, the death there not being her own of course, to give Jane her due.

It was not a matter of expertise, a word she'd learned to despise after a banker had gone on about it once, nor methodology, but one of rising to a fate, assuming the position, or playing that ultimate recapitulative role on the threshold of death. It was a matter of knowing one's situation in the empathetic field, like in a theatre, but here it was a response, and responsibility, to "us" Recap thought. She made it easy, from financial concerns to hymns to be sung. But it was not acting, in that fallen sense, it was a real coming to terms. It was waking up all those clichés like "it happens to everyone". She hated all the futile and pseudo heroic talk about courageous battles and she laughed at all the fuss over and stigma to the word 'cancer'.

She ate properly and exercized, in moderation, after her first breast cancer operation three years earlier. She'd taken these years as a bonus and then accepted her time. She spoke to them with full presence of mind right up to the last day, that horrendous last day when she was re-admitted, somehow not wanting to die in the house, again for their sakes.

The hospital was a complete fuck up that day and it reminded them of all the hassle changing rooms earlier and how easy it was to see for oneself and then with talking to nurses how the cutbacks were affecting the capacity for care. His mother had given substantial donations to this regional hospital but, of course, all they wanted to give and all she wanted was normal human care. She rose above all the unsettling moves, ignored all the distractions and just resumed the assumption of her dying.

She had been getting weaker and weaker but had calculated her energy and time. The extra hours in the emergency room on a stretcher bed, with no water but what his sister got from the drinking fountain, had almost undermined the choosing of her time. And though she'd been on oxygen for weeks they were going to take her up to the room without it. She wouldn't have made it, let alone the half hour trip into town they also suggested she could take without it. All the nurses had remarked on her wonderful attitude.

One could say it would have been more appropriate to have stayed at home. Who knows her reasons. The house she loved but it was after all Recap's father's father's house she would say and sometimes found it alien. She grew up in Lethbridge and that's where she would be buried. Recap had thought, still thought, it had something to do with making it easier for them. She would be there to the end but when it came she would make it clean.

Recap had sat with and touched his father's dead body but felt no need in her case, the ideal teaching death she gave them overshadowed, ironically put, any need for that touching of the body. His sister found it different. She had not been there when their father died and so she went to the obnoxious funeral parlour and somehow critiqued her way into its interior and looked at her dead mother, and was glad that she had.

Their mother in her hospital bed that last night, extremely weak, would yet toss her head from side to side every once in a while like someone staving off drowning. Then she would measure them sitting at the foot of her bed. She would smile and said a few little things they could hardly hear, to do with her position on the pillows, then she looked at the clock and as cheerfully as possible said they should be going. When they left Recap knew she would then let go.

He was almost back home from his home away from home. Recap: the time just before the war when his parents would go to Banff before they were married. There were photographs from the period and it all seemed so romantic. They stayed with locals, in their houses or in cabins in their yards. There were the stories of his father's mother going alone for treatment at the hot springs. She was very frugal and would say in both a sweet and defiant way "and it was quite nice", after describing her stay at the Y, and after describing the meal, fillet of sole. Every once in a while Recap and his brother would use the expression on the farm with the intonation their mother had taught them.

It was a period that was confused in Recap's mind. The hard times survived by his mother's parents and the period enclosed by a larger period that marked the dramatic career of his father's father. The ranches they owned, but farmed, and then lost. The Kilgannon Ranch and the Cameron Ranch, all the big houses he had built. The biggest farm in the British Empire back before the twenties and then losing it all to the punitive banks whose own lawyers said he was the "best damn farmer" they had ever seen. Then making a comeback in the thirties, at the forefront of the communities fighting the soil drifting. Farming big again and working with soil scientists, and then proclaiming that small farms were the way to go. Recap thought of the toll it took on his father, trying to hold it together and keep things running. A stroke at forty-nine and a heart attack two years later.

Recap: the photograph of his father, just before the stroke, that Recap liked and his mother hated. He looked tortured and thought-laden, and Recap romanticized it. Then there was the photograph from just before the war on the grass around the pool at the Banff Springs. He looked a little too romantic and dashing, sitting but leaning toward a strange woman while over his shoulder you could see Recap's premarital and pre-maternal mother looking, not tortured in her long, dark red hair that didn't show red of course in the black and white, but a little left out as she typically squinted into the sun. There was no projected anxiety when he looked at the picture, but rather the nice feeling for them as young and free, or undetermined, albeit mixed up with a time-capped feeling.

His mother told them about driving down the road in an open car to Johnston Canyon and his father spitting cherry pits at the oncoming cars and saying things like "and the muscles on his arms stood out like sparrow's knees", referring to no one in particular. Recap could hear the pits being spat by hearing his father spit out bits of tobacco from the filter-less Buckinghams he used to smoke. Recap used to steal those Buckinghams and smoke them in one of his many huts, underground or once up on stilts as if an outhouse for the swamps. Recap was precocious in an odd experiential way back then before school. He had a girlfriend in grade two. They used to sit together during National Film Board films. Then he went all puritanical sports, and would get saved from time to time, either by a local fundamentalist or by travelling evangelists.

Recap: his mother and father were part way up Mt Norquay and then started running down toward the road. They ran out of control, got the giggles and were scared at the same time as their legs flew and could barely keep up. (Rock: all his "I told you" stories, the primal mountain accident, the Ararat founding and "the race to the bottom".) Had Recap begun from the *arrêt* and splat on the road? Was Recap the new race of childless and jostling Zarathustras, kicking himself, and as he tried to get behind his moral[e] in the Nietzschean, genealogical sense?

He would ejaculate purely and as overproof, say "well", and would go back to it with Rousseau and the desert tribes, and found or would found rhinos. What kind of a move was this? Surely not Ionesco over again. Well again, it was — "over again". And how could you make the absurd farcical? Recap had no intention to. After Benjamin, his dialectical imagism, his blasts from the past, he sought to open up the present. Not a Hegelian dialectic here, which is not however mere recapitulation, but a recapitulation of a past moment-position, ie one loaded with argument and structurated event, but, again, from a new present, which would make the recap different and make the moment-position different.

It was not that, it was simply a skimmed-off blast that achieved such dislocation that it became a very un-Hegelian blank, in itself, but as an opener it presented, not represented, a very Hegelian moment, the ghost of the future that was free and recallable, in both senses, just like the past, if you consider the commutative action of the kite/anchor, and again consider old moments recapitulated from different new moments as also different.

Recap just wanted rhinos for the time being, and maybe even the absurdity, not for some neo-modernist tragic sense, just for a little kite/anchor flip-flop of the hemispheres, a touch of alienation on new terms and high ground. The Rockies as rugged rhinos and as sheer blanks in the post cardiac picture.

To him the town of Banff was riven, not by the river and not by the ecologists vs the developers, though those of course, but by the idea and fact of work, and the idea and fact of leisure. The ideas of the facts interrupted Plato's swing of futility, that is, after a few swings, the idea would get to the reciprocal fact before that idea's fact, as it were, got there, or passed (out!) into it. In the larger interrupting geographies, the national and international points of view separated-off and blocked or blanked Banff into the leisure position, the strange and made-strange playground for the "aways". But the locals were a good study. They inhabited the play with their work.

Recap once observed that the tightest circle was the bartender who got off work and simply went to the other side of the bar, or on a technicality, across the street to another bar. This tiny circle is of course the abstract universal. As the circle widens and detours just locally it puts the bartender in the woods hiking or on the mountain climbing. Can any of these activities be a truly Aristotelian activity, that is can they call on a complex tradition to invite a complex psyche, call on its deepest faculties?

In other words can these split-off or abstract activities, in Hegel's sense of one-sided, even though pre-eminently empirical or factual, be anything but symptoms of the lack of a really concrete world, in Hegel's sense of whole and not a master-slave lopsidedness? Ironically it's the waiters/waitresses and bartenders who have evolved to businesspeople who come closer to Aristotelian activity. Business draws on higher faculties than skiing. Of course the way out of a lopsided business reality/unreality could be through skiing or hiking, smelling the flowers. Scientific engagement with the flowers would be a greater activity again, keeping in mind Aristotle, greatest biologist for two thousand years. And there is lopsided science too and again actually smelling the flowers can be its antidote.

The ideal would have the integration of play and work. Not the marriage of Heaven and Hell, rather that of Frost's vocation and avocation from, in his case, a grudging New

England mud. In such a world as ours, of abstract dominances, it is not normally possible. In the meantime there is this history's and this nature's now still positive alienation. There is smelling the flowers, amateur botany and geology, all swung for by the elsewhere job. Recap chose the alien position, the bad Banffite with a closet naturalist's dream and sympathy, even as he was more drawn to the smelling of flowers, and to the reading of names, to the ghost of Jon. The farm swung out slightly elliptically, if not in real astronomical time making for the seasons at some anchor or cultivator shovel level, then in his psychically warp-mapped time. It swung out like some benign edenic asteroid that blasted him out of his mountain slumber each spring.

Back in FoxHog, (after a hedgehog up from Russia, with the thistle, and some desert fox from the Palliser Triangle) or Jena, or Kant's Scottish Humeland, before field work got started, he rented the video *River of No Return* and watched Aunt Marilyn and Robert Mitchum raft down the Bow in Banff National Park. The good Mitchum, a man's man but who took some falls, was a farmer in the mountains! After Recap's heart, but not his head. Mitchum went on to say nobly that "we cleared this land and now it is ours" re resisting the marauding and bad Indians.

And yet hidden in the ideology, in the noble savage as worthy enemy and as tenuous but implied judgement of the rest of the white men sinners and gamblers, over against the mountain farmer, were the counter signs that snuck around and out when the movie came round in Hegelian history action, that is as the movie embedded history with its cropped screen and sweeping, under-the-rug, cameras, *and* as it in turn is embedded in the open, now absurd farce that new history generally and film history give us. Of course the absurd farce was there for the culture and ideology critics of the fifties and there too at the portrayed period and there before the period, with say Rousseau, if not there precluded by his extreme *other* romantic ideology.

It all adds up to the River of Quite a Bit of Return. Unless it's the eternal return, which is not the same as "nothing ever changes". It rimes, on the one hand, with the fact that the old movie is not, in two senses, universally an absurd farce: there are those who simply willingly suspend their disbelief and there are those who politically will the disbelief away, underwrite the embedded "no return". On the other hand, below the politically correct reflex of simple idealism, the chances and obstacles to justice are just as challenging and unresolved as ever. It's just that eternity has found a new corner in which to present it all, even as the representations bury it. In memory and anticipation Recap pushed his imaginary hat back, let the breeze play the sweat on his forehead.

Recap: in Banff at the writers' retreat a poet from Edmonton thought about the photographs of Marilyn Monroe that the local photographer Eddie Hunter had taken. From a reading of the photographs she surmised that there must have been some electricity between them. Recap wished now perhaps there was too but thought it would have been like photographing a photograph, but then thought about the lore or gossip or Marilyn's own local history that would have her vulnerable and ordinary, approachable surely, and smart, and one would think that would be augmented by that oddly privileged, in the middle of her great under-privilege, position, in the centre of everyone's gaze, in everyone wearing her, the turning of the tables of the emperor's clothes. And besides, she was a friend to Canadians, great electricians of the dammed rivers of no return, but yet of great returns, both profits and prophets, those voices of the repressed who allegorize edens upon lost edens. And then there was the [Henry] Kreiselian almost meeting when Jon might have sold her a *Calgary Albertan*.

Recap: Hunter's daughter, the photo journalist, who had been in South Africa and got caught in a crossfire at a crossroads in history, but also caught the moments with her camera. She was honoured at the Banff Centre in the Mountain Book and Film Festival and she gave a lecture that proved she was not just an air brusher for a pretty *ugly* out of context.

Recap: the Banff Centre: anti-Matterhorn* of plenty: all manner of musician, artist, writer, and dancer from around the world. Bruce, wormholed from the Big Apple, officially assessed the visual arts, scoffed at the virtual reality program. Later, on the radio, praised the art of a prairie storm, as taken raw from the airplane window, slinking over Lethbridge, where he was from, brought up.

---

* Rhino-ceros: *nose* + *horn*: metaphor for the artist's strange growths (W. Lewis on how the artist evolves new organs in response to the terrible needs of her life). Rhinoc-eros for the arrows of the deep-skin beautiful that returns through itself, thick and thin.

Rock, Playcefire and Recap in the Mall

Recap walked into the Book and Art Den and went up the spiral staircase to the second level. Through the stairs he saw Rock looking at books through the window from the sidewalk. He picked up the books that had come in for him and on the stairs going down he saw Rock in the store bent over looking at books on a lower shelf. Recap walked over and gave him a friendly insult to the effect he didn't know Rock could read. Rock took it kindly, with a detectable moment that said he wished he couldn't, it would save him a lot of money if not offer a certain simplicity. Recap thought with this counter evidence against how Playcefire would call the two of them penny-pinching or tight, to use his word.

Recap: Rock's money-saving do-it-yourself projects. Recap knew that it was Rock's comment on the structural stupidity of the world and equally a way of diverting it into his own back world, cobbled-up and hands-on. Playcefire of course on another scale knew the same interventionist logic. He had founded a business and it had evolved into his theatre or dramatistic offering in a corner of the world of historical commerce. Recap thought of the seamless, almost too seamless, suggestion in Richard Ford's *Independence Day* that the fiction writer was a real estate agent. Then there were Alice Munro and Henry James and their houses of fiction, Kroetsch and his puppeteer, the strings and the construction showing, the puppets deliberately foregrounded as wooden. Rock would fit in here with his behind the scene sense of things. But of course he said he didn't read novels anymore.

Recap and Rock were about to leave when Recap saw Playcefire suddenly emerge from the travel section, so he proffered the same friendly insult about reading but let it trail off, even though the strong irony of Playcefire being a natural-born speed reader would more than have suffered it. He just didn't have or take the time that much anymore. With Rock, whose house was made difficult to move around in by the books, his insult was absurd. With Playcefire it might have hit a nerve.

But Playcefire heard the comment and no nerve was hit. Recap (a flash): the log house beside the post office that Jon had "lived" in. But had he? He had, Recap had been in it with him, but the boxes of books that covered the entire main room were never moved. There might have been one feeble effort to install some book shelves, but Recap could just remember the careful footing required and the few jumps you had to make to get to the kitchen for a coffee. Talk about a house of fiction!

Playcefire had in his hand a Mexico travel book, which he ended up buying. The three of them went into the little mall in the Clock Tower Village. Playcefire asked about the late winter snowfalls down on the farm and how that would do for the moisture situation. As an old standby they asked about one another's dogs and while they sentimentalized Rock looked bored.

Recap told them about the comedic pollster he heard on the radio who said how he learned that the manipulative techniques in polling he used for his comedy were the exact ones used by the serious pollsters. Rock had seen the complete story on TV and picked up the story from there. That got them laughing enough that they started telling

Clinton jokes, pace the professional comedians were trying to go a night without telling any. Recap had not yet read Gloria Steinem on the matter nor Salutin's review of the differences, and seeming irony, in the respective male and female coverage of the sex thing, so he just listened to the jokes as they lifted into a sheer, prescinded pleasure.

Finally Playcefire told a joke about the Pope and a rabbi. The rabbi was visiting the Vatican and was alerted to a special phone. "What's this?" he asked. "Oh that's a direct line to God" the Pope replied. "Can I use it?" the rabbi asked. "Sure". So the rabbi made his call. "How much will that be?" The Pope said "a hundred thousand dollars". Then the Pope visited the rabbi and saw that he had a similar phone to God. He asked if he could use it. He did and then asked how much it would be. "Oh nothing, it's a local call" the rabbi replied.

The three of them laughed and then went their separate ways. Playcefire to Mexico Recap assumed sometime soon while Rock continued down the street to his user-friendly world, his choice (but rimed) Ulyssesesque course. Playcefire used to exhort Recap to do some travelling. When Recap went to the UK and phoned his relatives in Scotland, they asked if he were in "this country". Not thinking, he had said "no, I'm in London" and they laughed and gave him an extra special welcome to their Edinburgh. Recap went home to his mental junkyard and house of out-of-order cliché. The clichés had gone blind from his playing with them too much. He sat down in this blind light and just enjoyed the Pope and the rabbi out there slinking down all the real and all the Dennis Burton faces of Cascade Mountain.

Alice and Recap Go to Dinner

Alice came in from Canmore and she and Recap went to dinner, prelude to a movie. Across from each other at the table in the Bistro under the theatres Alice asked why Recap got a new name and she didn't. Recap felt for Victor Frankenstein's rescuer locked in an ocean of ice, up around Greenland. "Frankenstein" was kite/anchor-slinkied to the monster who exceeded in hapless caplessness the original Victor. Recap: his own name[s] and then the polar ice caps and the lid he had on his mother's life/death, the one that opens and closes with a tear-triggered blink.

Recap marked his place in the never ending indices of his anchored and landlocked self and then he broke his silence with a tack in the wind above the ice. He told her that with his new name, "Recap", he was ironically left open and could therefore fly over the ice, stop at will at a floe, make it flow. Alice said "well I can put a stop to that!" And Recap said "you sure can and that is how I will be preserved, as a third person whose ghost is only a vortex or empty nest in the very latest robot." "But what about me?" Recap: "Thou bookstore owner through the looking glass, what about you?"

They went to the movie, a film noir in which the hookers were look-alike famous actresses. After, they walked out with the rest of the crowd, crooked smiles on their faces but silent movies in themselves, like invisible rivers riven into rivers within rivers, changing rivers in mid river, till they spoke and the horse gave the barn door its head. Inside the horse they returned to the movie, slipped out inside but their conversation just horsed around and the movie repressed itself, wouldn't give them its head, slipped in and went "off!", with theirs. Patroclus went by in drag foreshadowing Hector's by and by.

They stood in the parking lot and then Alice said "I'm outta here" and a week later she was in Mexico staking out places for a twin to her bookstore in Canmore. Recap went into his cabin Walter called his woodshed and, like the monster in the dark, looked, but to the parking lot light in the slit, in his case, vertical, where the bedroom section joined the main structure. He was too far away to see anything but the light coming in, so he shrank to sloppy-thinking homunculus in a forgiving, because delaying, Cartesian theatre.

Recap Is Captured

Recap stood at the head of the Fenland trail, leaning on the tall spruce his hand clutched as if it were a pant leg. Child of the forest. Rhino stick-in-the-mud. He was circled and barred, posted. He was branded and did a high swan dive into a dammed-up diamond. Without a hitch he was broken. He packed up and left — the quarks to shift for themselves in the original riverrun.

To be stopped in one's tracks by a capping off, by, say, drinking in the stars, is a consummation devoutly to be wished. So Recap, with one foot standing on the other foot, prelude to an allusive, famous piss, bladder full of pointless territoriality, ended up on the arête* of Rundle,

---

* Recap didn't know whether he preferred the arête over the summit, or even if this Rundle ridge was the arête proper, preying on Gadd on the reverend's mountain: "... how the southwesterly dip of the bedrock†... has given [it] a characteristic writing desk shape."

† Layers of which, after the whittling of glaciers, slid into the valley.

high above its sandwiches, contemplating the *arrêt* of time in the lifted sediments. And then he contemplated *arete* (virtue), highest of *aretes*, ie of contemplating, whereupon he lost his footing and toppled back down to town.

What to do in consummate Banff, meaning "the little pig" according to Ernest G. Mardon, when you're undone, like Banff itself, by a guilty geology that flatly dissembles its recap, simply presents its heavenly faults? Before the glass was a crowd looking in on the young woman stirring a huge vat of chocolate. Recap: his niece when he told her what he'd read of the new concerns of parents re chocolate containing traces of cannabis. Science reassured them and winter kept them warm. It said it would take about twenty-five pounds of chocolate to get the equivalent stone of a joint. His niece had said "can you imagine then getting the munchies?!"

Recap ended up in Africa in the movies, as in the retro "see you in the . . . ", popped into a big pot of water listening to himself degrading into bubbles, and then "pop", he heard Sid sing "down along the Livingstone", beautiful, original displacement — thanks to Captain Blakiston, already out of his earth checking the magnetic field every hour, at times every two minutes. In the haunting voice of Hamlet's father, through Henry Kelsey, in the Grizzly House of a Sunday evening, Jon intoned, intones "ungava".•

• All the aspiring musicians, writers and artists had "ungava", the great weight, in *Homage*, Henry Kelsey, Jon put on it, echoing in their heads in the seventies and *beyond*, the meaning Jon would have of "ungava".

AFTERWORD

I would like to acknowledge the use of the following books: *Homage, Henry Kelsey* by Jon Whyte (Turnstone Press, 1982), *The Fells of Brightness, Vols. I & II* by Jon Whyte (Longspoon Press, 1983 & 1985), *Indians in the Rockies* by Jon Whyte (Altitude Publishing, 1985), *Mountain Chronicles*, Jon Whyte, edited by Brian Patton (Altitude Publishing, 1992), *Jimmy Simpson* by E. J. Hart (Altitude Publishing, 1991), *Columbia Journals, David Thompson*, edited by Barbara Belyea (McGill-Queen's University Press, 1994), *The Palliser Expedition* by Irene M. Spry (Fifth House Ltd., 1995), *Tales from the Canadian Rockies*, edited by Brian Patton (Hurtig Publishers, 1984), *Community Names of Alberta* by Ernest G. Mardon (University of Lethbridge, 1973), *Handbook of the Canadian Rockies* by Ben Gadd (Corax Press, 1995), *The Canadian Rockies Trail Guide*, sixth edition — revised by Brian Patton and Bart Robinson (Summerthought), *Men For The Mountains* by Sid Marty (McClelland & Stewart, 1978), *Lost Harvests* by Sarah Carter (McGill-Queen's University Press, 1993), *The True Spirit and Original Intent of Treaty 7* by Treaty 7 Elders and Tribal Council, with Walter Hildebrandt, Sarah Carter, and Dorothy First Rider (McGill-Queen's University Press, 1996).

I would like to thank Hilary Putnam for being "delighted" and letting me use the two quotations from his essay "Why Reason Can't Be Naturalized" which I read in *After Philosophy* (MIT Press, 1987) but which originally appeared in *Synthese 52* (1982) from The Netherlands, and so also the two quotations are used with the kind permission of Kluwer Academic Publishers.

And I would like to thank Walter Hildebrandt for reading an early version of the manuscript, Marlene Ménard for her patient computer trouble-shooting and fomatting, Jim Swanson for his printer earlier on, Ernie Kroeger for his photograph, and finally Seán Virgo for teaching me how to drink Irish Whiskey, out of necessity, and out of a wine glass in his case.

MEMBER OF SCABRINI MEDIA
Quebec, Canada
2001